WANTING RADIANCE

WANTING RADIANCE

A Novel

Karen Salyer McElmurray

south limestone

Published by South Limestone Books
An imprint of the University Press of Kentucky

Editorial and Sales Offices: The University Press of Kentucky
663 South Limestone Street, Lexington, Kentucky 40508-4008
www.kentuckypress.com

Cataloging-in-Publication data is available from the Library of Congress.

ISBN 978-1-94-966914-5 (hardcover : alk. paper)
ISBN 978-1-94-966915-2 (pdf)
ISBN 978-1-94-966916-9 (epub)

This book is printed on acid-free paper meeting
the requirements of the American National Standard
for Permanence in Paper for Printed Library Materials.

Manufactured in the United States of America

For Pearlie Lee.

Dauncy
1973

She was my mother but I called her Ruby, and I believed her hands were magic. She knew how to read cards and runes, how to find meanings in the shadows in photographs. Some people believed she could cast spells for anything from bringing a missing lover back to healing sickness, but I'd never seen the proof of any of that. The only thing I knew for sure was that my mother was afraid, partly of her own fortunes. The prophecies she claimed were enough to scare just about anyone, but I knew she was afraid she'd reveal the truth I wanted most—my own father's name. She'd look at me, head to one side, and laugh when I asked about our past. "Just tell yourself we come from a long line of tale-tellers and fiddlers," she'd say. She also said you couldn't trust a thing like love, but I loved it anyway, a highway at night with the car windows down and the radio playing Jim Morrison. I loved not knowing where we'd end up, or for how long. I was fifteen, but I did the driving and studied Ruby's hands while she surfed the air.

Once we lived in two rooms above a dry cleaner's in Swannanoa, North Carolina, a place that smelled like a just-ironed dress. After that we headed west because Ruby loved the way a turquoise ring could look on a man's hand. Six months later, I drove us back east and we ended up in Dayglo, South Carolina, where the factories made paint that Ruby used to draw sad-eyed women on our walls. I made the sign for the front door, that time. *Ruby Loving, Prophetess and Fortune Teller*. And then it was summer all over again and we rented a trailer near a spring outside of Dauncy, Kentucky.

It was the hottest spell on record in Dauncy. Ruby said it was a miracle the spring hadn't dried up in the heat, so the minute we got up that day she set about making a potion. I helped her mince the stinging nettles and pawpaws. Helped her rummage through her things to find the rattle-tails from snakes and the bones of critters she'd found in the woods. Steam rose from the stove, and the kitchen was full of songs about wild horses and a man who loved some woman way too much. The potion simmered and I painted her nails red as she gave me a sip of her sweet wine. Then I slipped a look at that notebook of hers. *On a night of the full moon*, I read, *whisper your beloved's name three times to the night wind.*

I wanted to be a blues singer in a nightclub in a city with a name I couldn't pronounce. I wanted kohl around my eyes, chocolates from Paris, France. Some days I wanted to stay put long enough for a boy to love me, but the only love charms Ruby ever gave me were don'ts, little daily spells to make me safe or to make me bitter. Don't look at them boys like that, she'd say when we went someplace they had a jukebox. But it was her doing the watching, her hands shoved deep in her pockets as we watched hips touching hips in time to the Eagles or Johnny Cash. She'd reach into some man's pocket to feel around for a five-dollar bill. She disappeared for days at a time, and when she came back again, her eyes were heavy with want.

By late afternoon Ruby was antsy, and she paced beside the long shadows on the wall by the kitchen window. I sipped cold water and wished I could hold the ice in my palm, pretty as diamonds, pretty as Ruby, her black hair tied back with a red scarf, her face shiny from the stove's heat. She draped a shiny cloth over a lamp, lit incense in the neck of a wine bottle. She set a record going, some woman singing the blues. *Love me in the morning, love me at night.* An hour passed, then two, with no one in sight, so she poured another inch of wine and flipped through her notebook till she found the lines I ought to know on a palm. *Girdle of Venus. Line of Intuition. Line of Mars.*

"There's always somebody by now," I said.

"Just don't you mind." She set the record going the dozenth time. *Love me in the morning, love me at night. Love me, Radiance, honey, till long past midnight.* I'd remember that song all the years ahead and with words that changed with every remembering, but I'd always see her behind the words, her head lifted to the open kitchen window.

The trailer's heat let go a little, and I took the kettle off the stove, poured it into jelly jars with the lids off so the potion would cool. "Just don't you mind," she said as she turned the pages of her notebook, writing down the day.

Seven o'clock, eight, and coal trucks shifted gears and headed past. I thought about how some nights it was women who came to our door, wanting to see how it felt to sit across a table from somebody with hands as wise as Ruby's. Her eyes were full of love affairs and the foreign places they believed she'd seen, but they were afraid of my mother's hands, and they ought to have been, the things she knew. Men weren't afraid at all. When my mother sat across from them, their faces hard, I knew they were ready to take what she had, whether she knew their futures or not. They thought they knew exactly what my mother was, a traveling woman with her strange hands and her fortunes. False prophets and liars, every one of them, Ruby said. When my mother told their futures, she looked straight at them, knowing more than they ever would.

By ten o'clock there was far-off thunder, and from the trees at the back of the trailer came whippoorwills and the scratch of June bugs. Somewhere a dog howled, high-pitched and restless, and a car door slammed as I hurried to the window. Out by the road a tall shadow stood and cupped a hand around a match's flame.

"Who's out there?" I asked.

Ruby turned her head to the outside sounds and waved me out. "I need to be alone for a spell," she said. "Go on now."

I went, just to the chair beneath the mulberry tree where I could see the kitchen window, her shadow moving from stove to table. Feet kicked gravel as someone made their way around the trailer. The back door slammed, and I thought I heard the small sound of glasses clinking down.

The only thing I really know about that night is what I still imagine. Her scarf sliding off, her hair falling as she moved. *Dance with me.* The record going full blast and Ruby reciting love charms. *Three silver spoons of brandy wine and you shall be mine, you shall be mine.* Behind the curtains, shadow selves leaning toward one another. For years I would think of her hands held out, a card balanced there. In my imaginings that card is The Lovers, and I see my mother's face, the smile there. *See the card I drew for you?* Then the shadow stood in front of Ruby, reached for her. How many nights I'd seen her want just that. *Hold me in the morning, hold me at night.* The record, playing and playing. *Hold me, hold me.* Their voices crossed as lightning streaked the sky.

I pulled my knees into my arms and wanted the storm to start, wished the world would be cool and fine, but it was only heat and it flashed and quit.

From the open window, voices arguing. A chair crashed down.

The truth is I remember some things and nothing at all. I remember boots running out the back door as my own feet carried me inside. I remember a floor strewn with glass and paper torn from my mother's notebook, gone missing as hard as I looked. I remember touching my mother, the place on her throat where a pulse would be. Her skin was still so warm.

Hours later, questions filled the trailer. I sat at the kitchen table with a sheriff, saying the same thing over again. "I heard footsteps. I saw shadows." They said I had to have seen something, and I wanted to tell them more. Wanted to tell how I ran inside, hero girl, how I pushed the chairs aside and picked up a broken bottle and held it out, saving us both.

From where and who I am now, I want to reach back and tell the truth, Ruby's, and my own from all the years since. I want to tell them about lovers who are only parts of themselves. One man, nothing but a boy who loved music so loud it hid our voices. Another man nothing but the feel of a rough face against my own face, how raw the heart can feel. Men and years passing, and myself slipping through the spaces of years like they were a left-open door I was never brave enough to shut. Most days, I no longer know who it is I am describing, and to whom. Whose future is it that I am now living? Have I become her, Ruby Loving, become my own lost mother? Or am I only myself now, a woman who long ago learned how not to love? The truth is this. I can't separate then from now, can't describe the difference in lightning and thunder, my mother's death from the sound of a shot. And that gun. That they found, mid-kitchen floor. A lady's derringer, they called it. A fancy handle made of abalone shell.

The room was full of her blood's scent and that song. *Hold me, Radiance, honey.* A needle scratched as the song played down and as I knelt beside her. She bled from her chest, and I wondered at it, how small the hole was. How to tell it, the way a body bleeds from a wound into forever? I held her, my ear next to her mouth and listened. "Sweet girl," she said as I hushed her, made her promise not to die. How cool her fingers were, cold as rain. What I remembered forever was the sound of her breathing, and love, taken for good from the underside of my heart.

Miracelle Loving
Knoxville
1993

1

Spirits and the Two-Step at Dill's Five-and-Dime

I'd like to say things were easy after my mother died. That whoever shot her was found and that I became a good woman with a nice yard, one where I danced a jig in Ruby's memory every summer. The truth is, whoever shot Ruby disappeared like a ghost before sunrise and I never could get my own story straight. Twenty years passed. Towns and roads and faces passed, and I spent way too many nights sipping lemonade and vodka at whatever bar was handy. Tonight it was Dill's, a country-punk fusion in downtown Knoxville, Tennessee. The crowd was small for happy hour, but it was a Thursday. Some business-suit guy was winding a skinny tie around an index finger and pointing it at a kid with fishnets and a pleather skirt. The place had promise, but the truth is, I was tired before the night even started. I was thinking about the room I'd rented at the Red Sari, whether I'd asked for pillows that were nonallergenic. I hadn't much thought about my mother in years.

A woman in a sweatshirt with a kitten on the front sat by herself at the end of the bar. Blonde-headed, with hair she'd cut herself and none too well. Spotty makeup and take-care-of-me eyes as she watched me shuffle my cards. There were lots of women like her out there. Ones with windows open to springtime, them listening to night sounds, afraid but still wanting love and not sure how to get it.

I was there to tell them love was a possibility. I'd pick a table for myself and lay out my business cards and my sign. *Miracelle Loving. Fortune Teller Extraordinaire.* I'd nod after I traced a lifeline on some palm over coffee or a quick beer. I said yes and yes while they went on about wedding rings lost in the weeds or husbands bad as the day they'd married them. Ordinary cards were twenty bucks. Tarot was thirty. For fifty I'd hold hands with them and wait until one or the other of us said they felt vibes.

3

What should it feel like? some mascaraed woman would ask, and I'd tell her to keep her eyes shut. Sweet pea, I'd say. It's all about touch. I'd hold on tight to her hands or the tabletop, whichever came first, and she'd later tell me it felt like a cross between an electric fence and revelation, and I'd say, okay.

Telling fortunes had rung a little hollow the last couple of years. For one thing, right over in the corner of Dill's was one of those quarter-for-a-swami vending machines, with a lot more customers than I had tonight. I would have been better off with a nice night job telemarketing cemetery plots or sex, but I liked the mystique. Woman alone, traveling the roads here and back and yonder. No kids. Too many boys from before and now not enough of them. Always looking for another night of drinking and more palms to read and other people's secrets to unfold. But boy howdy, me and my shitkicker boots had sashayed myself around dance floors aplenty, and I was beginning to look like I felt. Rode hard and hung up wet.

The blonde was fiddling with a napkin wrapped around her drink, waiting for me to ask her to sit down at the table I'd claimed. "I loved him more than anything."

I wanted to ask her what "anything" meant, but I said, "Honey. I've been there."

She began to cry, but I took it slow. I reached inside my brain and picked around some and found a couple sweet young things and a few cigar-toting elders to offer up as commiseration.

"Anstor," blonde said, like she hadn't heard me. Like I knew exactly who Anstor was, and I sort of did. Anstor was like anyone else I'd heard about from women whose fortunes I'd told. He did this, he did that, he did nothing at all, and still they wanted their Anstors, these women whose lives I told.

I bent my cards nearly double shuffling them, but I was gentle with her. "Oh, girl, I've been there. Late at night on that phone. I know how it is." I fanned the cards out in a nice arc and looked at her. "Calling some 1–800 number and waiting on someone you don't know from Adam's housecat to tell you what might happen or what won't."

Her eyes were teary-bright.

"Sweetie, what you need's a little dose of truth."

I laid one of my business cards on a palm that felt all lotiony and damp.

"I don't know."

"Just give it a try. One card, on me."

Pink lights flashed above the bar, signaling two for one on the drinks. Anstor, blonde-headed was saying, had gambled away everything he owned but his skivvies, and I was kind of listening but I also wanted another lemonade and vodka. A song started up, one about a fortune teller named Madame Rue, her and her gold teeth and love potions. Blonde was telling a story about Mr. No Good. How he'd bought her this really nice diamond ring and it was too big but she wore it in the shower and next to her heart on a string. It near about turned her finger green. Cheap and no good and didn't that prove itself every dang time?

That was the very second when it all happened and in a way I would have said was mystical if I was into such things. I felt this itching, low down, at the back of my neck. The itching turned to words, and then to a voice way too familiar, one I hadn't heard in years. *Miracelle, you oughta have more heart for women like her.* I nigh about fainted.

The voice had a pleased-with-itself sound. *Look at you, fortune-teller girl.* I shrugged and concentrated as I told blonde how I'd seen my share of smooth talkers and Bad Men and, why, look at me.

By that time she was poking in her purse for the twenty bucks for half an hour's card reading, though I'd already talked with her that long, minus the cards. She was telling me about how Anstor had moved in, moved out, taken over everything in her life from her Grand Prix to her calico cat.

What're you doing, girl? the voice said. My heart rippled.

Smoke rings rose from the bar crowd and I followed their trail to the filthy ceiling. Felt up under the table and found wads of old gum, like they'd tell me what was what. The voice was inside my ear and it had taken a seat. *Just when you think I was gone for good, Miracelle Loving.* A voice like Southern Comfort at the bottom of a glass.

"My name's Beatrice," blonde said, her eyes pleading as a little dog's. She handed me a twenty folded up into a neat little square.

"Hush," I said. "I got to listen."

Come on now. The voice was so close to my collarbone I shivered.

The blonde looked a little scared, like maybe one of us was crazy. "Listen to what?"

I didn't answer because I sure didn't know. Haints, they use to call them. Ghosts. Stray souls. Nothing but leftover voices from too many times before, and I'd had my share. Voices down long empty halls, like that time I was cleaning cabins at a state park in the swamps of South Georgia. *Hey, Miracelle, you done Number Four yet?* Another time, working the register and renting a little RV camper behind a store beside the highway to the Grand Canyon. Mothers and daddies and kids stopped for pop and chips. *Hey, you watch them kids at that edge,* the store owner would say, every time. A woman alone, why, she could hear just about anything, good or not.

I stuck the twenty in my shirt pocket. I wasn't ready to leave yet and I wasn't ready to stay, and I sat there while the jukebox played that fortune-teller song again. Love potions and ghost voices from some past I'd just as soon have left in the dust. What did I expect on a Thursday night in a no-account bar?

Dill's had country style and lip rings, plus enough rhinestone-shirted women and toupeed men to fill up every DeVille in a used Cadillac lot. I pushed my way past a bunch of pretty girls with brand-new cowboy boots, stopped in front of the mirror next to the bar, and checked myself out. My dress was a blue so deep I could taste it. I told myself I didn't look a bit crazy.

"Feeling lucky tonight?" The bartender was Indian, and he nodded his head in that back and forth and all at once way.

I laid down a ten. "I've been luckier, mister."

"That so?" He handed me my drink.

A tattooed boy drummed on a tabletop as I headed out onto the floor. I sipped and danced by myself for a little, then found some quarters. I needed some George Jones bad, but even with his twang and croon, I found myself humming another song I couldn't quite remember. *Hold me in the morning, hold me at night.* The music climbed up my arm, settled in the hair tucked behind my ear.

"This dance free, sweetheart?" A cowboy-looking guy, gray haired, with a stomach traveling over his belt buckle, loomed next to me.

"I'm not into dancing, tonight, mister," I said, but I sized him up. Tall, with snakeskin boots that looked real and a checkbook stuck in his front pocket.

"You should be rocking somebody's world tonight, sweetheart." He wrapped a strand of my hair around a finger and I shook my head no, but he followed me back to the bar.

I ordered a beer for the bottle since, I'd recalled, spirits and bottles attracted. You hung them on your trees in your yard, blue and green and red ones, and they caught all the spirits, all the kith and kin, and held them, forever if you wanted. I drank the beer quick so I could sit there and see if that voice would curl up in the bottom of the empty like smoke and leave me be.

Cowboy wasn't leaving anybody be, and neither was Beatrice. Blonde had followed me over to the bar, waving my *Miracelle Loving, Fortune Teller Extraordinaire* card and asking me did I also read palms. Before I could help it, her and Cowboy were sitting on either side of me downing shots two for two. I had one, even though I hated the taste of anything straight. It was like fire.

"What'd you say your name was, sweet thing?" The cowboy wasn't choosy, ordering tequila once, Jack another time.

"She's Miracelle," Beatrice slid the business card over to Cowboy and he peered at it.

"What's this here?" He pointed at a pyramid with beams of light on it that I'd had printed on the cards.

I mumbled something about Masons and the new age of light, though I didn't actually know.

"Miracelle's a prophetess," Beatrice said. She smiled like this was a joke, but then got serious. "She told me some things."

"What kind of things?" Cowboy asked. He leaned in close, lit me another cigarette.

Smoking was a thing I didn't usually do, but Beatrice kept feeding me Lucky Strikes as she started into another story about all the nights she'd spent waiting up for Anstor to drag-ass in. She drew a heart in the sweat rings on the bar.

Cowboy was as drunk as Beatrice.

"What was your name again?" His turquoise ring made his hand feel heavy on my arm.

"Miracelle."

"If you're a prophet, what do you predict for me?"

He ordered me another drink and I settled back. A stray ten had fallen out of his wallet and sat there on the floor until I scooted it under my boot for later while I traced my finger down the center of his palm. He'd give up cowboying, I told him. He'd buy himself a forty-acre farm in West Tennessee and he'd meet a neighbor lady.

"Didn't I just meet you, sweetheart?"

I brushed his question aside, turned his hand from left to right and examined the lines on the edges of his fingers. "Now, this." He leaned in as I pointed to the lines on the edge of his hand. "I'm not too sure, but it looks like children are in the picture. You got kids?"

His breath was smoky and stale and he looked annoyed, then smiled. "Guess I'm not too sure either when it comes to the kids," he said.

It was ten or eleven o'clock by then, and the place was filling up with leather fringe and spray-netted high-rise hairdos and a few Goth types. Somebody had picked Kitty Wells, a song that slowed the crowd down, left them tight wired.

Beatrice was crying and drunk dialing on her cell phone and headed out onto the dance floor. I went with it, him and me. We circled the floor, a stumble-and-hold-yourself-up kind of thing between table and bar and jukebox and back, a spoof of every dance he knew, which wasn't much. A feeling settled over like there were eyes on the two of us as we did a clumsy two-step. A clumsy do-si-do toward the jukebox. Five solid minutes of clogging to Hank Jr. left Cowboy's face red, and I led him back to an empty table.

"I could use me someone like you," he said.

"Use?"

"Don't fine-tune my words." He coughed into a handkerchief embroidered with roses.

Beyond us, the dance floor spun with lights. Blue and neon pink pulsed across faces. Mustached ones, pockmarked ones, a clean-shaven head covered with blue tattoos. The place rocked with heat and cigarette smoke as I studied him. Cowboy was spit shined, with good leather not broke in yet, but he had places that were soft, a paunch and the lips he lowered to my level hoping for a kiss. "I could take care of you, sweet thing," he was saying as I sighed, considering my options just as the voice spoke up all over again. *Don't just remember what your mama taught you, girl.* I flinched enough that Cowboy looked concerned. He raised my hand up to a mouth that looked like a little boy's.

Truth be told, I could remember plenty my mother taught me. I could tell whole lives by looking at eye color and the shapes of irises. I could read cards. I could use a poker deck for fortunes, with the one-eyed jack for good luck and the queen of hearts for love. And just like she had done for ones like Mister Cowboy, if they looked at me just right, I broke out a fancier deck I'd ordered called Poets and Planets, cards with writers and musicians. But between you and me and the salt on the rim of a glass, I couldn't live on any of it, and I'd learned ways and means my mother would never have dreamed of.

It was easy, watching all of them smoke fancy cigars and fall all over themselves to buy me another round. Businessmen. Women in suits and high heels. Farmer-men you'd see bellying up for a beer or three at a dive bar way more country than this Knoxville place. I'd follow them out to a parking lot and a big fine car. We'd roll up the windows and smoke a little of this, snort a little of that. I'd tell them just enough about me and what I knew and how. Been spinning fortunes, I'd say, since I was knee high to nothing. Yes, one of them would say as they reached over and touched my nose or my lips like they were testing the waters.

I'd pull out just enough fortune-teller rigmarole to be convincing. The ten of wands, I'd say, a release of all the energies you have built up over time. By that time we'd be staggering out of the fine car, a Corvette if I was lucky. They'd zero in for a kiss tasting like mint and gin, and soon I'd see myself in the mirror in an elevator headed to the top of some fine tall place with so many floors I could have gone out on the roof and seen forever if I'd wanted to. In the room, I'd help them unbutton themselves, help them unbutton me. Massage feet smelling of old leather, read soles, follow their empty roads of skin up and up to the planes of their backs and bellies. I was Miracelle Loving and I had the power of the future, power of the past. I had the power to taste their sweat as I rode them down. I let them read me too, their hands following all the lines, a map to everywhere I'd ever been, everyone I'd ever touched, if only they'd known how.

None of us was lonelier than anyone else, and one night was as good as the next when it came to comfort. Touch never lasted. And love? Come the end of the night, the most I could count on was just enough money and a little more to take me to the next town.

Right about then, rockabilly took over and Cowboy pulled me to my feet for a dance, but the voice was louder and peskier. *I'm still here, girl,* it said. *Ready or not.* It wasn't just a voice this time. The words had a cold edge, and they moved down the back of my neck. They tickled their way underneath my right ear, made the shape of a circle on my cheek. A rodeo song yodeled from the jukebox, a skip and hop of a song, and a whole bunch of them were trying their best to do a drunk line dance. *Don't the fools abound, girlie?* The voice shook me hard, and I turned around so quick Cowboy spilled his drink down my front.

He dabbed at me with his handkerchief, and his hand lingered.

"Give me a minute." I felt the room tilt, and I steadied myself and pulled away from him. He put both arms around my middle, a strong hold, and we stood that way. I could see a shape of myself across the way in the mirror behind the bar. The glass was speckled with tiny blue stars, and there was a giant photograph over there too, some country music singer with wide white teeth in a smile that went on and on. Beatrice sat, blonde head down and in her arms, and beside her was a young girl in leopard skin tights and motorcycle boots. She was laughing fit to kill.

"I think I made a mistake, mister," I said.

"What'd you say?" Cowboy spun me toward him but I could hardly hear him. The voice was as jangly now as car keys on a metal ring. *About time you listened up, girl.* I wanted to swallow and hold my breath. To cover my ears and say, *No.*

I broke the hold his arms had.

"What was that?" He looked at me like he'd been bit.

"Leave me be," I said, but I didn't know if it was him I was talking to or the voice. *I should have told you more.* The words inside my head now were as loud as glass breaking, and I was scared.

Cowboy looked taller, the round edges of him hot and mad. "Leave you be?" He laughed and the sound was hard. "I'm a night of standing drinks the other side of leaving anyone be."

I wanted to run, toward my motel room or at least to the first street out. Wanted to run until my lungs hurt or until I could hold my head over good dirt and empty myself out. I headed through the tangle of arms and faces and dancing.

The voice ran too, pushing its way with me through the crowd. *Should have told you about the power of fortunes, girl.* The voice had the taste of chalk. *About time we told the truth, you and me,* it said. The voice was full of midnight sounds. Bottles falling into a trash can in an alleyway, tops ripped from sweet cans of Coca-Cola in the heavy heat of summer.

As the room wove and spun, I knew that voice once and for all, whether I wanted to or not. I remembered some night and a drink or two. I remembered her. How she stumbled out into the street after a night of drinking, me with my arm around her waist. *What would I do without you?* Ruby Loving. And here she was, the first time in nigh on twenty years, making mother sounds, telling me to hold still now. *Listen, listen.* All I wanted to do was heave until I was empty, of her and Cowboy and everything that came before.

The next thing I knew, I was standing on the sticky floor of the closest restroom. The place was empty and it smelled like cheap cologne. I held my breath as I steadied myself against the sink. Stay put for a little, I told myself. Check the hallway. Find a back door out. I needed a minute, that was for sure. I was a sight. I hadn't combed my hair all evening, and in the mirror I looked like a wild woman down to my eyebrows, which needed plucking, bad. I looked like what I was, actually. A thirty-something hangdog woman with a cowboy waiting for her on the dance floor.

I turned on the faucet full blast and then forgot why I was there. The water sounds made everything else drift off, the bar noise and out beyond, car horns and sirens. And Ruby's voice was now so clear she could have been sitting at my feet on the bathroom floor. *Miracelle Loving. You need to get on with it.* Clear as when I was little. Her fingers combing through my hair and telling me and her both that everything would be all right. What was I supposed to get on with? A cowboy palm, open on my knee? *Get on with it,* she said again, and I touched my own face, and that made me so sick again the room turned. I realized I was holding my breath, but I wouldn't cry. I would not.

Suddenly the door swung open and somebody was standing there. The first thing I saw was an arm tattooed with a circle that had two words inside it. *Harmonic Convergence.* The arm was attached to a young man, who wanted the men's room that, I now saw, I was standing in. He had about the gentlest face I'd ever seen, a face like light so soft it wanted to soothe me.

"Excuse me, ma'am." He looked embarrassed. He put his hands in his pockets. "You don't look so good."

"You think?" I asked, but I could see what he did. I looked pale and sweaty. I looked haunted, and I was.

Ruby's voice was inside me like I was nothing but pieces of myself. She was inside me as I started to fall and as I took the only hands there were to hold on to.

He helped me look for my things, then paid my bar tab with a twenty I handed him out of my pocketbook. I stumbled as we stepped down from the curb, headed across to his car, though I told him I was fine, that I could call a cab.

"I've got the time." He waved me toward his car.

I didn't much care where we went as long as we just went. There'd been odder things on the roads I'd traveled, strangers who'd loved me and fed me and taken me in.

"Can we just drive?" I said as I rolled the window down, stuck my head out, breathed and loved the street-scent of old oil and asphalt.

"You look like you've already ridden somewhere and back." He uncapped a water bottle from between the seats and handed it to me.

We rode past power lines and office windows lit all night while he skate-boarded with his open hand against the air out his window. "Then there's the who-are-you question."

"Card Reader Has Been." I reached a hand across to him. "Miracelle Loving," I said after that.

"Miracelle," he repeated, like he was tasting my name.

We took a way he knew through the late-night Knoxville streets, took exits and ramps, drove until the suburbs gave way to open fields and fireflies.

"In there just now," he said after a bit. "You looked like you'd seen a ghost."

He pulled over at a wide spot and a sign. The Starland Drive-In.

Ruby Loving was a ghost, all right. *This is a little better now,* she said. She was riding shotgun on the hood of a car belonging to some man who'd saved me.

The drive-in was playing a late-night marathon of old movies. They were halfway through *The Snake Pit*, and they were just at the part where Olivia de Havilland is being straitjacketed as we parked across the road where the two of us and Ruby too could watch for free. I could have sworn I felt her tickling the back of my neck and laughing a little as he and I began to talk.

"What brought you to Knoxville, Miracelle Loving?"

"The road. Fortunes now and again."

"You tell fortunes? What kind do you tell?"

"I'd read a chicken bone if I had to."

"Do you figure out much people really want to know?"

"I aim to please."

"Ever find out much about yourself?"

I tucked my legs under me on the car seat. "I'm the teller, not the told about."

"Don't you have to figure out where you've been," he said, "before you can tell anyone else where they're going?"

"How's that?" I started to say, but I didn't. I said, "Maybe you're the fortune teller."

"Just saying what I see when I see it." He flicked a match out the window. "Really all I know of late is a good day's work."

"What would that be?"

He folded his arms like I wouldn't believe him. "I work at what you could call a museum of freaks, though I myself hesitate to use that word."

"Do they have live freaks or just little plaques?"

He raised his eyebrows. "It's the largest museum this side of the Mason Dixon. It's full of wonders otherwise overlooked."

There you go, I thought. Mermaids with cardboard for tails. But that wasn't what he meant.

"A kingdom of the dispossessed," he said.

I had no idea what that was, but I nodded.

"It's called Willy's Wonderama."

We drove along a length of deserted building, past coal piled high in a railroad car. I could see the city lights in the distance, and I closed my eyes a little, studying him. He had a smooth, shaved head and a thin goatee. He was good looking enough, but it was some kind of knowing in my belly that unsettled me. If I'd believed in past lives, or even the one I was living right then, I'd have said I'd known him for years, but I hadn't even asked his name yet.

Her voice came to me one more time at the end of that long, long night, as we drove past a truck-stop sign. The sign flashed yellow and red and blue and I wished for a minute that was where I'd ended up. Roadside waitress, white shoes all spit polished and a starched, new uniform. *Running away isn't about highways, girl,* Ruby said. She tickled my ear. She stomped on my heart. *What would being happy look like,* she asked me, *if you painted it like a picture?*

    I wasn't really a fortune teller, and I knew that well enough. I mean, glimmers of this and that came to me. Moments from what might be, but more often moments that had been. Mainly I could see a whole long line of blonde-headed women ahead of me in other bars like Dill's, all of them wanting to feel better about love. What did I have to give them but my own nights full of cowboys and empty palms waiting to be read?

    He asked me if my head was clear enough now as he let me out at the curb near my car. Then he gave me a card with a number to call. A job, he said, if I wanted one.

    "You never know," he said. "You might like staying put."

    "Maybe."

    I watched his car pull into a far lane, watched the shark eyes of his taillights disappear. *Willy's Wonderama,* the card said under the streetlight, with curlicues and a drawing of a little man with a fox head. On the other side was a scrawled name. Cody Black.

    The voice came to me one more time. *Joy abides,* it said. Was there such a thing?

    Once upon a time, my mother held her hands out the car window and surfed the air like we were flying. I was happy, a long time ago. I remembered that self like I was a ghost riding shotgun down a highway. All I knew for sure right now was that I was lonelier tonight than I'd ever been.

Ruby Loving
Radiance
1941–1957

2

Then and There

Her first memory was reaching out of darkness toward the faces of the women ready to receive her. She held back, safe in the damp, warm inside, her eyes open and already not sure of the world she was about to enter. *Wait,* her heart told her. Then they took hold of her hands and pulled her out into the light, into a room that smelled of tobacco and herbs, a room where her mother cried. A beautiful child, the women said, but Esther saw right away that her daughter had more than her share of mortal flaws.

Why, just look at your hands, Esther said when Ruby was six or seven, and sure enough, they were rough from mud in the yard, her palms threaded with fine cuts from the broomstraw and catbrier she plucked behind the house. Maybe Esther had wanted a son instead, Ruby grew to believe, and so she took the broomstraw and wove it into things that seemed more solid than herself. She filled tiny baskets with hatched-out robin's eggs and stones as smooth as she could find. Or maybe Esther had wanted no child at all. Ruby worked to disappear, hiding inside quilts at the end of the bed, vanishing inside closets and coats in the summer heat. Her hands were so far from her own body, she saw them as two lost things she no longer wanted. If there was such a thing as a mother's love, Ruby saw it fall through Esther's fingers like rusty water. And if the world held beauty, Esther kept it too close.

She pulled the clothes all clean off the line and breathed their scent when she thought no one saw, and she kept bottles in all the colors she could find. Blue and red and brown hung by twine across the kitchen window to catch all the light coming in. Late evenings, she sat at the mirror by the dresser, her own slender hands parting strands of her hair to make a

17

long braid. Tell me about love, Mama, Ruby said as she wound stray bits of thread on a spool.

There's no such a thing, Esther said. There's only God.

God decided how cold that winter would be. He fixed the summer days so hot you couldn't touch a doorknob on the outside of the house. He made autumn so lonely Ruby stared far off at the sound as she sat on the porch while her daddy sang songs so beautiful they melted the air.

Her daddy, people said, played the fiddle like it was shady roads and a pond in August. Made her want to go walking in the dark. She held on to the songs when he went riding the roads. Poker and bootleg. Gigs in juke joints west of Radiance. They drove for miles to hear him, but it was his nights at home Ruby loved most. How he'd start out with nothing but silence. Like clear canning jars and liquor. Fire turned low and blue on a gas stove after supper. She'd make herself a cup of instant coffee and sit next to him.

He'd tuck the fiddle underneath his chin, sing songs from deep in his belly. They were ones he wrote. *Love goes around and comes back,* he sang from his belly. *Flies out and brings me back to you.* Ruby wished it were so, wished love was the way the world was. The air in the house was thick as water, and underneath that water she tried to breathe. He fiddled songs late into the night while Esther slept—never, she said, remembering her dreams.

By the time Ruby was ten, Esther looked her daughter up and down as if she should be hidden inside a coffee sack before they went to town. As they walked the streets of Radiance, she gathered Ruby against her hip. She covered her with scarves and sweaters even in summertime. Ruby grew acquainted with it, the way the ground looked when she kept her eyes down. She knew the far reaches of pockets, the feel of her underarms as she held her own self tight. When she studied her face in the mirror by a window at night, all she saw was yearning.

Ruby held on to thunder as it traveled over top the ridge. The light from Radiance. The streets and their houses. Stores and their shelves filled with movie star magazines. Days, there was school, but that taught her shame, the way they taunted her for the sweaters she wore, buttoned up tight, a scarf covering her head. *Ruby, girl, strange Ruby, coming down the road like a secret hid.* Books didn't interest her much, so what she did those nights her daddy fiddled was teach herself to read in a way that mattered. She laid out rounds of aces and hearts from her daddy's poker deck. Cards had power. Cards could tell your future, if you just learned how. Ruby turned the cards one by one and let them tell her about places and times she'd never seen. She held a card balanced on the end of her forefinger like it was something she'd someday need bad at the end of a long road, and she knew already what it was. Love, a prize for the longing that grew in her heart.

Esther said Ruby loved things too much. Lingered too long over the ripe smell of garden tomatoes. Loved the feel of her bare feet in the dirt. The shape of sweat on her daddy's back as he fiddled. Ruby held her hands out to the night air, lightning bugs settling there with their thrum and thrum, a fire she felt in her own chest. She shuffled the cards and laid them down, aces and queens and jacks, and believed her future was fore-told there. Long highways going to a place she'd never been. It was wanting made her hurt the way she did. Some days she could hardly breathe for it, the wishing after a thing she couldn't name.

Then one day in the garden, Esther drew her breath. She grabbed Ruby's hand and guided it down inside the neck of her dress. Underneath her mother's breast was a thing round as a banty egg. Like so much else, this was a secret, this roundness, and they told it to no one. Esther drove the hours west, and from a hall Ruby watched her mother lying behind glass. A theater, they called it. A training place for doctors who answered nothing. Here, they said, and they pointed at her mother's body like the diagram of a steer. They scooped and dug and left a place where a breast once lived.

After, they spent three days in a family-owned motel, and Ruby went out for milk shakes. For cans of orange juice and saltines to settle her mother's stomach. The room, Ruby thought, smelled of feet, and the sounds outside made her heart skip. Cars sped up and stopped in the mid-dle of the night, and men laughed and argued about whiskey and fought over the scatter-roll of dice. From inside the motel walls came skittering mice sounds, and from the next room Ruby felt the voices there like the scraping of nails on skin. A woman called out. "There, Frank. Now." In the morning Ruby saw a woman in the motel office, her dark hair in pin curls, her mouth a smeared slash of red, behind her a man who looked like a

Frank, his lip fat with chaw. Back in the room, Esther was pale, her eyes fast shut, a blue map of veins across the lids. Ruby held her fingers across her mother's sleeping face and wished, for what she wasn't sure.

Back home, her daddy had never known about the breast and the days they'd been away losing it, not that Ruby could tell. But when the front of Esther's dress hung empty, how sad he said it made him. After that he'd be gone for weeks, a month. At first her mother mourned. Played songs on the radio meant to call him home again. *Come awake, little my own true one. Come awake and come back home.* She sipped shine from a jar to still the pains she said traveled from her missing breast, underneath her bones and inside her blood. Once Ruby brought out the card deck and said it, that one word. "Fortunes." Esther swept the cards off the dresser like they were a bad-tasting prayer.

The years until Ruby was seventeen passed, and she grew used to it, the things that went missing. An old man at the church house had half an arm shot off in a barroom brawl. A little child up the road had part of her face burned away where she fell through a coal grate. But Ruby saw Esther's missing soul clearer than any of it. Her mother stood at the well and leaned against it, the water bucket in her arms, and looked in and in. Let me do that, Ruby said, but Esther made a shushing sound, looking down like the well had a bottom past forever. I reckon I can do for my own self, she said as she took hold of the chain and hauled up with all her strength. Her eyes and mouth winced with the pain of it.

Esther harbored a ghost inside, a ghost that howled and begged and then grew bitter. A ghost-woman, her mother suckered tomato plants and hoed hills of beans. She scrubbed iron kettles and boiled taters and beans. Her eyes turned from sad to nothing, her half-breasted chest proud of its own lack. Ruby sat some nights wondering what it was they did with a breast when it wasn't yours anymore. Did it flush away down a drain or lie lonely and no longer part of anyone at all in the back of a truck going west?

Ruby knew what she never wanted to be. The women she grew up around, why, they were stronger than strong, knew how to raise an army of children, through years of getting by. They knew how to till and mend, to clean and send their family fixed up nice out into the worlds some of them never saw. What did the verse say? *A virtuous woman . . . She riseth also while it is yet night, and giveth meat to her household, and a portion to her maidens.* Ruby wanted none of it. None of the women who spoke through the mouth of God. The ones who took it and took it, the backs of hands, the fists against a wall, the dust from a car scratching off down a road.

Esther quit braiding her long hair and winding it neat around her head. Quit caring what her daughter did, and where. She sent Ruby to town to buy herself a grilled cheese at the drugstore lunch counter, and she gave her dollars to buy herself pretties. Jean Naté. A Coke with ice. Red polish. Take those hands and make them useful, she said to Ruby now. Get you a good man, she said, laughing a laugh not kind. Maybe a good man would take Ruby to all the places Esther had never seen, all the places her lost breast might be traveling all its lonesome.

When her daddy traveled the road with his fiddle, their land lay fallow. Catbrier and trees of heaven grew, claiming space. Her daddy had never been good at the farming. He tried, on his trips back home. He sawed and split and his palms grew calluses. He'd be hoeing a row, and before he knew it he'd have to stop and look at birds roosting or the mountains he loved, and Ruby could tell he was thinking a song.

Nights he played every song he knew for Esther. Love songs. Sad ones—"Little Polly," "Barbry Allen," "Little Maggie." He sang all the songs he knew about women lost, women strayed, women stolen or disappeared, and his voice sighed. It cried and begged and grieved. It drifted away, then remembered and came back again. And one of those songs he sang, he said, was Ruby's. *You know miles and miles you've never seen,* the song went. *Your heart knows plenty before its own good time.*

When he sang that song, Ruby watched the notes rise into the sky like bats and night birds. And while he sang, Esther stayed inside. She shut the windows fast, pulled the curtains, shut off all the lamps. Ruby could hear the way she took off her shoes and dropped them one by one by the bed. The way Esther threw back the covers and slid herself inside the bed, her hands folded over her chest, the place where her breast had been, healed and glad in its emptiness. It was on those nights he sang, Ruby told her first real fortunes. The cards she set down began to know truth the way only blood knows it.

Queen of hearts. That was her first card one night, a crown all royal and those proud eyes. That was who Ruby wanted to become, though she did not yet know the ways and means of it. Her next card was a deuce. The roads she'd take someday, ones beyond their hollow and all its mountains wrapped around, roads she could not yet imagine. All she knew was how she sat on the porch in the dark, long after the fiddle was laid in its case, long after the last of the night birds quit calling.

The last card she drew was a one-eyed jack, and her gut told her the meaning. Shadow man. Out there somewhere in the far black night filling up with rain. It was summer, and the day had been so hot, and there'd been nothing at all but flashes of light over top the hills. The light was hot its own self, and it was trying to push through the skin of the sky. She held her hand out, palm up, beyond the porch's eave. And then Ruby heard it, the first tiny whisper of rain on leaves. She trailed a finger between her lips and tasted the rain like it was him.

Miracelle Loving
Knoxville
1993

3

Willy's Wonderama

Late at night in the streets of Knoxville with a tattooed younger man, just about anything made sense, but not so much by good daylight. I rolled over and looked at the trail of shoes and underwear leading across the floor, but that made my head ache. I closed my eyes and opened them again, focusing instead on the things I'd put here and there for home's sake. Taped to the dresser mirror was a photocopy of a palm with all the lines marked for readings. *Hepatic Line. Saturnian Line. Double Line of Life.* And on the dresser top itself, a ceramic statue of the Holy Mother, a blue wine bottle with a candle in it, and, like in every place I ever stayed, Ruby's derringer. I'd set it with the handle propped between a thick astrology book and a paper encyclopedia of seashells, which seemed to suit.

The gun, Ruby always said, was part sea-dream, with the fancy gloss of abalone on the handle, and part for show. She'd carried it in her shoulder bag and put it in every kitchen drawer in every place we'd ever rented, and I'd done the same thing. I'd carried it with me to the Northwest that time I had free room and board for canning salmon. I'd carried it to Kansas City, too, and I'd been glad of it when I heard some man praying in a bathroom stall next to me. "One more time," he said. "One more time and that's all there'll be if you help me," he said, on the edge of desperate. I reached into my bag and gripped the handle of the derringer even though, like Ruby, I kept the thing unloaded. A yellow silk flower stuck out of its muzzle now.

I tossed and turned, lay with a pillow over my head. *It's about time, Miracelle Loving.* Her voice again. *Time for what?* I said back, but she'd gotten what she wanted, I reckoned. I was awake, but I lay there remembering. I could see her just as plain, listening over and over to that song on her old record player. *Love me in the morning, love me at night.* On nights like that, she couldn't stand the sight of me. It hurt too much, she said, to see what she was and what I'd likely become. A woman by her lonesome on another Friday night, the only cure for anything a cheap bottle of whiskey and the blues. *Love me, Radiance, honey, till long past midnight.* Desperate. That was what you called a night like that.

I made coffee and stood bare-ass by the open motel window like I could care less. A diner across the street was called The Pelican when there couldn't have been anything more landlocked except for maybe my own self. In the mirror above the dresser I had drugstore burgundy hair with the roots coming in, a hole in the side of my nose where a nose piercing hadn't worked out. Would Cody Black have liked what he'd seen if I'd asked him up here last night? Him all shave-headed and smooth-cheeked, except for one little patch of midnight black hair in the center of his chin. And me?

I paced. I flipped on the television, but there was nothing but ads for a mattress discount store, home shopping networks, and a movie about a woman with a black heart tattooed on her back. I turned the volume down and clicked through the channels, watched faces and eyes open and shut, mouths sending out words I didn't care about. In the shower I cranked up the hot water and stood under it, trying to let the night before and her voice wash away. *Get on with it,* Ruby had said, but the best I could do for now was tarot.

I dried off and sat on the bed with my deck. The tarot I owned was cheap-and-good, from some Miami head shop, but if you looked at the fine print on the back of the box, the deck came from a printing company in San Francisco, California. If they knew more about the future than I did, I'd eat the cards. There wasn't a fortune I'd ever told that didn't require me looking something up in a tarot book and memorizing some phrase to drop in at the best moment. Every now and again, I took the cards out and held them next my chest and wished on them, like they were stars. The first card I drew, for the past, was the eight of cups. A woman knelt by a lake reaching back into a dark cave, and the eight cups floated inside. *An unconscious kind of change taking place on the very deep feeling level.* I'd been down the deep feeling road and it sure hadn't worked out very well. Once in Houston I'd lived for almost three months with a half-rich preacher I'd met at a rodeo, but he turned out to be the farthest thing from preachering I'd come across, so I left him behind in a cloud of Texas dust. I'd made an art of leaving, if I was honest about it. Doors slammed shut.

My present card was a black-robed woman watching three golden cups spill out along a dirt road heading up a mountain. *A loss and wishing for what might have been. Being crippled by sadness, grief, and vain regret.* No one would know the difference if there'd been a reversal, so I flipped the card and looked in the book again and it was a little better. *New prospects and new projects are about to come into your life.* I'd only been in Knoxville two days, and who knew about prospects. Some days I felt like I was floating above some memory I didn't want to reach, some city or little town I couldn't name. And that far up in the air it didn't matter much, the day or the time or where I was headed next.

The future card, another cups card. Cups were for emotions, and this one was an ace. A hand. A long, embroidered sleeve. A cup with the dove of peace. *The seed of a new direction, a relationship or spiritual journey, perhaps as yet unseen. An opportunity for joy, contentment.* I'd told fortunes for DJs and hairdressers and waitresses in coffee shops and bus stations and in the front seat of my Dodge. I'd read cards and felt bumps on heads and laid little cellophane fish in palms from north to south and west and back east in more places than I could shake a stick at. A new direction sure wouldn't hurt.

I dumped the whole deck on the bed and stirred around in it, thinking about drawing a final card for good measure. One of the cards stared out at me and I picked it up. A tall young man with a crown walked near a river, a rod held up to the sun. It made me think of Cody Black, though that was a stretch. Cody was no prince. He was a tattooed-up boy with big old holes in his ears and, lordy, him coming in the door of the men's room and me about laying on the floor, ready to heave my guts out.

Beside the tarot cards I laid the card Cody Black had given me with the little fox-headed man and the insignia. *Willy's Wonderama.* I dug the phone book out of the bedside drawer. It showed Willy's under both Tourist Attractions and Miscellaneous Sales. *Willy's Wonderama.* I pictured myself dusting shelves or shoveling gravel in the parking lot, at worst. I pictured myself back at the Red Sari some night soon with Cody Black, waking up with him, drinking motel room coffee. Maybe I'd read a card or two for him. I got up and paced the room again, thinking. At the dresser mirror, I stood looking at myself. I ran my fingers through my hair and wondered how I'd look with it darker or with a henna rinse or at the very least some lipstick, maybe a nice, deep red.

I wished to hell Ruby would speak up when I needed her, but her voice was quiet as I dialed the phone at the bedside. *New prospects and new projects,* the cards had said. Worse come to worst, I was here for a few weeks, and an adventure or two with Cody Black sounded about right. A recorded voice came on the line. *Willy's Wonderama! Museum under re-construction! Grand reopening, Summer 1993! Emissaries wanted!!* Hmm. I rooted around in a suitcase and pulled on a jacket and slacks and shoes with little heels. In the Red Sari lobby, I jotted down some general directions from the desk clerk and headed for my car.

I laid the directions on the seat beside me and took a bypass around the city, then a couple of exits until I found myself in front of a boxy-look-ing place in the center of a charred lot. There'd been a fire, all right, but most of the building was still there, the weird offspring of a southern Civil War mansion and a warehouse. I sat thinking about how soon I could be in North Florida if I packed up quick, but I made my way inside to the main foyer. A room on the left bore a plaque that said Office.

Inside, a middle-aged man was blowing his nose and two teenaged girls were wearing jelly sandals and matching sweatshirts that said *One Way! Believe!* By the time I got an application, my stomach was gnawing after the breakfast I hadn't had yet, but I figured I'd be out of there in a half hour. Back in the foyer I found a folding chair and set to. Loving, Mira-celle. Then lots of blank spaces for dates and towns and education. *List all relevant experience.* Not till the last page was there a whiff of anything at all exotic. *Tell us,* the question asked, *about any visionary experiences you have had.* I nibbled at my eraser.

On the road, I'd slipped inside Holy Roller churches to listen to god-music. Once I'd worked for a few weeks as a janitor for the Tallahas-see House of Faith, operated by a pastor named Barbara with tall perox-ide-blond hair and a shiny suit. I liked that job best late at night with not a soul around. Streetlight shone into the sanctuary room, a plain place with a slap-hazard cross above a podium like they'd use in a high school gymna-sium and no stained glass anywhere. That kind of holiness appealed to me.

"Glad to see you made it."

Cody Black was toting a mile-high stack of manila folders spilling out of a cardboard box. He set the box down and leaned over my application. No longer in bar light or car light or night light, Cody Black had two tiny star tattoos beside his eyes.

They hired me, and I went in the next morning to learn who was who, what was what. I was ushered to a room on the second floor where a woman with a gauzy dress and sparkles glued on her fingernails told me the basics.

"I'm Marvis Temple." She pointed and I took a seat.

Willy's, she said, was the South's most famous museum. Had bitten the dusts with three fires, most notably the Armageddon of 1989 and the suspected arson in 1992. That last time, they'd lost a good majority of their strange phenomena.

My job was finding talent for when Willy's reopened. She gestured toward a small desk stacked high with piles of unopened envelopes.

"Here's the main thing about this place." She handed me a three-ring binder labeled *Recruits: What to Do and Say.* "You'll be what's called an Emissary," she said.

"What's that?"

"It means you're supposed to know what you're doing." She laughed. "Or sound like it, anyway."

I flipped through doctored-looking photos of four-horned this or that, chickens with no beaks.

She polished her nails on her sleeve. "You're a lookout for new talent."

There were people photos, too. Some with not but one eye, others with no nose at all except a flat place with holes for breathing. A note was stuck to the photo of a woman with a shag hairdo. *Finds places no longer there.*

"Study up, your first day or two." Marvis handed me a stack of more notebooks. "Then see what you can find."

"How am I supposed to do that?"

"The public library, when you need it. And there's boxes of old stuff down in the basement." She paused. "And there's letters."

She passed me one last notebook. I opened it and read the first page.

Letter. Dated December 16, 1990. Photographs (images of conjoined baby elephants). Origin of letter Northern European. (Of interest. Big box. Possible shelf life.)

Dear Sirz:

I was in the attic yesterday and there was a box, a maho-gunie one with a big lock and I broke it because the house is mine now after all these years and from my grandpapa, who once was a big-game hunter and is now dead, not from any rifle wounds, but from apoplexy. Anyway. The house and this chest are mine. And so are all the photographs, like this very one I hold out for you now.

"You read and you take notes, and if anything strikes you right"—she waved ceilingward—"then you send it on up."

I assumed "up" meant another office and a person who wasn't just a wonder-finder, but I looked at the photo that went with the letter. A boy stood beside the joined dead bodies of the two elephants, their small tusks pointed at the sky.

All of it made me sad. The piles of paper—letters and envelopes and who knows what—covering all the small desks in all the cubicles. I imagined swiping it all into the trash can, but I reckoned I'd hold out for a few days.

Those days were soon full of claims to wonders—three-eared dogs, mocking-birds that wouldn't mock, conjoined miniature this, legless miniature that. I stayed somewhere between tickled and nervous, but other than that, the job meant gray walls, gray particle board partitions. On one side of my cubicle was a woman named Cynthia, and on the other was a girl named Joan who wore so much eyeliner and lipstick she would have been a marvel next to a Kewpie doll. The three of us spent the days divvying up the mail, which was packed with more letters about people with most of themselves there but essential parts gone in one way or another. Wonders of the World, Willy's called them in the advertisements they sent out here and yon. What they got back were letters.

Letter. Dated November 14th, 1992. Typed, to all evidence on an old manual typewriter. Copy is carbon-papered. Origin: Puera-les, New Mexico. (No interest. Too much god-stuff.)

Dear Willy's Wonderama:

Twenty years ago, I was called upon by a young couple to

perform the Sacred Rites of Baptism on an infant with pupil-less eyes. Is this boy a Wonder of the World?

In between mail runs, there were leads to follow, meetings and brainstorming sessions, phone calls to take, calls to return. The mail was the main thing, and I'd had only one letter that took my fancy.

Letter. Not Dated. Handwritten. Female. Mid-forties. Origin: Babcock, Kentucky. (Maybe.)

Dear Willy:

I have a daughter, just the one, and she is a soul beyond reason, and I do not mean cruel, sirs. She is a gift, and I have worked long to know how to receive her.

She is a seer, my girl, and her name is Maria. I named her that because it sounds almost like a miracle, and it sounds like the smallest thing inside us too. And together the three syllables of her name make heavenly music. I believe that. But at first I did not believe what is really true about my girl.

My Maria has seen what others have not. Once she knew there was a chest inside a wall in a house down the road, knocked on the very place they opened to find it and a lost deed, right inside. Another time she woke and all she said was, look there. And she told about a barn three counties over, how they'd find a missing child there. Oh, but Willy, she sees more than all that. Maria sees ghosts.

She sees souls inside souls.

Yours,

Mrs. Dauphine Murdy

I read that letter over and over. Souls within souls made me think of an old black-and-white television Ruby and I once had, how all you could see on it were shadows of movie stars. When Ruby was gone all night, I held my hands across the television's snowy screen and told myself I was touching ghosts, telling lives better than my mother ever could. At the library, I searched phone listings for Babcock, Kentucky, and Dauphine Murdy. I dialed and the tone was from one of those old-style phones, then silence.

31

"Hello," a sleepy-sounding voice finally said, and I launched into the Willy's script. "Ma'am? Is this Mrs. Dauphine Murdy?"

"Last time I checked."

"I'm excited to be phoning you with some good news."

"Could use any of that you got."

I scanned the letter, searching for the way to start. "I see here," I said. "I see you've got a girl you're real proud of."

The phone went quiet again. I could hear dogs in the background. "What you know about Maria?"

"You wrote us about her."

A throat cleared. "Who are you?"

"Willy's, ma'am." I paused and tried to sound more official. "I'm a representative for Willy's Wonderama. The museum you wrote to here in Knoxville."

"That place that wants stories?"

"Yes, ma'am."

"Well, we've got enough stories around here lately to keep us."

"Is that right?"

The woman sighed. "My girl knows more things than she ever did, here of late."

"What kind of things?"

"Why, honey, it's got so she knows the color of the weather before I open the drapes."

"She does?"

"And she knows more than that."

"Like what?"

"She knew two weeks before the fellow down the road showed up for the revival."

"Yeah?"

"He was a preacher and you couldn't trust a word out of his mouth and Maria said so. Right up in front of everybody. Told him what was what about believing what you believe and bearing false witness." I stopped her, but she went on. "And she'd know about you, too, honey, if you looked her in the eyes."

"That's what I called about," I said. "Meeting her, that is."

"What's that?"

"I believe Willy's Wonderama would like to meet her." I hesitated. "Make her the wonder she is."

"She is a wonder, that's the truth." The woman laughed, a thin sound that broke and put itself back together. "When I got up this morning, first thing she said to me, she said, Mother." She cleared her throat. "She said somebody would be calling us today."

"She did?"

"Somebody with the name Ruby."

I held the phone with my ear and shoulder and rubbed my arms. I felt cold.

I heard the shifting of furniture, the slamming of what could have been a drawer.

"Ruby's an old-time name, and I wouldn't likely forget it."

"I guess that's a fact," I said. I held the phone and my mouth was dry.

"And another thing," the woman said. "She said something about fiddle music. It playing so pretty."

"She said all that?"

"I don't know. Let her tell you her own self."

She laid the phone down. Chairs shifted, and there was urging. "Oh, talk to her. What could it hurt?"

More scraping, then breathing on the line.

"Maria Murdy?" I asked.

"I am."

"I read about you," I said. "About your miracles."

"I wouldn't go so far as to call them miracles." Her voice made me think of sad eyes, ones sure of what they knew.

"What do you call them?"

She laughed. "Just a little seeing and knowing, I guess."

I thought about the name the woman had said. Ruby. "Was that your mother?"

"It was."

"She said the name Ruby just now. How did she know that name?"

"I told her it was a name that come to the person who'd call. A name that come as a voice."

"I don't know about any voices," I said, my voice faint.

"Listen." She got quiet, and the line hummed. "Listen to what the voice says to you. To the stories it tells."

"And if I do? What comes after that?"

"Well, I feel like I've seen some sign or something."

"Signs? Like God, you mean?"

"No. I mean like a sign with lights, and a purple cat."

A purple cat? That was a little better than God. I was ready to hang up, but I waited for her to say more.

"The only thing I really know for sure is there's a town with a name like light."

"That should be easy enough. Is there more?".

She laughed. "Onliest thing you don't know how to do?"

"What's that?"

"Love, I'd say. But I don't know enough about that to tell you much."

"I don't either," I started to say, but the line went to static and then I held on awhile more until I was sure she was gone.

Ruby Loving
Radiance
1957

4

Shadow Man

Ruby ordered a deck of tarot cards from a magazine advertisement that promised the real deal. *Prophecies. Answers.* Her favorite card showed a young woman in a robe covered with foxes and dragons. The card was called the Priestess. Ruby thought of walking in the woods whenever she could, gathering herbs for the potions she had begun to make. She wasn't sure what her potions were for, but she loved their hot, bitter tastes. She read in a library book about charms for love. About an undoing—a spell for making sure what someone believed in most got undone. The Radiance diner had to be full of souls who wanted spells like those.

At a diner booth, she tasted sugar from the bowl and ordered coffee with extra cream. Another piece of chocolate pie. The waitresses weren't afraid of her exactly, but there was the small downturned smile when they saw the cards she laid down. At first she practiced for her own self with three cards and Celtic crosses, but then a big-handed carpenter man stopped and asked what she was after with all those cards. She noted the calluses on his palms as he shuffled and split the cards into the three piles for his past and present and, his fingers fumbling and letting cards go by then, his future. Some of the waitresses brought her coffee refills, lingered as she told them about the possibilities for marriages, for jobs, for lost faith in God. One waitress brought her every kind of pie on the house, lemon and banana and coconut, until she finally got up the nerve to sit in front of Ruby and ask. "I need you to tell me about how it would be," she said. "About heading up to Indianapolis and getting me a place and, you know, singing at night somewhere fancy?" The girl's hair shone, fresh washed and hopeful. They were all hopeful, the ones who sat with her for their futures, and Ruby liked that, the imparting of hope.

That was how she met him.

He stood a long while by the register, reading the menu. His body had an ease about it, a coiled energy she already wanted to see unwind. He shrugged, took a seat at the lunch counter, and gave the redheaded waitress his order. She watched him as he drank from his water glass, the swallow, the way he spit ice cubes back in. He cut his sandwich into neat parts, poured pools of ketchup, eating his fries whole. She watched his black eyes and his full mouth as he glanced around the Monday-empty room. When he looked at her for the first time, she memorized his face.

Esther had said Ruby's hands reached out for a body, as if her fingers could climb inside you and turn your heart over. It was true enough that Ruby's hands seemed to reach toward the man as she watched him. He stood, kicked the toe of a muddy boot against the lunch counter. Took his black felt hat off and shook it, looking puzzled as he set it back on his head. Could he hear her all the way over there, across the diner? *Who are you, mister?* Her tongue went dry and she felt her hands laying themselves down, the fingers drumming on the table. She laid one hand over the tarot deck, sure she felt warmth rising from the cards.

As he made his way over to her and stood there, that hat in his hands, she laid one hand out in his direction. Palms and cards, mister. She said that and turned one of her own hands over, palm up, waiting until he laid his own hand there and she touched the warm, rough feel of his skin.

She didn't see him again until a week later when her daddy was on the street in Radiance. He was playing along with a man with a washboard strapped to his chest and another one with a guitar he made sing so sweet. It was a song about wanting and not-having and Ruby held her fingers against her face, hoping there was some scent there that was still his. She memorized the crowd, looking for him.

Him with his felt hat and his black eyes. He made her want fire.

At night she took to dreaming of mountains opening up, swallowing other mountains, one by one by one. She dreamed herself swallowed up and disappearing inside love. Dreams, he said when he lay atop her and looked down into her eyes. Her fingers, he said, were like dreams their own selves, moving down his back. Dreams, she said, were like birds that took wing at daybreak. Dreams weren't real as him, he said. She dreamed ravens as big as storm clouds, and they made her afraid.

They stayed in Radiance, him and his logging crew. After they'd been here awhile, mountains were split open like hardwood, and the scent drifted in the open windows at night. Musk. Tearing. A scent of blood and birth. And behind them the coal men left their machines. Earthmovers. Excavators. Extractors. Big machines with names of companies bold across them. *Smyte. Black Diamond.* Ruby would walk home from town some nights and see a huge shell of a thing that had taken a mountain's insides in its wake. Prongs of a forklift, held out like empty arms in prayer.

And when they are finished with us, her daddy said, they will spit us out and go on like we never were.

He will be that way, too, that drifter man, that man you say you love, her mother said. The world, Esther said, used to be a circle of earth. Mountains and trees and water so sweet. Then it became a circle of camp houses at the foot of a mountain chipped away. It was him who made the world crash open.

Men like him reached inside the mountains and pulled out their hearts. He did this and Ruby loved him anyway.

Miracelle Loving
Knoxville
1993

5

A Mirror and Some Songs

Late afternoons, I drove the streets, circled blocks, memorized the short cuts to grocery stores and clubs until the town made sense. Nights, I drove 640 around Knoxville, took exits I'd never heard of and let myself get lost just for the hell of it. Most times, I ended up at Willy's like it was some homing ground I couldn't forget. I was sitting there now in the empty parking lot, sipping cold coffee and ready to head on back to the Red Sari, when Cody Black's car pulled in too. Music was jacked up, some song I didn't know. *Love had wings that spread across the sky at night.* A woman sang and bass guitar sounds spilled across the parking lot as I got out of my car and went on over.

A cigarette with a hand attached to it hung out his open window. I said hello, but there was no hearing anything above the song. *Love had wings and teeth to hold on fast.* He tapped his hand against the side of the car, then seemed to think better of it, and turned the music down a tad. He shut off the engine, just as the song was starting to crescendo and I'd tuned in to the lyrics a little more. *Wings and teeth and love that stings no matter how hard you try.* What kind of love song was that for 8:30 of a Sunday morning?

"You here on a day off too?" I leaned against his car.

"Catching up on a few things while it's quiet." He tapped his cigarette against the rolled-down window and I moved back.

"Had breakfast?"

"Not yet." He forced his glove compartment shut against a wad of papers and a big plastic cup.

"Found some good biscuits and gravy at that place across the street."

43

"I've got coffee and peanut butter crackers." The car door screeched as he pushed it open. "I'll share."

A ceiling-to-floor tank was on one side of the hall, sharks swimming there. They were big, burly-looking things, one of them missing an eye, the other an albino, both of them a long way from an ocean. The sharks had survived every fire and destruction Willy's had known, Cody told me as we watched them swish by.

He sat cross-legged on the ratty carpet. Light settled around him, and it could have been like hallucinogenic tracers, but Cody Black was finer than that, I'd come to believe. "Thinks he's smarter than the rest of us," one of the cubicle ladies said when I first asked around after Cody Black. "Him?" Marvis Temple said. Tattoos and music loud enough it'd break your eardrums. From East Tennessee, somebody else said. In New York City for a couple years, then right back home again, his body covered in tattoos. "Thinks he's after God or truth or whatever." A turn or two in Peru or Venezuela and enough vision medicine to remind himself he was lost and belonged where he started from in the first place. Light, though there was none in this dank hallway, settled somewhere behind his left shoulder, drifted down and touched his face, lingered in his eyes. A week back, I'd asked him for supper at the diner beside the motel, but he'd turned me down. I was nervous, so I fished around in my pocketbook for my poker deck and shuffled, laid down three cards. "Let me tell your future."

"You believe in fortunes?" Cody asked.

I turned over the ace of hearts, which seemed like a fine card for anyone's past.

"Depends on what you mean by believe."

His next card was the two of diamonds.

"I'm giving you three cards only. Past. Present. Future."

"How long you been reading cards, Miracelle?"

"About as long as those sharks look like they been in that tank." The sharks trailed each other like they were pacing a floor.

I turned over the third card. The queen of diamonds.

"These three cards together." I paused, thinking about possibilities. "They're about new beginnings." I wasn't really sure about that, of course, but it was as good a riff as any, especially on a poker deck.

"What beginnings brought you to Knoxville, Miracelle?"

"You know the score on that one, Cody. Told you about it that first night we met."

He shrugged. "I don't know two red cents about you, as a matter of fact."

I shuffled the cards again, thinking one more card couldn't hurt. I drew out the ace of spades. That ace couldn't equal anything to do with hearts, so I slipped it back in the deck. "What do you want to know?"

"Where are you from?"

"Lived in Maine one winter, and the cold about did me in. I'm a creature of sun and sand."

"Not much of that in East Tennessee." He smiled. "Do you have a home base?"

"You saw my car. Dodge Dart. Slant-six engine."

He lay back on the carpeted floor, arms beneath his head, and stared at the sharks. "What's a woman with a name like Miracelle Loving doing here, now?"

"Let's talk about your future, not mine," I said as the sharks dove, nosed their glass.

"I told you that first night I'm not convinced where fortune-telling is concerned."

"Fortunes are a million years old, I'll have you know."

"What I know about my future I don't need cards for," he said. "I figure I'll work here till I've saved up enough."

"For what?"

"My own business."

"Doing?"

"Doing what I love." I could see the underside of his one arm and words tattooed there. They looked red and tender on their edges, like they'd just been drawn there. *We must believe.* "I'll call it Visionary Tattoos. Something like that."

"Knoxville doesn't lack on the tattoo places." I laughed. "But I reckon there's money to be made in faith?"

We were quiet for a little.

"Don't you ever just want," he said then, "I don't know, just to stay put?"

"Staying put sounds too much like a stuck door to me," I said.

He sighed. "What about love and somebody knowing you inside and out?"

45

"Love?" I shook my head. "Been there and back."

"Miracelle." He got up, shoved his hand in his pockets. "I guess you'll tell me about yourself when you're ready."

Days off from Willy's I hand-washed my underwear in the motel sink. Ordered pizza for breakfast. No matter what I did, I was antsy. *What would being happy look like?* Ruby asked me some long nights. If I was honest about it and looked myself straight on, I really had no idea. I got two cents' worth of happy out of brushing my hair, my teeth, and rolling lint from my clothes. On my days off, I cranked the motel windows open and lay there until nigh on eleven o'clock. I paced my room, paced downstairs to the lobby, paced to my car and back. Hell, I was pacing in my dreams. Dreams were the house of the soul, those self-help books said, but helping myself sounded like a family dinner and I'd never had many of those. Happiness? *Just look,* Ruby's voice said to me again and again. I'd tried looking, plenty.

Once I'd rented a slate-shingled shack out in the woods and stayed put until spring. Another time I cuddled beside the ocean and a woman with wild red hair whose bitten fingers were rough as she touched me and told me that this, more than anything I'd known, was what love felt like. Staying put, Cody Black had said. I'd tried that one north and south, east and west, and here I was trying it all over again.

I covered the beat-up motel dresser with a violet headscarf and set my decks of cards on a saucer. I bought plastic hangers and hung up all my shirts and dresses and tacked up a net shoe bag on the back of the closet door. I had two or three diner cups I'd snuck out of the place across from Willy's, packs of ramen noodles, and a plug-in kettle to boil them in. I even bought a tube of lipstick and dyed my hair, a new color they called Moonlight that came out a chalky-looking black. I lay awake at three in the morning and looked at the ceiling, listening to time pass on a wind-up clock from the dollar store. *Got a love spell for me now?* I whispered to Ruby in motel room dark, but by then she'd been quiet for days.

Cody began to wait for me at the end of work at Willy's and we went to this diner or that one for supper. After, we haunted downtown Knoxville, walked along the river and the shops that sold things neither of us could much afford. We parked across the street from the fancy-schmantzy apartment building that used to be an ordinary old bank. We parked ourselves at dives with walls painted like the sea, listened to poets with lip piercings. I trailed my fingers through the wet rings glasses left and told myself a fortune lay there inside the circles. *Taste the fire of now,* they sang. *Taste the fire of nothing at all.* We sat in a parking lot for two hours one night as a steady, soft rain fell and we listened to the local radio station play Kurt Cobain.

Cody asked me about myself again and again. About the jobs I'd had, the rooms I'd rented, the family that raised me. I told him about Ruby Loving, dispenser of love potions, teller of fortunes. I told him about the jobs I'd had and a lover or two. I told him next to nothing about my life, and nothing at all about the night Ruby died.

"And what about the rest of you, Miracelle?"

"What rest?" I punched him on the shoulder, pushed open the car door. "Take me dancing, Cody Black!"

We ran, our shirts soaked as rain set in. The Knoxville air felt almost like fall. By autumn, I could be standing in a doorway at night watching lightning bugs with a person I had yet to meet asking me to dance to music on a radio in the next new room I'd rent. I didn't want to think about that. Not yet.

Ruby and I danced plenty when I was a kid. She'd braid my wet hair to make me hippy curls and she wore her red lipstick while we danced to the radio. We played "Ramblin' Man" and danced slow. We turned up the Rolling Stones and danced until our T-shirts stuck to our backs. Love was in every song she liked most on the radio as we drove through one more town and stopped at another place where we'd set up shop. She made sure there was a new bulb in the lamp at the window and I tacked up the sign one more time. *Ruby Loving, Card Readings. Ten Dollars. Your Future Guaranteed.* She put up crystals in the windows and the bleached-out bones of birds on the sill, and word got around plenty. Cars passed by late at night, windows rolled down and bottles flying out, breaking on the road. My mother, a cross between a prophetess and a red-light wonder. "That Ruby Loving," they said behind my back in the halls at whatever school it was, that time. "*Ruby Loving, ten bucks a fortune, a trip around the world.*" Their words buzzed in my head, both wrong and right. Her love charms followed us, town to town.

Many the night I sat with her, her in a blue satin thrift store bathrobe.

We shared plates of leftover chicken and bread slices dipped in gravy and I shuffled her cards for her, an open bottle of red wine between us like we were friends, me the one who knew the end game was always the same.

"Pick a card for me," she'd say, her eyes all bright. "Just one."

If I drew something she wanted—the Lovers or the Magician—she'd say a rhyme in my ear to make me laugh. *Three silver spoons of brandy wine and you shall be mine, you shall be mine.* If I drew the Tower or the Crone, my mother was just what she was. Her hands wrapped themselves around her wine glass tight enough to break it, and conjured Tom or Fred or Rick. All of them who'd loved on her and none them loving enough, all the names filling up the room so fast it was a wonder I could breathe.

"Tell me, Miracelle," she said. "Tell me why he doesn't love me."

I'd dip polish out of the bottle, her fingers spread across the kitchen table so I could paint them and tell her all I knew, one more time. How pretty she was, beautiful as the blue glass bottles in our windows, the cobalt shadows dark made. Her hands and the fortunes she told, why, they were wise as wise could get. It was them who were the fools where love was concerned, not her.

One time it was a preacher. He wanted his fortune told as long as no one saw him there to ask. He'd put his soft palm against my forehead every time he stopped by to see Ruby. "God loves you, you know," he'd say, and I'd nod my head like I agreed.

Another place we lived was so cold we left the oven door open to keep the heat. A carpenter came to fix the window frames in that place. "Take me dancing," she said, and he sat with me while she went to do herself up, his rough fingers snagging in my hair.

Some nights Ruby was gone so long I'd give her up until there she'd be, bringing me a tiny present, a dime store surprise. A little box of Jean Naté cologne to rub on my wrists. A bright blue band that held my hair back so tight it hurt. In somebody's book, these were the things good mothers did. I know she believed that, but there were whole days lost. Her staring off down the street like she was waiting for a car to come that hadn't yet. I got her to tell me stories, those times. Stories and memories of a past I wasn't in to get us through the night.

"When I was little," she'd say, "they'd braid my hair and rub my cheeks with mullein."

And she'd tell about what they called Quaker rouge to make your cheeks blush. Or cucumber slices to bleach a face. Barley water for wrinkles. How to hold your lips when you smiled, how to lean in just enough when you read a fortune in the iris of an eye.

"I still want a wedding like they used to have."

"Like what?"

"A wedding and a shivaree," she said.

She poured me a little more wine in a metal cup and shuffled her cards while she told about it. A yard full of music and a bower made of petals. Fiddles tuned and liquor passed one to the next after the vows were said. Some of them would throw pebbles at the window glass, keep it up until a light came on and the man who'd wed was at the window, leaning out. Come down, they shouted, come down, and before you knew it, he did. And the dancing went on and they passed the jar again and the cars started up. You could just imagine it, her alone in the bed, waiting for him to hold her again.

But why, I asked later as Ruby turned back the sheets for the bed we shared most nights. It's what folks did, I reckon, she said. Her body was cool and damp from the bath she'd had. "Love," she said as I snuggled beside her. "Why, it's enough to make anyone shiver, on and on."

Her one hand lay across my chest and I held it.

"Tell me more about love," I'd ask.

She'd tell me, like she always did, about the highways I'd see, the lovers I'd know, the lands and foreign places I'd leave behind.

"But how come," I asked.

"Which how is that?"

"How come we're alone?" I had questions and questions she never answered about who my father was, where my people were, who made us, me and her both.

"They always say love is patient."

"Is it?" I asked.

Her lips were soft and bruised looking in the low light from the lamp still on in the kitchen.

When I looked at Cody Black as we sipped whiskey in a dive bar or stepped into the doorway of a diner for breakfast at the break of dawn, I saw in his face a kind of map of places I'd never seen yet, and I felt my chest tighten. *Love.* The world was full of it. A window display in Old Town Knoxville, where I walked late at night when I couldn't sleep. The window was hung with netting threaded with red heart sequins, and bald-headed manne- quins wrapped their slick mannequin arms around one another. Love was in the air, a sign promised. Love. The word made me feel such sadness I had to shake it off me like rain.

Falling in love. Falling was the world from a height so great no one had ever seen the like. Falling was a place from which any of us might nev- er make our way back. Falling was the memory of my mother's breathing, how it sounded almost like my own as I lay awake at the Red Sari those nights. Love was moonlight pouring into one more room. How I laid my head against my mother's shoulder and said, Ruby. *Tell me who we are.*

Ruby Loving
Radiance
1957–1958

6

World, Come Open

One of his last nights in Radiance, he sat beside Ruby on the motel bed and opened a road atlas to the state of New Mexico. He pointed to a town. *"There's where I'll become who I am."* The words were jagged and sharp, but she said nothing. *Willette.* A town in small print, it had no stars or boxes and was surrounded by a long, flat space of brown.

Two afternoons each week she met him at the Redbird, where they let rooms and never said a thing about who was who, though they knew everyone in a place so small. And who would not know her? Ruby the fiddle player's daughter, and more it seemed. The woman at the motel desk had narrow black eyes that said what she thought. "You the one that reads cards?" And Ruby allowed it was true. She told lives and unhappinesses and how things could be good. "Dark wonders that better belong to God," the woman said. She dropped the room key on the counter and turned away quick, her fear larger than any spell Ruby could ever have wrought.

The first time in that room, Ruby stood on the scatter rug just inside the door and couldn't think what might happen if her feet went further. The walls were tongue and groove, and she said that to herself. *Tongue and groove. Tongue and groove.* Her own tongue clung to the slick top of her mouth. How hot it was. It was summer that first time, and the room was damp, its concrete floor and a fan the only cool, but she shivered as he spoke to her.

"Come here," he said, but she stood another minute, looking.

The windows set high in the walls made the room like some cell for a saint or someone glad of their starving, and that was what she felt as she looked at him. *Hunger.* She wore loafers with coins in the toes and she kicked them off, stepped away from the scatter rug onto the bare floor. She unzipped her skirt, pulled the blouse over her head and felt her hair snag as she ripped it free. She felt how slight she was, though she could not have named where the slightness lay. Not slight in her body. Not even in her youngness, though she knew she was. Her fingers stroked the long muscles of his thighs, the pale flesh of his naked self, and he reached too. He took up her fingers and pulled them one by one through his lips, tasting her. Nothing lay between them but the sweat-slick of their own skin and how they fit against one another.

That was the dark wonder of those afternoons, how nothing else existed at all. Not the house she came from nor her cold-eyed mother, not his wife, not the thin cotton of the blankets he pulled over her, not the mountains beyond the room. Two hours were nothing, though she wanted them to be as large as more. She was the sum of everything he had known before her, and he was nothing of what she had ever dreamed of wanting.

She lay still and listened to the tick, tick of the clock beside their bed. Soon the weeks became months. Soon summer let go. By then she had taken the best of him and inside her was planted a life she had never dreamed.

The day he left, Ruby laid out her cards and drew the Tower. The earth catching fire. That was the way his hands had lain upon her body, like revelations from God. By then the earth itself was catching fire, burning away to slack. They could all hear it. Exploding sounds and the way, she later believed, the mountains cried.

The company-owned trailer at the end of Main Street had all its windows open, and tall spring grasses sprouted beside a crooked porch. They tossed things they'd never need right out into the yard, canning jars and milk crates, and under the porch a little dog hid itself, afraid.

The engine cranked and his truck pulled away, leaving everything changed. Her belly tipped and churned, though the child inside was nothing but a kernel, a child-to-be. She imagined a line from her belly to her future. The angle of the world had changed.

Winter came. At night, when Ruby dreamed, she dreamed a daughter's face, a bud unfolding in snow. Esther stood on the porch and Ruby watched her. How thin she'd become, sick again, lowering herself against the porch swing's cushions. You're carrying a child, her mother said, and looked at her belly so hard Ruby flinched. Don't you know, Esther said, a child will tear you open, now and then on from there?

World, Come Open

She wore sweatshirts and stretched-out sweaters and cut the waist-bands of her skirts to make them looser. She got up in the night and stood there, looking out at the empty road like she used to when her daddy was away making music. But now he stayed home. Sat out in the yard and played the fiddle and that sound. It was mournful. It held long and sad in the dark, and it settled at the middle of her and made her want.

Ruby could have married this one or that. The man who moved to Radiance and opened a store where they sold coal things. Candy statues like miners and their empty buckets. Could have laid herself down all over again in the wake of some passing others. Instead she dreamed girl babies not yet born. Dreamed one night of a woman standing in a doorway to a house she'd never seen, flashes of purple neon light splashed across some steps leading up. And all will be well, the woman said. But nothing was well or easy. She roiled with child, her navel a button to press for what was living inside.

Esther's guinea egg had grown back and was rising to the surface of her skin, pushing itself out with pus and blood. She laid her hands flat against Ruby's belly, held them there. If you tell such good fortunes, she said to Ruby, tell me mine. Ruby couldn't stand it, how her mother's hands felt cold as the winter earth.

The card she drew every time then. Six of swords. The women come together at a central point, carrying red roses of passion.

It's him, isn't it, her daddy said. That travelin' man who took the mountains away and you too. And now look at you. Just look.

And she did look. Did nothing but look back, trying to remember the least sign. As if a sign was needed since, after all, he had told her the truth. What he thought about love. Love, he said from the start, ties you down. Ties you to things. A house. A car. A one-eyed cat or a driveway with trees and why would anyone want that? A life that could just about make you forget being alive. Tell me about her, Ruby said. Your wife. And he said, hush.

As the child grew inside her, she wanted the flight of birds in a blue, blue sky. Wanted desire like honey on a spoon. Wanted water on the corner of a rag to chew, but that was later on. The child wanted too. Made her want the taste of clay or blood. Kicked so hard inside, Ruby woke up shouting a word she never remembered as hard as she tried. The word felt like flight. Felt like unweight. Felt like nothing at all.

On the day the baby was born, everything tasted of rust. The hours ticked by with gray sheets of rain, the window glass bowing in, out, each time she breathed. Esther was so thin by then she was a taut wire standing by the bed, and Ruby did not know which of them held up who. Her mother's hands pushed against her stomach and Ruby called upon the Lord. The Lord, Esther said between the knives of hurting, the Lord had nothing to do with it. And for this you loved, her daddy said. He peered in the doorway, his eyes like steel.

Her whole self tore open, and she saw herself reaching inside the tear. The world was a card that turned into an open palm. The world was a tower, a lightning bolt cutting through the cloth that is the heavens. The world smelled like blood, alive and red. The world became a revelation, a before and after. A dream of what had never been but might, and in that dream she reached across the far space of the room. She reached into the far space inside herself and felt other hands there, her daughter's hands, her child waiting to come alive.

Ruby dreamed about gods. A god of pomp and circumstance, a god of thrones and angels. But as time passed, the dreams shifted. God became a woman, not Mary, neither the mother of Jesus nor Mary Magdalene nor anything in between. In her dreams, God was a woman with hands that had worked hard, thin hands, strong and sure of themselves. As she gave birth, Ruby's hands became songs. Her fingers became slender strings stretching across some sky paler blue than heaven. She reached up and plucked the strings, and the sound was pure as it had never been before. Pure as slivers of glass. And thus Ruby was born on the same day as her own flesh was born. Mother bore daughter and daughter was born, both of them seeking the same roads out.

Her daughter was a way and a light all its own, and she named her after that. A name that sounded like miracles. *Miracelle.* The name was a way and means, and the child was so beautiful Ruby wanted to lick her clean, but she held her instead. Washed her in a kitchen pan. Remember this, Esther said. There are only so many ways to baptize in this world.

Then it was spring, and they took Miracelle to the Church of Jesus Christ of the Heavenly Mountains. How Ruby's heart ached when they lowered her daughter into the waters of faith. Above them, sheered-back hills held them all like sore, crucified palms. The god Esther loved was so big he seemed to cover the sky. Faith was consolation, her mother said that day, but Ruby wondered who was consoled, and how.

In town, Esther had made up stories that stilled rumors about Ruby and her daughter. Soldier husband dead, although there was no war. Husband working in Detroit and how he never came back again. At home there was the Bible, with underlined verses about good women, how they rose up at the break of day. At night her daddy sat on the porch and fiddled hymns about thorny crowns and glassy seas before they all went to sleep.

That fall, Esther fainted, the guinea egg full to bursting, her face white as a plate. Faith was miracles and deeds. It was giving in, giving way, lying down for it and saying nothing. It was the laying on of hands, but when Ruby stood by her bed with cool things, with rags and apple slices and her own cool fingers, Esther pushed her away. You and your hands, she said, see what they have wrought. And Ruby remembered like it was new again the day she was born. How Esther held her and imagined palms that had no lines at all. What to do with a child with no lifeline?

A scent rose in the rooms. The scent was of Esther's decay and, Ruby feared, her own. Praise the Lord for the miracles He has wrought, Esther said as she turned her face to the wall.

Praise was memory, of that much she was sure. That time she stood in the garden and put ripe tomatoes in baby's small hands. Or the time Miracelle's hair in sunlight had threads of gold. She remembered it, again and again. The way his mouth tasted of tobacco and all salty. The way he'd pulled the long threads of her fingers through his lips, savoring the taste of desire and naming it her. And this child that was his, was she not the reward of such praise? All those afternoons of want and want, and here was the celebration, the hymn of rejoicing. The face, looking up. The child, saying her first words. Too much time was passing, and how quick, how quick. The flame of desire, a red ember flaming down, and Ruby longed to catch it before it disappeared.

In town on the street a man said to her, "*No telling what a woman like you might do.*" Ruby allowed this was true.

What she did not say was that now when she thought of God, she thought of the power of her own hands. She laid her hands out flat and reached and reached. What would happen if her hands blossomed into pathways, ways out, highways she could follow to places she could now only imagine?

She began to think of the world that way, as a possibility. Go with me, little girl, she said as she reached to touch her daughter's hair, made her laugh. So she began to plan it. The dresses inside the suitcase. The tiny folds of socks and blankets and baby things. What to take and what to leave behind. Her tarot cards in a box in a drawer, left behind, a future she might come back to if she ever came home again.

Take after him and don't you ever come back, her daddy said.

The night before she left, she sat on the floor in the corner of the room and cried for it. The girl she had been. The self she had never been and still wanted. She saw herself beside him in the far reaches of those afternoons, how she had named it, the thing between them. *Love.* It was for that she would give up everything.

Miracelle Loving
Knoxville
1993

7

A Tattoo and Afterwards

It was Sunday night and I felt aimless so I fixed myself up like I knew where I was going—a fancy red dress I'd bought at a thrift store a few days back. It was almost dusk as I drove through Knoxville, down Broadway, then Ludlow, heading to Willy's, where I didn't see a soul anywhere. Sunday evenings were one of the few times the hubbub of renovations died down. I liked those times and often found myself headed over there, walking the quiet halls. Weeks had passed and Willy's was on its way to a grand opening, or so the sign taped to the outside of the main door said. My time here was almost over, and I wanted to memorize the oddities.

At the top of the steps leading from the big entryway a display case held giant luna moths, green and gray and gold ones pinned to a mounting tray. A taxidermied sloth and a huge bat, its wings spread and tacked to a cork board, completed a display dedicated to Exotica of the Farthest Reaches of Rainforests. I drifted past other cases filled with knives and bones, arrowheads and pottery bowls. Paraphernalia of Lost Tribes! I pushed aside a curtain to a room next to that one. I flipped the light switch, but the room was dark, black-painted shades drawn. I flipped another switch and a spooky recording played something that might have been wings swooping. "You have entered," a voice-over said, "an exact replica of a cavern deep under the earth. Are you ready?" I was not.

I passed through the Lost Tribes room into a narrow hallway that ended at a small room lit only by candles you could get by the dozen at any local bodega—St. Christopher, mighty angels. I walked the walls, touching things, first a large mural made of cross sections of trees. *Heartwood. The hardest part of the wood*, a sign read. There was an aquarium, too, filled with pale white frogs, their skin so transparent you could see their tiny hearts pumping blood.

The ceiling made this my favorite place. I sank onto the floor and lay back, staring at my reflection, hundreds of me in cutouts from tin, mirrors cut to the shape of hearts. I'd seen mirrored ceilings before in motels that also offered auto-massage beds and a bar with aphrodisiacs and cinnamon-tasting drinks, but nothing like this. Every square inch of this ceiling was covered with shiny hearts—and my image was everywhere, small, large, thin, my neck as long as Alice's in her Wonderland. *Hearts aplenty,* she said. It was Ruby, talking at me like she hadn't for a spell.

I raised my hand and waved as a dozen reflected hands waved back, all of them mine. I lay still, listening to the silence of the building. I tapped my fingers against the floorboards and made a radio song of it, a Tom Petty song I'd have played over and over driving on a highway as the wind cooled off a summer night. Then a long-gone song, a tiny square of memory music, gathered inside me. *Hold me, Radiance, honey. Hold me in the morning, hold me at night.* My heart beat fast as I remembered Ruby's hands trailing in the air, telling lives, conjuring lost love, letting love go one more time.

In the mirrors the lines beside my mouth were making their way down the center of my chest, furrows into my skin, waiting to open into some other me, these next years ahead. *Hell for leather.* Some lover or other had called me that, once upon a time, and I'd liked it, the way it sounded like biker boots and a Harley both. But what did strong mean, when you began to reach the other side of your own self with no hands to reach out for you on the rocky way down? Would I be raging or just sad as I packed my car the next time and headed east or maybe west, looking for my own horizon? *Love's been here and gone,* Ruby'd say. In the mirrors overhead, I looked pale and tired and I knew the truth. It was long gone, my heart.

"You don't look like you, Miracelle Loving." Cody Black stood in the doorway, a coil of electrical wire looped over his shoulder.

"Who do I look like?" I stood up and ran my fingers through my hair.

"Like a word left out of some sentence." His eyes traveled the length of my dress and back up.

"That's one way to describe me."

"What are you doing here by yourself, anyway?"

I shrugged, then suddenly felt light-headed as I remembered the hundreds of mirrored images of me. I took the can he held out to me and sipped Coca-Cola, pure and sweet.

"Let's get you some air."

I followed him downstairs, then outside to the gazebo where he and I often had lunch. From there you could see a little rise a couple streets over from Willy's, one with a billboard of an angel and Jesus. I leaned next to the good sweat scent of Cody, my head on his shoulder.

He reached inside his jacket and whipped out a paper bag. "Miracelle," he said as he unwrapped a cheese sandwich and tore off half for me. "What're we going to do with you?"

"I didn't know we were doing anything with me."

"What are you going to do with you, then? What'll you do after the museum is finished?" he asked.

"Find a new road out of Knoxville, I reckon. What about you?"

"Get a dog." He laughed. "Can't you see a big dog hanging out my car windows?"

"Pretty well."

"You got another plan than a highway?" he asked.

In the distance someone had set a boom box going with a spacey fusion of night-sounding guitar and drums.

"Before I get a plan," I said as I ate and swallowed the now-warm cola, "I'll have to ask the stars about it."

"I'm still not much on the fortune telling, Miracelle."

I took a chance, reached for his hand. His hands were blunt fingered, a boy's hands. But they were a man's, too, broad-veined and strong.

"Maybe I'll get one of these." I traced the inked petals of a tattoo on his wrist.

"I didn't think you were the tattoo kind."

I finished the last of the sandwich, then held my hand there still, against his arm. Ruby would have done that. She was there now, on the tips of my fingers that strayed up his, trailed along the soft hairs that rose from the lines and paths his tattoos made.

"Looking at you is like looking into a valley," he said. "Or a well, maybe. Someplace that has no end at all, but you want one, over and over."

"I just wanted—" I began, and then hushed.

"Wanted what?"

"A stopping point." There were other words inside my mouth but I wasn't sure how to say them. Instead I looked at his face, the boy-cheeks, the one little earring he had in the side of his nose. Boys. I'd loved some of those, and I liked it, usually, how I could love them from a spot that felt so way up high. Me, taller than them, older and wiser and here, there, gone when I liked, with Ruby's voice riding along beside me on some highway west, who knew how far. What would a stopping point look like?

Then I said the thing he least expected. "Where do you get a tattoo around here on a Sunday, Cody Black?"

We drove miles outside the city, then on from there, and I thought about Cody's tattoos. Some of them must have hurt good, the way country songs hurt when you were dancing with one lover and wanted another one you couldn't have. His new ones must have hurt even more, them fine edged and next to the bones of his hands and wrists, but if I had to guess, I'd have said he'd liked tattooing for just that—a pain he could name some nights when he couldn't sleep.

"You sure you want to do this, Miracelle?" He'd tried to convince me often enough to go with him, see the tattoo places he loved, and now he was trying just as hard somehow to persuade me to head over to some juke joint for a bluegrass band instead, but I was set.

"Do you have any idea why you want a tattoo?"

I'd thought about it many a time as I lay awake at the Red Sari, but I had no idea how to tell him about that. Always before I'd been like wind blowing in the open window of a car, I'd been like cigarette smoke blowing past as I traveled two-lanes that turned gravel. I wanted what Cody Black described, that moment when a needle traced a fine-cut line on your body. Surely a tattoo would fix me to the earth in a way I'd never been before.

"Might as well take you to a place you'll never forget," Cody said as we pulled over at what was once a Texaco station. Christmas lights were draped over the former gas pumps. A sign lit up with more lights read *Maura Swain's Herbary.* From a cage to the side of the building beagles bayed at us, their eyes red in the lights of the truck.

"This is the place?" I pictured the tattoo parlors Cody loved in Knoxville, their neon lights and lava lamps and juice bars.

"You really sure about this, Miracelle?" He held his arm out, underside up, and I saw a moon and a star hiding behind a cloud. "These last awhile."

I followed him out of the car. "Ink can be my rite of passage," I said, not liking how scared my voice sounded.

He knocked until a door was opened by a woman in foam curlers who must have been in her eighties.

"What you want this time of night?" She leaned out the doorway, peered close.

"Hey, Maura." He grabbed her hand and shook it.

"Cody Black. You were just here a week ago." She coughed into a bandana while she studied me.

"Brought you another customer."

She eyed my red dress. "A looker, too, I see."

"This is Miracelle. She says she likes your work."

Cody held out his arm again and we all stood looking at the moon and star while Maura told about the night he'd gotten that tattoo. There'd been rain all day and she needed the moonlight, then the star, one Cody could make a thousand wishes on.

She folded her hands across her chest. "You got an idea what you want, Miracelle?"

A white cat with one ear rubbed at her legs as I nodded. "I know it in my head, and I brought a thing or two to remind me."

"All right, then. This way," she said. "And you." She nodded at Cody. "And you fix Miracelle here the drink she'll need."

I went with her past the curtain into a narrow room with a long glass case full of sewing things. Big spools of thread. Yarns. Half-knit afghans. And on top of the case, enough needles and jars and colors of ink to tattoo half the country. I took a seat and she folded her arms again, looked at me.

"You got a picture in mind?" She smiled.

I fished around in my pocketbook and found what I'd brought. Ruby's tarot deck. "This." I drew off the top card. "And a photo."

She drew the edges of her housecoat together and sighed. "I got a whole slew of designs in there. And a bunch on that poster yonder, too." She shuffled to the other side of the room, picked up a yardstick, and pointed at some of the patterns on the poster. "What about a dream catcher? You look like you could use a few dreams."

"If I'm gonna do this thing," I said, "I've got to do it right."

I sat with the card and the photo in my lap, sketching on a pad of paper Maura gave me. I was no artist, but the card was easy enough. A woman walking past a mountain. Priestess of Wands. The photo was the hard thing. Though I knew my mother's face as well as any I'd ever seen or would, making the tarot woman into my mother was tricky. I wanted tattoo hands that reached out just as Ruby's hands had for me, time upon time when I was a girl. As I sketched, Cody came in, handed me the drink he'd made, and mouthed words: Was I sure? I tossed the drink down. It burned like whiskey could, and it tasted sweet, like honey and almonds, and it came clear to me. The tattoo I'd wanted all along.

"Sure hope I can please you," Maura said.

"What was in that drink, anyway?" I felt calm and sleepy.

"Just a few herbs," Cody said as he smoothed my hair, massaged the back of my neck.

"Herbs?" The word floated out of my mouth as the road I was drawing began to flex and straighten. It became ribbon-slick, asphalt in the rain. It became every road I'd traveled and all the ones I still wanted but could not imagine I'd find. The woman I drew started out as me, but then it became Ruby.

"You'll have to let down that pretty dress, honey," Maura said as she took the paper from me, her forehead wrinkling. "Pleasing you is going to be a task."

I unzipped, let the dress slide down to my waist as Cody handed me a sheet to drape over myself.

"Close your eyes. Think about relaxing." Cody's voice was warm in my ear as Maura dipped into jars, filled small shallow plates with ink.

My skin felt slick as oil, and the drink was a silk path I followed, feeling myself slide and ease along. My eyes closed, but not before I remembered a little road behind the woman on the card. Gray. I hadn't told her about the color gray I wanted for that, but it was too late. I was drowsing as the drill started up and Maura's voice soothed me. "Just you relax, now."

Other voices stirred in my head, some of them I knew. I heard Marvis Temple telling me what was in the new files she handed me at Willy's. The more odd, the better, honey, she said. Cody Black told me that tattoos rode an invisible line between pleasure and hurt. Then a voice I didn't know at all curled around me as I slept in my car at rest stops and under streetlamps in the parking lots of service stations shut down for the night. You'll be okay, girl, it said. In my tattoo sleep world, voices came and went, begging me to guess who they were. They became Ruby's voice. *Be careful,* she said, her laugh ice in a glass. *Be careful what you wish.* Her hands held me above the shallows of a river smelling summer hot. Maybe God will make the difference, she said as I was lowered into baptismal waters that had never saved me at all. Memory voices washed me further back to the shore of a past I didn't know. A torch singer on a record Ruby liked. *Love me, Radiance, honey, till long past daylight.* Blues at a raunchy bar at midnight where I was drunk and sad. A truck-stop voice. *Order up,* a waitress said, scratchy-throated with cigarettes and cheap whiskey, but that wasn't it, either. The voice belonged to a street-corner preacher I'd seen back in Bucktown, West Virginia. *Love ye the Lord.* Some other voice, another time. That voice inside me as I'd ridden waves of drugs and nothing down streets and alleys where music crashed, ridden it all high and mighty into towns where no one knew my name. It was every sad woman or man I had talked to on the phone at Willy's Wonderama, every voice trying to find out if their oddness was odd enough. And her voice, my mother's. *God help me, all I want is love.* Her voice, or mine, full of every time and place and longing I'd ever felt. All the voices followed the lines of a tattoo as it crossed and cut onto my shoulder, made a picture of a woman looking for home.

A few hours before dawn Cody Black and I were at my door at the Red Sari, not bothering to turn on the lights, not saying good night and goodbye like we had done before on other Knoxville nights. I invited him in for coffee and he shook his head at first.

"When I look at you, I see the places you want and can't reach." He tilted his head to the one side like he did.

"Cleveland, and Fairbanks and then some." I meant this to be funny, but all he did was trail his fingers across my face.

"Your eyes," he said. "They're the main part." He followed me inside, shut the door behind him.

"About two parts wore out?"

"I'm serious, Miracelle." He touched my hair this time, let one long strand of it wind around a finger and fall against my chest. "Sometimes when I look at you I kind of see myself."

"You don't know the first thing," I said, and I meant about me, but by then he tasted like smoke.

He was warm and steady as he backed me against the wall, his arms moving around me and my knee moving up. My legs looped around him and we held on to each other, balanced, waiting to see what we'd do and how, though I thought I knew everything about how it would be. Thought I knew it inside out, the dance from door to hall, from fall of a dress on a floor to the length of a bed. I'd thought being with Cody Black would be a movie I'd rehearsed again and again in a hundred other places, with lovers whose faces I could no longer recall.

I'd thought I knew everything, the scents and tastes, the first moment another body founds its way beside or into and then away from my own. I'd believed nothing could surprise me, but I had never rehearsed this, the way my hand would touch Cody's face, his chest, the warm stretch of his bare stomach. I thought I knew it like some script, the way we shed our clothes and forgot them. I knew nothing about the way I led him into the lukewarm waters of the Red Sari shower, how we washed each other clean of this night. His hands were gentle near the rawness of my new tattoo, and my hands were surprised by the surface of his skin. He was real and he was asking me to be real right along with him.

He lit a candle beside the bed, pulled back the blanket, smoothed the sheets while I wondered at how the boy he'd been was a ghost I could see so well in his man's face. I folded my arms against my chest, too aware of the young woman I was not.

"Let me see you, Miracelle." He pulled me to him and brushed my forehead with his tongue, laid his hands on either side of my face. As he touched each part of me, he named it. The crook of an elbow. A foot's arch. The back of a knee. He said I had the scent of gingko trees as he stared up at me from between my legs.

"Look at me," he said, but I closed my eyes and reached for him and let touch carry me. I went where I often did, to other rooms, other hands. Remembered wanting, more distant and safe. Towns east and west and south and north, places that weren't here, were more here than now. Cody's touch was fire on my skin and it warmed me, even if I held back, afraid of how easily I could crash and burn. I was with him and I was not, this lovely boy-man and his tattoos of the world, the spirit, the stars.'

Cody lined himself all along my back, his knees tucked in next to mine, his arm draped over my side. He rubbed a warm foot along my leg. "I wondered if we'd ever be this close." He lifted the hair from the back of my neck and blew cool air there. "Close enough to feel each other breathe."

There was a space between the words, just enough of one, and I knew he was waiting for me to fill that space in, but I didn't. I rolled away from him and got up, walked around the room, looking at my own things like it was the first time I'd seen them. I picked up the snow globe on the dresser next to the bed, shook it. "My mother told futures from a globe like this."

We watched glitter settle in the tiny street inside the globe.

"What fortune did she tell for you?"

"It's all one more rented room," I said. "That's what she would have said."

The long fluorescent lights from the hall hummed beneath the motel door, but morning wasn't too far off. I settled back on the bed, put my arms around him. "There's a lot you don't know," I said to him, but I wasn't ready to fill in any of the blanks.

I want to say that in that one night, that one occasion of touch, I opened myself once and for all, that it was a tale told fine and good, how Cody reached inside me and fixed what scared me as good as magic. I want to say that we soared like the backdrop of a sunset in an old, old movie. That we made love and made it right and then smoked cigarettes from a pack beside the bed, drank the last of the wine in a bottle, made coffee so strong it burned our throats. That we got up at dawn and got in the car and drove away together, following our hearts along all the highways and byways they could possibly take. I want to say that I trusted everything from that night forward.

What I did was lie awake a long while, listening to Cody breathing and talking a little, quiet, sleep words. *Here. Up there.* Dreams of moving shelves and boxes at Willy's, but I couldn't sleep. I lay and counted things in my head. Road signs. States. Towns. The boxes I'd packed often enough in the back seat of my car, them all laid along the seat and the floorboard, an open map beside me on the empty passenger's side. I counted the things that fortune-teller girl I'd called at Willy's said. Love, she'd said, was the only thing I didn't know how to do. There'd be no sleeping for me these hours.

As I wandered the room, I knew what I needed was a potion. I needed jasmine. I needed rose. Cinnamon. Saffron. Ruby used to steep all those, a tea for passion. Is that all that love lacked? Potions and charms. Spells against the world and its highways and byways and all the places I'd been and things I'd done that had never left me satisfied. I stood by the window, my hand on the bandage over the tattoo. It stung as I peeled back the tape.

All my life I'd seen map lines. Interstates heading west and east and back again. On my shoulder, the road Maura Swain had etched was clean and simple, unhealed lines leading ahead with a woman standing there, her arm held out. The woman's face was just a shadow, but it was Ruby and I knew her as well as I ever had. I touched the raw edges of the tattoo that made her part of me in this new way, made her part of me all over again. Suddenly I didn't know of what I was more afraid—roads out or all the roads leading inside.

8

Subterranean Worlds

The summer was winding itself down. I'd always liked that place between seasons, a time that had always before been about knowing
where I was and not knowing where I'd be next. Now the highways west
I'd imagined before coming to Knoxville made me think of spirals of dust
vanishing over a horizon. I tried not to name it, the ache I felt inside as
Willy's tall shelves filled up with bird skulls that claimed Outer Mongolia,
wooden flutes labeled Ecuador. We were only weeks away from being finished with the renovations. We ducked under ropes, stumbled on plastic
drop cloths and half-full cans of paint, all signs of final touches ahead.
Always before, I'd save little souvenirs of a place I'd been, reminders I
wouldn't throw away when I left. Menus and junk store price tags. Lately,
even peeled-off labels took up too much space.

I stayed late that Thursday afternoon reading up on towns with
names like Wind and Rain, Wyoming, and Silky Falls, Idaho. Marvis Temple had assigned me a Willy's display that had been begun some time back
but never completed—towns with reputation for their ghosts—and I'd
been doing my research. The town called Wind and Rain, so articles said,
had storms where the wind was like the forlorn cries of abandoned children, while in Silky Falls the entryway to a cave had been found behind
the town's namesake waterfall. In the cave were the bones of two women
missing for a dozen years, but investigators had been able to remove only
scraps of cloth and buttons from their clothing. *When we tried to gather
the bones*, the article read, *the air filled with intolerable weeping.*

There were some boxes down in the basement I might find of use,
Marvis had told me. "Plenty of leads about ghosts from Emissaries before you, if you find the right box." She'd given me a key to the basement's

padlock, but I hadn't been down yet. Basements in general had always had an aura of spiders and mold to me, let alone what the basement of Willy's might hold. But now, just as I finished the last of the articles I'd printed, I felt the itch and shiver in my ear I hadn't felt for a while. Ruby's voice.

Ghosts, she said. She seemed to be laughing. *I reckon ghosts are as good a place as any to begin.*

I bit my lip, put the articles in the file I'd started, and began to gather my things, but Ruby whispered again, louder this time.

Ghosts and things can leave a trail mighty curious if you'd just take a look.

I sighed and laid my hands over my ears. She was haint enough and plenty.

Ghost stories, she said. *Why, they're the least of it.*

So I found myself putting on my sweater and heading downstairs, past the shark tank, around two more corners, past towers of crates, past a bathroom with an open door and a sink on its side, its gutted pipes littering the tile. Just past that was a crooked panel in a wall with a padlock. "The lock's a little stiff," Marvis had told me, "but jiggle it, and the panel's easy enough and you're in."

My only flashlight was the one on my key ring, and I shone it down some steep wooden steps, letting my eyes adjust. It was damp as a vault with something unnamed buried in it, and already I could smell the creepiness. I made way my down and stood feeling the damp through the soles of my shoes as I aimed the little flashlight toward the ceiling, located a chain, and pulled it. What was likely a rat skittered off. The subterranean space took shape.

The one bulb lit a room piled to the nines. Narrow windows near the ceiling proved there was an outside, but it was late-day and a dusty light had draped itself over the boxes that were everywhere. My eyes adjusted more, and I made out stencils and stamps and scribbled codes. *Fragile. G33.* Sitting atop the boxes were some of the Willy's Wonderama oddities themselves. A dull-feathered bird with two heads, wired to the top of a box as tall as myself. A mangy cat as big as a Great Dane, the thin fur spotted with gray, naked areas of hide. There were plenty more things with extra legs, missing wings, and dozens more dated boxes. I was standing in the middle of leftover wonders, all the things that had survived Willy's fires. I lifted the top off a file box of photos. A black-and-white one of a hand with a large stone in its palm: *Moon Rock Found in Back Yard.* A girl with a long, thin neck and a smile so shy I wanted to cover her face: *Alice in Our Times.* Another photo of twins, their webbed fingers joined in a coffin large enough for two.

I made my way past shoulder-high stacks of books that looked like they'd seen floodwaters. One storeroom gave way to another, and I ducked through a round stone arch of a doorway into a yet another room smelling of pine straw. More skittering. A tiny, high-pitched animal sound. I trained my light on box atop box, these with inscriptions. *Moon Stones, Outer Reaches Beach, 1982. Facial Reconstruction Plates, Eastern Shore Tribal Centers.* The place was rife with ghosts. Behind the boxes the glass eyes of birds and foxes and things with no names watched me.

I felt around for a switch that spilled more weak light into the shadows. I thought I could hear faraway footsteps from overhead in the museum rooms as I breathed in, out, in. Silence. Boxes on a shelf with dates. 1899. 1872. 1839.

If you want to know who you are, you might just find a clue here you can use. Ruby's voice nearly licked my ear as I scanned box label after box label. *Flood Records, 1946. Stars and Planets, 1927. Secret Desert Military, 1901.* My eyes settled on one that read *Small-Town Ghosts: Towns N–T.* I pulled up a crate and took a seat, lifted the lid on that box.

You're heading in the right direction, she said as a scent of mothballs and flower petals flooded my nose.

I turned the beam of my key-ring flashlight on folders inside the box, those too labeled. The first one was *Nickelback, West Virginia.* An envelope containing photos of empty houses and a body of water. *Ghost town submerged,* the envelope read, *beneath lake made by power company.* Another photo was a shot of an elegant building's skeleton. On the back of that photo was a short, handwritten notation: *Apparition seen in early morning on the porch of this famous home.* Another envelope. *National Bank of Nickelback, 1938.* A photo of an open bank vault and the handwritten line *Ghosts of famous outlaws said to revisit Nickelback bank on the anniversary of shootout.* I sat reading folder after folder as the names of towns amazed me—Piquant, Tennessee; Quietude, Kentucky—and I felt the ghosts these towns named hovering near me as the light from the small basement windows deepened into evening.

You be patient, now. You're headed home, Miracelle. Ruby's voice was soft, and I had to strain to hear it. Home, she said? What home was that? The homes I'd had with my mother had been roadside motels. Juke joints. Apartments for rent by the week. And my idea of home was none too high and mighty. A few mementos set out and a thumb-tacked postcard or two. Home, I'd always told myself with what passed as hard-won knowledge on the fly, was where my heart was at any given minute. *You don't know what you're looking at yet, girl.* Ruby's voice was lonely as a fog on a river.

I picked through other folders piece by piece, town by town. Rose-bloom, Ohio. Smyte, Kentucky. There were photos of women in coveralls on the steps of a boardinghouse where an enormous woman had visions and laid on hands. And in Thurmond, West Virginia, were coal cars spewing soot and beside the tracks children so gaunt they could have been haints kneeling to gather slag.

I never had the words to give you, Miracelle, Ruby said as I looked through folder after folder. *You and me, we were haunted right enough. But I never knew how to tell you about the past.* Her voice grew small.

Then I came to an "R" folder, misfiled but labeled with the name of a town I kind of recognized, a name that warmed me in the damp basement air. *Radiance.* I traced my fingers over the letters and imagined spirits in a town with that name. Ghosts the size of fireflies or ones like the aftertaste of whiskey. The name was familiar, the more I thought about it. What had Maria Murdy said? *A town with a name like light.* As I rifled through the contents of the folder, Radiance had hauntings aplenty. There was an article from a book about a variety of Radiance ghosts. A shut-down five-and-dime where the ghost of a salesgirl was said to wander the aisle, winding up all the jewelry boxes. Foreclosed businesses haunted by their former owners. One photo showed some dead man with sunken cheeks and a note on its back read: *Wince Turner still visits his homeplace.*

Then, mid-folder, there was a stapled group of papers that I almost flipped past, thinking it was one more ghost story. *Right there,* Ruby said, her voice as excited as I could ever remember it.

On the front of the stapled papers was a blank sheet bearing a label with a tiny fiddle in its corner and what seemed to be a personal note. *Shaun,* it read, *for you and your love of songs and ghosts. A ballad.* Below that, in delicate handwriting, was a verse to the ballad called "Long Black Veil." *She walks these hills in a long black veil / She visits my grave when the night winds wail / Nobody know, nobody sees / Nobody knows but me.*

Above me in the museum more footsteps sounded, quick ones that died away as I flipped to the next piece of paper. That was a news clipping. *This is what we came down here for*, Ruby whispered. *Part of what you always wanted, girl.*

A town long known for its share of tales of hauntings and for old-time music, Radiance these days has more than it likes going on. Veins of coal mean someone is striking it rich, but landowners fear it's not them. "The wrong decision will haunt you the rest of your life," says local musician Leroy Loving. "Watch which dotted line you sign on, is my advice."

My heart skipped a beat. I read the clipping again, then again as I settled on the name. Leroy Loving. My mouth went dry as I said it aloud. Loving. My own last name. I held the clipping underneath my flashlight, reading the words backwards and forwards. Maybe he was a cousin, or maybe it was a coincidence, that name. But Ruby had told me more than once how it was. We come from a long line of tale-tellers and fiddlers, she said, but had never told me more.

There was one more item in the stapled group, another news clipping. This one was a photograph with a note taped to it in the same delicate handwriting. *Nary a ghost on this porch, Shaun. But there right ought to be.* The photo was taken at night, and its black and white was grainy as smoke. A man was seated on the steps of a porch, a fiddle tucked beneath his chin and his bow raised. The caption: *Kentucky Fiddler Makes the Music We Need.* Beyond him were a group of people. Two women dancing, photographed mid-spin. Children and a ridge-backed dog. An old woman, a washboard strapped to her middle. And behind all of them, nearly hidden, a face that stopped my breath. My mother. Ruby Loving. How young she was, her face full of hope and something else I couldn't name. Was it love? At the bottom edge of the clipping, one word. *Radiance.*

I stood so quick I was light-headed. The key-ring flashlight clattered near my feet, and its light went out as my head swam with names. Leroy Loving. Radiance. And my own mother, too. Was it this easy finding the father I'd never known? I studied the rest of the Radiance folder like it was the *World Book* encyclopedia. No further mention of Leroy or any other Loving. More ghosts in more towns than you could shake a stick at. Cards

75

with handwriting on them—charms to cast out spirits. Homemade remedies for those who had lost loved ones and now suffered from broken hearts.

What I had seen this night was real ghosts, that much was true. In late-night movies, ghosts floated out the open windows of beat-up motels. They were the thing scientists wrote about in their notebooks. Ectoplasm. Lost souls. Ghosts in those movies were a gray something or other drifting across spaces like this basement and, somewhere you couldn't see, chains rattled to see if you were listening. If ghosts were like in the movies, I could have thrown down my flashlight and run back up the stairs to Willy's and been back at the Red Sari quick enough to hit the road before daylight. This was no movie, and these ghosts were as real as it got. I had just seen proof my mother had a past, and him too. My father, fiddling his tunes like they were a spell holding sway over her and over me, my whole life long. These were the ghosts that had always haunted me. Mother. Father. The past I didn't know.

Ruby's voice had fingers now. It touched my cheeks, traced along my eyebrows and held still. *Everything you want is there if you know where to look.*

I turned my little flashlight on again and held my hand in its beam until I saw the barest red shape of my own bones, an x-ray of the past. I seemed to remember myself, little and waking from some dream. Was it Ruby who bent above me, telling me to sleep, sleep now? She brushed strands from my eyes, then a bedroom door shut. How dark the room was. Times long gone were in my heart now, and I could hardly breathe for the sadness of it.

Cody stayed with me that night. I made us frozen dinners in the microwave while he walked around the room, studying the postcards of deserts and mountains and lightning and the photograph of my car that I'd taped to the closet door. Where's this, he asked. I named the places I'd been for him like I never had before. Reno. Miami. Saudi Daisy, Tennessee. The names and names of times fell out of me, not like music exactly, but like—what did they call it?—a litany. I closed my eyes and listened to the hum of remembered bar light, the clink of coins in a jukebox, the clink of glasses making toasts to this time, that place, no place I'd ever been very long. And then I fell asleep, listening to the sound of Cody's heart and his breathing. Did I imagine it, him saying that to me before we drifted off? *You're safe now, Miracelle.*

In the night Ruby sang to me, that song from long ago, and as the words took shape, they made a song I knew. *Love me in the morning, love me at night. Love me, honey, till long past daylight.* The Ruby singing inside me was hoarse with cigarette smoke and whiskey. Her ghost-self cut decks of cards and told stories about lives not her own. Her feet danced inside my heart, slid sock-footed across one more barroom floor, across the floor of one more kitchen we never called our own. She stood by one more long-ago stove top, making the bittersweet of a love potion she never believed in. Love, girl, she'd said then. Why, you can't trust that old thing.

Old men in their wool jackets of a summertime. Married women in their brush rollers, their worried faces. All of them come to us to settle up their accounts, the tangled-up places inside their hearts that her fingers knew how to unravel. Ruby held her card deck balanced on her palm, offered it up like it was something holy, and they'd shuffle the three times, cut the deck and lay out the three cards. Past. Present. Future. She summoned them all. Summoning or conjuring, I was never sure which. Calling forth was the truth of it, and what she called could have been wind outside, or a storm not seen in weeks, it had that much power. She'd tell about messages from kin long gone, about missing this, long-lost that, deeds and records, photographs and street addresses, phone numbers and even the names of almost forgotten songs. But mostly what my mother told was about hearts. Hearts torn open by time, hearts forgotten and lost in a gnarl of memory, hearts hurt or changed, stolen or damaged. Hearts almost beyond saving, she'd say.

Which was real and which was only memory? Me, sitting in the yard, the rust and creak of a metal chair as I rocked and listened and watched their shadows pass back and forth on the other side of a curtain in that trailer's kitchen, then. The sound of boots out the back way and a motor revving, quick, and Ruby calling to me. *Miracelle. Miracelle.* My name from inside my mother's mouth. Her in my arms and her blood on my shirt. A red shape on her chest like the wings of a bird, a shape that would never wash out. Ruby's dying had a scent not hers, the scent of salt and blood, strange as snow in summer. Bits of torn paper surrounded her. Letters and halves of words. Rips and tears of paper from her notebook scattered beside her and edged with her blood. They never found the notebook when they searched the place later. Ever since, I'd been looking to fit the pieces together like they'd tell me my very own name.

When I was little, I'd search through drawers like I'd find my own self there. Drawers full of stockings and the silky feel of underwear. What did I think I'd really find? A photograph of some man, his face hidden by a hat's brim. Some man I'd imagined again and again and again. A man with a father's face I could never call my own. You can't trust love, she said. Love was a worn-out toothbrush someone left behind. An empty bottle you'd pitch out a car window as you drove alongside a steep, steep bank. Love was a page from a book, ripped out and torn into a million pieces and thrown away. Love was a no-name father, a man I wanted to know and did not want and wanted more than anything. What did it mean that Cody Black told me I was safe now as he drifted off to sleep? What did it mean to be safe in this world or that world, none of them ever entirely my own?

Toward morning, I thought of the things from my past I knew for sure. Strings of love beads, red and orange and green, hippie beads on a string hung from a rearview mirror. Love songs on the radio. *Help me, I think I'm falling, in love again. When I get that crazy feeling, I know I'm in trouble.* How we'd driven along highways and back roads, Ruby Loving and me. She'd stop and buy me syrupy drinks with ice, ones so sweet and cold they froze inside my nose. *Oh, you're too young,* she'd say. *Too young to think about love.* But I thought about it. Love was like fishnet stockings and skirts so short you had to pull them down again and again. Love was free. Love cost too much. Love was my mother, her face gone so sad, and I'd reach for her like I'd do this or this or this to make her better. *Wait,* she'd say. And I had. I'd waited forever and now here I was.

Here I was lying beside a boy so kind, a good, good man who saw right through me and might still like what he saw. Here I was, waking in one more motel room but readier than I'd been before to be still, hold on. Ready to give love a name and a face, ready to open my mouth and speak of love to Cody Black. Here I was half awake and half dreaming, remembering a love charm, one from all those years and years ago. *On a night of the full moon, whisper your beloved's name three times to the night wind.* Ruby Loving had conjured those words again and again, dropped them into the potions she made, hoping against hope for love, casting her spell, and it had worked, settled, made me who I was.

I sat up, rubbing my eyes, shaking the night out of my eyes. The bed beside me was empty. "Cody?" I said.

He came from the bathroom, his T-shirt and face damp from the shower, sat on the edge of the bed near me. "You slept some." He'd made us coffee in the pot beside the bathroom sink, and he settled beside me on the bed with the cups.

"Dreamed more than slept." The tip of my tongue burned from hot coffee. "I need to show you something, Cody," I said at last.

I went to the dresser drawer, the bottom one where I kept a few things I seldom looked at. I hardly noticed the reflection of my own naked self in the dresser mirror, though that was something I was shy about.

"There," I said as I took out a box, a small round metal one decorated with winter things. Fat little Santas, their noses red from the cold. A reindeer starting up from a snowbank, flying across the dark sky as I came back to the bed.

"Christmas in summer?" He leaned against the headboard of the bed and sipped his coffee.

As I pried the lid off the box, I felt the way my face was, the set of my mouth, the way my dreams had settled inside me. I scattered the torn pieces as if they were confetti, a celebration, but there was none.

He held a torn square up to his eyes. "What's this?"

The pieces were jagged puzzle pieces that had never fit, one against the other. Pieces of a map I had long not known how to read. Paper shreds with spatters of blood gone brown with time, gathered that night she was shot. I stirred the pieces on the bed beside him. Halves of sentences. Halves of words and letters. *A. By. If you only would.*

"What is all this?" he said again.

"I guess it's my mother, or what I have left of her."

"Your mother?" He set his cup on the nightstand, picked up more of the scraps, held them up to the light. "Sometimes it's hard to think you ever had a mother, Miracelle."

"Her name was Ruby."

"She would have a name the color of a heart."

I tucked my legs under the covers and we sat like that, the heap of paper tears between us. "She died when I was just fifteen," I said. "And she had hands that could tell a fine fortune."

He took hold of my own hand. "Hands like yours?"

"Let's just say they were fortune-teller hands more complicated than mine."

"How did she die?"

"I guess that depends," I said.

"Don't be so cryptic, Miracelle. Tell me."

"She died under mysterious circumstances."

Nobody said anything for a spell.

"All right," he said. "And what did you do after she died? You were a kid."

"You do what you have to, Cody."

"You do, at that. Who was this mother?"

"She taught me to read cards," I began.

"Cards are one thing, but who was she?"

The black hair. The long, fine fingers holding a glass of cheap red wine. "You know about as much as me." My voice felt small. "You want to know? She was shot."

His voice gentled. "Shot?"

"Killed and I held her while she died. I never knew who did it—all I saw were shadows and a pair of boots that might have been my father's."

He scooted next to me. "All these bits of writing." He sifted through the tears of paper. *Mountains. Eyes the color of sand. After he left.* "What are they?"

"My mother kept a notebook. And these pieces of paper are all that was left of it on the night she died."

"You were just fifteen. What did you do? Where did you go?"

"I did what you see me doing, Cody. What I've done ever since."

"And your father? Who was he in all this?"

"That I never knew." I went back to the drawer and reached in where I'd hidden it from myself at the bottom of the box. The clipping. I took it out and smoothed it against the blanket. "Until this. I found this in some research files in the basement at Willy's."

He took it from me and read it, let it lie on his lap, read it again. "Leroy Loving. You think it's him?"

I took the clipping up again, held it against my chest. I could almost feel it, the music on that porch, the way a fiddle's strings must have quivered beneath his fingers. But I shook my head, a silent yes, not sure I could say the words. *My father.* Maria Murdy had said as much that day on the phone. A town like light.

And then there's the bigger question, Miracelle."

"And what would that be?"

"Who are you?"

"I would have thought you'd know that by now."

He sorted through the torn paper like he was looking for what to say next. He held up a square to the lamplight. "You're like this," he said.

The bit of paper had one word on it, a word ghostly with years-old ink. *Radiance.* He laid it in my palm.

"All that light underneath your skin. Like you're full up to here, in love with someone or something you've never even met."

"I don't have the least notion what you mean, Cody Black," I said.

The paper word in my hand felt hot. Alive. *Radiance.* The word fit against the clipping from Willy's basement and I could nearly hear the sound of pieces falling where they ought to be. *Leroy Loving.* I studied the fiddle player's face in the clipping like I had known it all my life. Was it that easy, finding my father? My father, like a song from the past I couldn't quite recall.

"Don't love me, Cody Black," I said before I intended to say anything at all.

His eyes were startled, like I'd caught him being hurt before he forgot that I was looking. The soft down of his hair growing out. A tiny scar underneath his chin. How beautiful he was. A beautiful man who meant the best. And me? A woman without a clue about anything at all.

"I can't account for what I feel, Miracelle," he said. "I can't say why I feel what I do for you, and I don't even have a name for it yet." He sat raking through the paper scraps like they were something alive. "But I do know this. You aren't going to love another living soul until you find out who you are."

A car revved in the parking lot of the Red Sari, and I stood by the window watching the trail of smoke from its tailpipe. How easy it was to come to know things, to count on them. The bitter taste of motel coffee. The way a hand felt, held in my own.

"Don't love me, Cody Black," I said again.

It hurt to breathe as I said this, and I wondered what I meant. *Don't love me now? Don't love me yet?* I had no idea what he heard, or how, but somewhere day was starting up. In my hand, the one torn-away word. *Radiance.*

Ruby Loving
Willette
1958–1960

9

Thursday Afternoons

As far as she'd been was twenty miles the other side of Radiance with her daddy to see a man about a flattop blues guitar. Or that other time they rode to see the doctor in Morehead so they could take a picture of inside Esther's chest. Now the world was an x-ray.

The shadow-shape of cities. Lexington. Louisville. Columbia, Missouri. Cities passing like dreams she'd had and remembered in parts of themselves later on. The bones of tall buildings at night and oddnesses she did not know by day. Tulsa, the bus driver said. Home of the world's largest praying hands.

Mile by mile Ruby became someone she didn't know. Beside her, Miracelle was everything, hands so small Ruby could suckle them while they looked out the bus window at passing highway signs and heat rising from the asphalt. In a rest stop bathroom, she wet her hair in the sink and then stood in the parking lot, Miracelle's hands running through the cool strands. The world was blazing hot and she had no idea where she was going next and that was good. It was all there was.

All night in the bus seats behind her they spoke the language of birds. A big family with an old woman and a baby that cried more than Miracelle, and they had boxes and bags and baskets and picnic food that smelled of something hot. They were Vietnamese, a grandmother-looking woman with them said, and they talked to each other in singsong words Ruby didn't know but hummed into the late bus hours. When the grandmother saw Miracelle, she offered Ruby a pickled egg the color of beets.

How the body could fold itself into the bottom of a seat, head against an armrest, a jacket as a pillow, Miracelle next to her heart, holding them steady as the bus traveled into a late night of rain. Their bodies, resting, sleeping, awake, sleeping. Ruby carrying Miracelle into rest stops for vending machine coffee and Nabs. And all the while, Miracelle, a warmness against Ruby's belly.

A child-anchor in the moving world where sleep was deeper as it came and went. And all the while his voice in her head. He was where Ruby was going and where she'd been and all the life she'd left behind. Traveling west and west, she made up a story about him. Like this.

The way he rides up over a vista on a motorcycle in the dead heat of summer, he is a cowboy. The Marlboro Man, at the very least. How they stop at a little store for something cold to drink. She cranks the top off the bottle, hands it to him. He buys her Nabs and chocolate to eat. Look at it, he says. The desert and all those stars.

Miracelle is in a sling across her chest as she holds on tight and they ride down the highway, past cactus and scorpions and the trails of rattlesnakes. They stop for picnics of Vienna sausages and saltines. Sit atop boulders that look out over stretches of red sand and a shine he says is mica. He has a pistol in his hip pocket and he lines up bottles he teaches her to pick off, neat, from the back of a fence line. Miracelle laughs her baby laugh as they ride that fence for miles. Love. She says that word into the dusk as they stop, watching the sunset. There the movie fades to nothing.

She rubbed sweets along Miracelle's gums and sang half a lullaby she remembered from long before. *May angels keep you from harm as your daddy holds you, safe and warm.* Her heart was becoming so full there was no more room left, not a heartbeat's space. Like this they traveled mile upon mile. A hundred miles. A thousand. Traveled past the trails of lights of far towns. The names of all the states leading her away from Radiance, away from home. *Tennessee. Arkansas. Oklahoma. Texas.* She was miles and miles from herself now. Had traveled outside her own skin, the only skin she'd ever known, traveled toward and away from it, her own heart. Ruby shut her eyes and listened for it, the way her daddy's fiddle would sing them peaceful back at home, but still she traveled west with Miracelle crying and hungry. All she could think of was rust-colored earth.

Desert mirrored in clouds so neat they were cutouts in a blue like she'd never seen. Cactus so tall and the sharp needles of them. Not pretty, this red world that reached so far. Spires stretching up from the earth and she thought of mighty churches and the blue, blue sky of heaven. Oil, the bus driver said, and she thought of Mary washing Christ's feet with perfume. They were in the country of oil dredged from the ground at every turn. What looked like cities, a tangle of metal and steam, and across the sky a smudge of smoke that could have been the Armageddon from Esther's church. A land of smoke and fire and brimstone. Land of thirsty Revelation's creatures, tails like serpents and fire in their bellies waiting to be born.

That evening when they stopped, the air smacked her down with its weight of heat. She swayed between past and future, faint with the days of going and going and the hot sun that sent waves up from the pavement. She held on tight to Miracelle as the whole world spun. She tipped spoons of sink water into the baby's small mouth. How she had to believe in it, this long journey that took them there. To him and Willette, New Mexico.

He met her at the bus station with flowers and a bag of peppermints, a blue stuffed cat for the baby. He said, Ruby. He swept her up and swung her around so her shoes were off the bus station floor and he held Miracelle in the crook of his arm where she looked so small. But he was not glad. She could tell that much, though she had not told a fortune in months. He'd found her a place to live, and she'd find that work was easy enough to find, though all of it was just until. Until? she asked, but he hushed her with a kiss.

They went right away to the room he'd rented, one in a circle of other such rooms around a plot of grass. She took her shoes off so she could feel the good earth, but the grass was dry and sharp enough to cut. She reached down and took up a palm full of sand, let it trickle through her fingers. Inside he wet a washcloth and she sat on the edge of the bathtub while he washed her face and kissed her eyes, one and then the other.

Early mornings, plumes of smoke poured out from the nearby factory. If there was work here, she told herself, it could never be in one of those factories, places that lit up the skies so Ruby thought of hell. She sang to Miracelle as the baby cried, unsure of the walls they now called home. She sang rhymes and love songs. Torch songs and rock 'n' roll. She sang every song she knew as she bounced the baby along the lines of the yellow linoleum floors. *Hold me in the morning, hold me at night,* she sang. *Hold me,*

Radiance, honey, till long past sweet daylight. When he came, he brought them fresh orange juice and left Ruby twenty-dollar bills.

Mornings she took the baby to that woman who kept kids. Six of them, gathered around her feet like little birds with their hungry open mouths, toys and diapers across the floor. Miracelle looked afraid, but Ruby kissed her cheek and said, hush. She laid Miracelle in the woman's arms while she went out walking, walking. Making her way down sidewalks and filling out the paperwork for jobs as this, that. *Waitress. Maid. Checker at a liquor store.* She'd nod and answer their questions about what she'd done before. Sweeping up? She was good at that. Or counting down a register at night, not so much, but she could learn. She was a good learner, and she'd pick up quick on working the breakfast line, cooking eggs with a shake of oil and a flip, but she never got much farther than the application. They looked at her like she was swimming under water. We're full up, they said. Or, we're not hiring until next month, and maybe try back. But she knew she wouldn't. In the desert the tall wells pumped oil but she could feel it in her own self. Fear oozing from her palms as she filled out one more empty space. Her name. Her place of birth, a million miles from this place of dust and pavement that burned her feet. Like that she got to know the streets of Willette.

Some days she dropped Miracelle off and did nothing at all but go to a restaurant and order coffee with spoon after spoon of sugar. Or she went to one place that played old movies. *Casablanca. Dark Victory.* She loved the stars, their waves and pin curls, the way their men loved without question in the end. Often she stayed through all the showings, curled herself up in the seat and slept, deep and dreamless. There was no excuse for it. She couldn't seem to come awake at all, her body was so full of longing for the one long afternoon that was hers.

How he moved against her skin, light from the refineries sweeping like searchlights across the gray skies and across the bed. The sweat of them. His taste. The rich scent of after, when he'd hold her close and tell her about how things could be if only she was patient.

Don't you see, he said. A man could be anything he wanted in a world like Willette, New Mexico. He could live cheap and make his money fast. Start out at nothing, unloading trucks and emptying drums of chemical waste and then, who knew. In a few years, Civil Engineer or better than that. Save his dollars and head east. Big bucks in timber and coal back there, once you learned what was what. Once you became a man they'd listen to.

Ruby laughed when he told the name of the town where he wanted to settle. Smyte. Isn't that something the Lord does? she said. Taking an eye or striking you down for a no-good deed? He was serious. The desert was beautiful, how it reached for miles. Reached forever, really. But Smyte, he said. There was a river there, back east. Trees and coal and what-all.

Am I a plan too? she asked. She did not say love, though he knew what she meant and he danced his way around the word. He was a grace-ful dancer.

I love how we are. I love that red dress, how it makes me want you. I love what we have. I love what we could have been if.

She'd get up with the sun so she could work as a temp. Folding towels for a week or typing in numbers for pension plans and how many owed what. Once she weeded yards until the ground swayed and bent with the heat. Honey, a girl working beside her said. Her front tooth had a chip and she worried at the place with her tongue when she reached over and caught Ruby's arm. You look poorly, she said, and Ruby told her no. Well, she said, even so.

She was hungry and what she wanted was a miracle to fill her up. Winged horses out of the desert to pick her up in their mouths. All the desert's hidden oil, catching fire. She wanted all of it back again, before the bus ride and its miles and miles, before the sad fiddle sounds off their porch at night, before the egg in Esther's breast. Back and back and back to a time before she loved him or anyone ever, before love at all.

Three o'clock. Four o'clock of a Thursday, and when he left she couldn't help herself. She lay still, listening to nothing in particular. The sound of planes across the sky. Dozers fixing the pipes along the streets. It was six o'clock, seven, by the time she picked Miracelle up, though the woman who kept children warned Ruby again and again. Six o'clock was too late and she'd have to charge more, an extra twenty bucks, but Ruby lay on and on those afternoons once he'd gone. It wasn't his leaving exactly. She knew plenty about that. She'd left Radiance and those walls back home and their one sad picture above the bed of Jesus, in the garden, the night before he died. She felt like it was her own self who died those Thursdays afternoons, and that was how the time drifted on and on, as if she was herself some holy ghost rising and leaving her body, the body of a woman alone on a bed.

One afternoon there was a sign at the matinee place that said they were playing *Dark Victory*. She'd seen it again and again, loving how Bette Davis feels the sun but can't see it and flies down to die as the world goes dark. She was almost the only one there for the showing. A teenage couple in a back corner, their faces so close. An old woman with a grocery bag full of towels. And a man smelling of old clothes and a sad she could taste.

His thigh pressed against her leg and she should have said, Mister, and moved two rows ahead, but right then the picture started and she was so surprised. There wasn't a sign of Bette Davis and her pretty black eyes. It was a silent movie, and as near as she could tell it was a story about someone thrown out of a house, then walking the streets, then rescued and living in a boardinghouse with a woman with her wrists full of brace-lets and eyes so fierce they shone. A fortune teller.

Black scarves and a long string of beads. Her hands waving a warn-ing and pictures of black skies and war. And beside her a stranger, just an inch of touch, his movie seat and hers, his leg next to hers. Later she told herself it was then and there that she became who she really was, or at least then was when she took those words in and held them, turned them over and over on her tongue, tasting them for what they really were. *Fortune teller. Teller of lives.* As the stranger's hand moved from her arm down to her leg, stroked her thigh, she seemed to hear all the things in that stranger's heart, and what she saw frightened her.

She saw a door slamming shut. A woman calling out. Him saying he was never coming back. The next night and the next. A day becoming a year. The long dust of a street and then rain and night. Long afternoons of sun that burned. A hunger from inside out.

The stranger reached for her, touched just the sleeve of her dress at first, and she could smell him. He stank from his unwashed skin, but he also had a smell like leaves she remembered from a rainy night long before. She balanced between these scents, hardly breathing as his hand traveled down her leg, back up, inside her thigh. She shut her eyes and held her breath, willing all of it to go away. The world was made of dark gods, and this stranger beside her was one of them. Her lover was one of them, and he made and unmade her every Thursday afternoon, telling her about the beauty of her face, her hands. How beautiful she was, he said, and she floated above his naked body like she'd bring love alive. But that never happened. He owned it. He owned love and he parceled it out in his own good time.

She opened her eyes then as the film wound down. As strangers looked for the Gypsy fortune teller in the shadows of some street. "No," she said, and the stranger pulled his hand back quick as being stung. How pale and small he looked as the theater lights came on and she got up, ran outside into the hot, hot streets. Ran, wishing against wish. *A job. Magic. A spell. A potion.* Anything better than no-love in the dark.

What lives had she told before that moment? Surely not her own. She'd sat at a Radiance lunch counter flipping cards, promising things— names, possibilities, outcomes. What good had it done? What had she really foretold about the sound of her own wanting? *Ruby Loving, Fortune Teller.* Maybe the one true fortune was that the world was made of glass and it could break at any moment, her own breaking most of all.

Miracelle Loving
Towns along the Way
1993

10

My Own Sweet Girl

I'd told Cody not to love me, but I remembered his tattoos one by one as I drove east. On his upper arm, a spider's web. A spiral on his chest. On his leg, an eye of God. Those last weeks, Cody had begun to make sketches of other tattoos for me. His favorite was a heart with a thin knife opening it up to the air, a drawing that made me feel the beating in my own chest. My heart felt that beating now, a sad on and off and on. I'd left town with barely a notice for Willy's, left the Red Sari at sunset so I could follow the lights out of Knoxville.

And now here I was one more time, riding down my past. There'd been plenty of towns and more departures than I could name, but I'd followed the routine this time like it was written on my skin. The tin box and its scraps of paper. My dresses and shirts laid out flat in the bottom of a suitcase to keep down the wrinkles. My milk crates filled with bottles and little boxes and the book or two I didn't want to leave behind, beside me in my car's front seat. Snacks. Music. Road atlas. Before I rolled out of Knoxville, I tried to look up directions for a town called Radiance, but found little. Highways turned into two-lanes. Gravel roads trailed off into nothing on maps. I put the news clipping on my dashboard, a compass toward Radiance.

I took my time and more than my time. Stopped at historic markers. Sipped coffee at diners in little towns with names like Awe or Pelfry. I listened to the tales of strangers. A man whose wife had not come home for a week. A kid who'd hitchhiked two states away, just to see if he could. I lingered at the coffee pot and creamers in convenience stores and talked to no one in particular. A woman who'd spent her last five bucks on gas for the man who left her in a cloud of dust. The boy with big, dark eyes who looked at me like he might have known me, once. When I did drive, it was for an hour, two, loving the semis, the car lights. I made up a little song for myself as I drove. *I'm leaving, now, goodbye.* I rolled the window down and surfed the passing air. I tilted my head out like a little dog looking for the way home. My only direction was the sound my tires made on asphalt. I was heading toward a town called Radiance, and while I was eager, I felt a knot of fear in my gut. Father or none, someone was at the end of this trip, and so I took my sweet time.

I liked how some little place would appear out of nowhere. A sign for a truck stop. Some place with a jukebox at every table, one with lowdown redneck songs, maybe even that song Ruby used to play. *Hold me in the morning, hold me at night.* I wanted someone to hold me more than ever now. Someone to hold me, dive into me. Make me hurt. But not love. Not yet. Cody Black was right. Here I was all over again, driving toward something I didn't know.

I rode past smaller and smaller towns until signs for gas and lodging gave out and a marker promised *Historic Route, Mountains.* That road was lined by stone fences, then by mountains that grew steeper. The road gave out way before the atlas promised. There were still signs, but none pointing to directions. *Fresh Eggs. Jesus, One Way or No Way.* I'd seen all kinds of mountains, green ones near cliffs and the ocean up in Maine, ones with flat roads in between with buggies and the Amish, but these mountains tugged me along, pulled me deep into them until the gravel road got eaten up by dirt.

I pulled off at a wide spot near a woman in a headscarf, a bag of trash in a poke on her shoulder. "Place called Radiance?"

She cocked her head and came up to the rolled-down window. "Them up yonder might tell you where what is, but I don't know nothing about no road, lest it's near them Johnsons. They'd know if anybody knowed."

The dirt road led into a spread of evergreens until it narrowed to a wooden bridge I inched my car over. More signs. *Sweet Sorghum for Sale.* My tires skimmed dust and I thought of Cody, his hands loose on the steering wheel, the way his mouth and his throat and his chest took in the world. He'd have loved this world, my car the only one for miles until I met a long blue Camaro and another woman driving, two kids in the backseat, their faces pressed against the window. I slowed, rolled my window down again.

"You know where this road comes out or when?" Our cars barely made it past each other, my wheels sliding down into the steep ditch on one side of me, the blue sides of her car on the other.

"Ask at that store up there, they'll know what I don't."

It was late afternoon by then, and the mountains were soaking up the daylight. I'd have an hour or two at most before dusk and I still had no idea where I was, so I was glad for the country store where I pulled over at last. A big-handed man was running the register, and a trucker had just finished unloading crates of soft drinks. They were both leaning against the counter, listening to a wiry-haired woman in work boots talk, and they made room for me as I spread my maps, looking for the turns I'd missed, the way toward where I was headed.

In a room I took for the night at a motel called Timberlands, I opened the windows to air out the room's damp and I slept until a knock came on my door at about three. *"You took the desk pen, sweet pea."* I crawled deeper under a pile of pillows and blankets until they went away. I had taken the desk pen, and I huddled under the covers with it, scribbling in the empty pages at the back of the bedside Gideon Bible. I drew hands there. I drew faces and ghosts. Ghost hands and little box shapes that were the houses where we'd once lived. I drew ghost daddies, too, ones with blank faces and only circles for mouths and bubble shapes about their heads and in there I wrote what I wished a father had said to me, once upon a time. *You're my own sweet girl.* I took out the news clipping I'd found in the basement of Willy's and copied the long shape of the fiddle beside one of the ghost daddies I'd drawn. Which father would I have once picked as my own if I could have picked back then? Would I love the father I found, after all this time? Famous musician and, maybe, just maybe, the father I'd never known.

Just before dawn I made myself motel-room coffee and headed over to the office about six, wondering if the man behind the registration desk who smiled when I asked about Radiance was my middle-of-the-night pen seeker. He set about recommending back roads to get there.

"Let me think on it a minute," he said. He scratched his head, a balding mix of orange bristles and a variety of big moles. "The road passes something like Abbott's Creek." He shook his head. "No, that ain't right." He fiddled with a desk calendar. "Asa's Creek. That's the name. What you looking for up Radiance way?"

"Just some things to settle up." I filled another Styrofoam coffee cup.

"Radiance." He whistled through his teeth. "Used to be, on a Saturday night, wasn't a place to beat it. They had one of the best fiddle players up that way anyone could want anywhere, anyhow. And, oh, the dancing."

I stirred my coffee, trying to be calm. "Yeah, I heard there's some fiddle player up that way. Used to be pretty famous?"

"What was his name?" He tapped his forehead, trying to remember. "Leroy Something, if I remember it right."

I drank the coffee too fast, my tongue burning. "What's there now? In Radiance?"

He shrugged. "Still a dance now and again on a Saturday night, for one."

"Is that fiddle player still around?" My heart raced as I laid down two twenties for the room.

"Loving. That was his name." He winked at me. "You dance much, sweet pea?"

I handed him his desk pen so he could sketch me the way.

Asa's Creek wound up and around as the name played and rewound in my head. I drove past boulders like big, fat hands, one painted with a Bible verse, Ezekiel 7:12. *The time has come. The day draweth near.* On either side of the road a gully was strewn with cans and bottles and plastic bags and sturdy weeds. *Leroy Loving.* Would it be this easy to find him? I drove until the gravel became a ribbon of red-brown dirt. I parked and got out at a place that was like some end-of–the-world movie with nothing at all in it but bulldozers and gravel and heaps of dry sand.

It was already twilight, and dark gnawed at me, trying to make me afraid. I was tired and the night was warm, but I refused to listen to sounds from the dry leaves as I made my jacket into a pillow on the car seat. Outside the inch of rolled-down window was the traipsing of something or other through the woods below the rise. Words circled and echoed inside me. I remembered Maria Murdy, how she'd talked about fiddles. *Fiddle music playing so pretty.* This much was sure. It was too late to find my way back and around or sideways to another motel. I curled up across the car seat and listened to the late-day mountains until I fell asleep.

I woke sweating, Ruby's voice, as excited as it'd been. *You're there, girl.*

I got out of the car, rubbing my eyes awake as I walked a ways through the trees. My key-ring flashlight quit, and I ran full on into a rusted-out wheelbarrow near a heap of red dirt. I licked my hand and rubbed the banged-up place on my leg, then stared off into the dark. I cupped my hands and called into nothing as loud as I could. "Anybody around here?"

I picked up a short, thick branch at my feet and laid into the wheelbarrow, a clanging that echoed against nothing in the trees in the distance.

I varied the rhythm of taps and full-out assaults on metal. I imagined country songs. Blues. The rat-a-tat and wail of music I'd heard with Cody on the backstreets of Knoxville. I drummed songs I knew and ones I didn't and at last settled on my knees on the ground. *Hold me in the morning, hold me at night. Hold me, Radiance, honey, till long past daylight.* I imagined Leroy Loving fiddling until the wind in the trees hushed.

Dawn arrived like light through the bottom of a canning jar. Fog showed me just enough of a road, and I followed it to a town not a half mile from where I'd spent the long night. The town was a stretch of buildings along an empty street with partitions and signs everywhere for New Town Construction and You-Haul-It. There were heavy plastic bags and shovels and groups of two and three men with hard hats standing around some pickup trucks.

"Where'd you come from, sister?" one of them asked as I pulled over and rolled my window down.

"Back there," I said. "Asa's Creek, I think?"

He laughed. "Ain't been no such a place for right smart number of years, sis. Ten or twelve, anyway. That's a logging road and a coal road too you come in on."

"And what place is that?" I gestured toward the street.

He whistled softly. "You are lost, girl. That's Radiance."

I took in boarded-up buildings and a large billboard sign with an angel on it. Open Hands Church, Service Every Day. Sundays, All Day.

He eyed streaks of mud down the side of my car. "Dodge Darts'll get you one way and back the other, I reckon."

"Radiance, you say?"

He leaned in and took a look at my dashboard. "More'n two hundred thousand miles on this thing." He folded his arms like he approved.

Just ahead of us was a large tin-colored building with a rented marquee sign out front. *Festival. End O'Summertime Fun.*

"Could've come at a worse time."

"What time's that?"

"Radiance's still got one claim to fame. Music. You like music?"

"I do."

"Well, that's good. Music's about all around here's got."

I took a deep breath, remembering my dreams of the night before. *A fiddle playing so pretty.* I was in Radiance and all I knew was who I wanted to come next. My father. Leroy Loving.

11

The Radiance Midnighters

By late that day the sky above Radiance was a sunless gray-blue as I sat looking at store windows full of mannequins in dresses ten years out of style. I wandered, not sure what I would find or do, waiting for some sign. I filled myself up with Nabs from a machine beside a one-pump Mobil station, then walked the main street up and back without seeing a hint of a motel. A brick house with a caved-in roof promised rooms for rent on a sign hanging by a steel thread, a grocery store advertised dog bones and Bunny Bread, and past that a little boy with ripped sneakers was kicking an empty can, a rattle-rhythm against gravel and heaved-up concrete. I came again to the door of the warehouse-looking place I'd seen earlier. Couples held hands there, waiting at a sign that promised end-of-summertime fun.

I stood listening to a cowboy song as boots and dancing sounds floated out the open doors and landed right at my feet. Behind the song was a scratchy guitar strum and drumsticks stroking down.

"You want you a ticket?" A woman with a brown-gummed smile held up a tin can for my money.

Inside I stopped at a table with a coffee pot and bought a cup. A gymnasium floor was waxed to a glossy wood shine, bleachers laid out all along the far back. Against one side a table was set up with speakers big enough to come right out of a sixties dance, and they sent out shimmy-and-shake sound. On a stage an all-cowboy band was setting up a keyboard, a big bass, a set of drums. They wore matching ten-gallon hats and blue fringed shirts.

"The Radiance Midnighters," a woman in boots said, like she was introducing them. She knocked a cigarette pack against her wrist and pulled one out, patted her pocket for a light.

A few ladies in crinoline skirts and cheerleader jackets stood along the opposite wall, waiting for their dance partners. One of them was by herself in the middle of the floor, her leather boots scuffing time.

"Not much of a crowd."

"Usually starts that way," she said. "But I hear they might bring on a guest tonight."

"Who'd that be?" I took the cigarette she offered, twisted its end.

"Used to be, honey, you said the name Loving and the air in the room started dancing."

My heart skipped its beat, held steady. "That so?"

"Wasn't a finer fiddler to be found."

"You mean Leroy Loving?" The name came small out of my throat and I breathed deep, wanting to ask her all she knew, but by then big folding tables and cast-iron kettles were being hauled into the gym and she hurried over to lend a hand. Scents rose, smoke and fatback frying.

Onstage the cowboys were tuning up, the whine of strings sounding as pegs were jacked up a notch or two. Metal sticks scratched against the skin of a drum, fingers felt for a pulse, notes as close to right as they could get out into the air. "Nothing sounds sweeter than the sound of somebody tuning up to God's own key," said a woman with a bag and a ball of bright green yarn as I took a chair next to her. Then a hush. Someone up there pushed his hat back, wiped his brow, straightened a lean tie. A finger tapped against a microphone and then hands clapped and feet stamped and there was shouting.

"Welcome them back, ladies and gents! The Radiance Midnighters!"

A bent-over old man in a brand-new denim jacket with a bandana tied around his head grabbed my hand.

"Just let me do the leading," he said, but I waved him away.

"I don't dance much, mister," I said. "I'm more of a looker that way."

He shrugged and took the hand of a blonde-headed teenager with pale pink lipstick. They launched into some dance between a two-step and a waltz and swept away toward the stage. Up there, the cowboy hats were shiny with age, the felt worn to a gloss.

An elbow poked me in the ribs. It was the Timberlands motel guy, scooted up so close to me I could smell his hair oil. "Here you go." He passed me a jar, and I sipped as yodels led into rockabilly.

A farmer with overalls with a patch that said *Betty* took the jar from me. "What's your name, little miss?"

"Miracelle," I said. "Miracelle Loving."

"Loving?" he said. "Loving's a fiddle player if ever there was one."

"What you know about that fiddler?" I began, but he was up and gone.

I stood with the crowd, songs mixing inside us, ones about lost lovers and sick babies and moons behind stars. Notes collided with the soft catch in the voice of a woman in spiky heeled boots who joined the cowboys for a round or two. The crowd cheered. The room tilted and righted with sipping, dancing, yodels, light from ropes of leftover blue and green and red Christmas lights at the back of the stage. Names at the back of my mouth burned fierce as the moonshine. Ruby. Cody Black. *Love.* That word circled and settled and stood up again in the middle of my chest. My head circled and hummed with the crowd on the dance floor, its crinoline skirts and overalls, its work boots and pretty Chinese slippers.

"Happen to know a guy named Loving?" I asked no one in particular, but the no-tooth woman who'd been the ticket seller had stopped beside me.

"I know about every soul around here."

I went with it, dancing with her to the next tune. Patsy Cline, this time. I held on to her damp hands as the room whirled its skirts and dance shoes.

Then the stage went dark for a couple of minutes and the music we'd been hearing cranked down to the sound of chords slamming against chords and the crash of somebody into the drum stand, then voices. "I told you he'd drag ass up there again, and now look."

The no-tooth woman was holding on to my shoulder as she pointed at the stage and whispered in my ear. "Loving? That's him."

A heavyset man with snow-white hair was seated, a fiddle across his lap. The stage went dark except for a lamp sitting behind his ladder-back chair. A low-watt spotlight on a strong-jawed face.

"Leroy Loving," the no-tooth woman said again, but her voice was drowned out in a mix of applause and throat clearings and chuckles.

The band was doing a quiet tune-up, fixing all that was off kilter. A drummer trailed his sticks, testing the waters while another cowboy bowed and did the introductions. "Onetime greatest fiddle player these mountains has known, ladies and misters," he said. "Radiance's own."

The old man's fingers looped around the fiddle's neck, his bow raised and another song began, this one so gentle it made me think of wind settling in a field below quiet stars. Behind him, song words. Sounds from one short draw, bow to strings. The refrain again. He raised the fiddle to the crook of his arm, his body quiet with the notes his bow sent out, the song a fierce wanting I'd felt all my life.

The tips of his fingers found this string, not that one, and a note shimmied and jumped. A shrillness hurt my ears and shame settled on his face as he lost his way in the song and couldn't turn back, but I held still and followed where I thought he might have gone. If this was my father, the one I'd wanted all my life, where had he been? Here in these streets, their storefront windows broken and empty? When he fiddled a tune about loneliness, did he follow it down? Was I somewhere inside him at the end of a long road he tried to fill up with music? The stage stayed dark except for his face, its crags and hollows, and I held still, looking for myself.

The crowd tittered, then outright laughter was here and there. "Used to be the finest fiddler there was," the no-tooth woman said as she handed me the liquor jar and I drank, deeper than I meant. "Just some sad old man now," she said, but I didn't believe her. Ruby's voice was in my ear, soft as I'd ever heard it. *Go slow, girl.* He began to play again, and I listened like I was hearing about some home I'd never known so long and long ago.

12

Fiddling in the Dark

An hour or two later, Main Street led out of the dark and I drove until Radiance vanished into eaten-away mountains and night and stars. In my passenger seat was Leroy Loving. "Somebody needs to haul his ass home," someone said as the last song played, and I said I'd be the one. I scalded my tongue on the coffee someone brought me and then someone else tucked the both of us into my car.

"You with us enough to give me some directions, mister?" I asked.

He was scooted as far away from me in the seat as he could get. "Plenty in there to get me home, without you."

"I thought I might as well be the one." I pushed in the cigarette lighter.

"If I was a younger man," he went on, "I'd think you was following a rock star home." He laughed.

"Didn't seem like you were enjoying yourself enough up there for rock starring."

"I reckon you're right on that one." He drew little x's and o's in the breath he blew on the window. He pointed east. "That way," he said. "When you're of a mind."

We rode past the lit upstairs windows of a house, past shut-down stores. *For Rent. New Location, Highway 50 North.* The town by night shifted shapes. Atop the one red light and climbing along the wires on each side of it, thick vines, and the stalks of tall weeds between the cracks along an unrepaired road. And again, at the edges of town, like I'd seen at the construction area, thin-throated, abandoned machines, squat and mean looking.

We passed heaps of coal. Trash dumped at the edge of the road. Cast-offs from autos, fenders and ripped-out seats, flung down into the shallows of a nearly dried-up creek bed. A plastic bag flew by, a haint traveling skyward. I drove blind through shadows and the white of peeling birches, ghost shapes that marked the tree line. I turned a sharp right when he said, through a stand of trees where there almost didn't seem to be a road.

"How long you lived where we're headed?" I asked him.

He reached over to the dashboard and flipped on the radio, found static, clicked it off again. "I guess you'll have to come in for some coffee."

It was a statement, not an invite, as he set himself to humming some rise-and-fall song way deep in his throat.

For years I'd imagined a childhood home, and this was it, a bare-floored room, one room of three in a tiny house in the middle of nowhere. He shoved his fiddle case under the iron bed in one corner. There was a woodstove in the center, and a couple of rail-back chairs along one wall. I took one of those while he fumbled with matches, lit a kerosene lamp.

"One thing I like about this place," he said as he fished around in a box from under the bed. "Dark of a night and light of a day and not much in between."

There were scratchy fingers of light along the walls. I could see him in here by himself, old man hidden with twilight.

"Sleeping tonic?" He'd found a bottle, was unscrewing its top.

"Thought you were making coffee."

He sank onto the bed, and its metal springs gave. "Coffee'll wait." He pulled off his boots, dropped them one by one on the bare floor. He lay back, the bottle perched on his chest.

"I have the feeling you want to know something about me," he said.

I felt his eyes studying me, and I studied him in the lamplight. My sentences wouldn't finish themselves. "You live here by yourself?" I asked at last.

"They're mighty quiet if someone else's here." He blew down the neck of his bottle.

"You always lived alone?"

"You sure ask a lot of questions." He sipped.

"That's why I found this place." I looked full at him.

"What was that?"

"I found Radiance and you because I want to find some answers."

"Had any luck?"

"I'm not sure yet." I laid my hands palm up in my lap, traced the lines there. "You ever have any children, mister?"

He stared down at his feet at the end of the bed. "Do I know you or something?"

"Daughters, maybe?"

He shook his head. "You got one question too many after a night of music."

I got up, followed a trail of light across the floor. My footsteps echoed as I circled his room.

He watched me. "Well, maybe I want to know a thing or two myself."

"Ask away." I stopped a few paces from the bed.

"You always driving home strange fellers in the middle of the night?"

"One or two." I crouched on my heels and saw black cases poking out from under the bed.

"You look like somebody," he said then.

I touched a guitar case, then one small enough for a harmonica. "I am somebody, mister."

"You got a name?"

"Miracelle," I said.

He reached over, set the bottle on the floor. "That's a name I haven't heard in an age." His voice was soft.

"You play them things there?" I asked at last. "Or do you just get up in front of folks and act like you might?"

"We already covered that territory."

"Play something for me," I said. "Something for nighttime."

"I'm played out."

"Nobody's ever played plumb out."

"I'm about there," he said, and then he said again, "Miracelle. That's your name?" His hands rose and fell atop his chest.

"Yes, mister," I said. "Miracelle Loving."

The room was quiet and the flame from the lamp sputtered, faded.

After I told him my name, he shut down good. He began snoring lightly as I eased open a chest at the foot of the bed, found a wool blanket. Outside, the wind had risen, and I could hear rain hitting against the side of the house. I wrapped myself in the blanket and stood over the bed and looked down at him, remembering a song. *This old man, he played two, he played knickknack on my shoe.* An old man sleeping.

I'd imagined fathers aplenty. Father sounds. Tobacco spit into a can or maybe a knife shaving cedar. A fancier father than that, one with pointy shoes and a skinny tie to dance me around the floor. Or a kind man, a father folding my clothes fresh off the line, hiding a twenty-dollar bill in a pocket to feed me come hunger, come need. *You there*, he'd have said to me, *you stay safe now*, time and again, father-standing-on-a-porch calling out to me as I rode away.

Nothing is as it seems, Miracelle. I knew that, but Ruby spoke to me as I watched him sleep. White hair and pale scalp so tender, whiskers yellow at the edges of his mouth. Rain fell hard.

How did the house of a childhood you'd never known sound in the dark? Scratching of tiny claws inside a wall and the small ticking of a clock. I knew the sounds I wanted, sounds that had taken me miles and years to this house. Hands made a sound as they brushed your hair, touched your face. Whose hands? Ruby's, soft as cream. Cody Black's, calluses on his palms along my belly. Other hands, far, far back. *Rest now.* A grandmother, once? Memory showed me hands touching the leather cover of a Bible, touching the surface of water that would wash me clean. Oh, how I had wanted it. The sounds family made. *You get on home now.* Sometimes I remembered voices from a house calling me home before suppertime. Or quarrel words. A mother and father and their words striking sparks on the other side of a wall at night. I'd wanted even that. What would a father have said to me as I drove down one more highway and slept for a night in some strange dark? *Girl, get on home.* I took out more blankets, made a spot for myself, curled up in it like a critter finding its way back to a hearth.

I hadn't been asleep an hour when the sounds called out to me. Words about sweetness rose up from the center of the room, circled the high ceiling. Riffs high up and low. Music. The whisper-scratch sound of horsehair drawn against strings, and underneath that, words that pulled me up from sleep. *Come awake, little darlin', come awake and hear the rain.* Against those words, the rise and fall of chords, the gentle saw of bow and fiddle, the tap of a boot against a floor. His voice was gut-deep and hurting, real as earth and bitter too. Bow and fiddle, strings and rosin, a sound beyond ears and mouth, a sound that winged and circled, a holy bird, a ghost over the floor where I'd slept. Wings fanned my face, and I wanted the scent of roses, the taste of tears held back in my throat. Bittersweet sounds traveled across my eyes, found their way to the center of my chest. Beyond radio or love songs, beyond honky-tonk or blues. Music. Dreamed or not, an old man played to me as I slept. He played Song of Solomon and hymns, Holy Ghost and emptiness. I drank the music in as if I'd been thirsty my whole life long.

Come morning, I woke to him by that little woodstove. *My father.* I turned that phrase over in my mouth, swallowed it as I watched him lighting matches against damp sticks and wadded-up paper. I shook myself awake and went over there, handed him my lighter, and we knelt by the little pile of kindling he'd made. He lit and blew and lit until a flame took hold. The house was cool after the night, and the fire burned clean. We waited for water to boil and the way morning light began to feel its way in.

"I won't ask how you slept."

"Fits and starts."

"I played you a tune or two," he said. "Played like you asked."

He set a plate of crackers on a beat-up Formica table. A new jar of grape jelly and a spoon. He looked shy of the things he owned, but we scooted next to the stove as the sun came up.

"Thought I was dreaming those songs." I offered him a cigarette from my pack, and he lit one for each of us. "Thought I dreamed the rain too."

We smoked and the stove knocked and hissed. The day out was cooler than the days before, a low-lying cover of mist from the rain. He'd left the front door open, and locust and tree frog sounds drifted in.

"I like a song like a dream." He set cups for us down and two spoons. Instant coffee and a dish of sugar. "And dreams like stories."

We sat like that for a time. "I dreamed a story," I said.

"I know you did, girl."

"How's that?"

"I heard her name in your sleep."

Her name was on the table between us, a question that wasn't one. We waited to see who would speak first.

"I heard you saying her name again and again, like you were answering her and she wasn't holding still long enough to hear you."

I looked at the torn linoleum under the table. A dog, its coat dotted with rain and beggar's-lice, made its way in the door. He started to shoo it, but I reached out and laid my hand on the wet fur of its head.

"I thought to wake you." He fetched the pan from the stove and poured water into our cups. "But you looked peaceful."

The dog laid itself at my feet, and I stirred the coffee, sipped, liking the sweet and bitter.

"I never was much of one for singing a child to sleep." His voice was morning-rough, sad. "For gentling anybody with a song or holding them to make things right."

I looked at him then, and he didn't look away.

"I always wanted to gentle her." He looked at his lap.

"Did you?"

He laughed. "There was a time."

"And then?"

He took his flask out, poured a capful or two into his own coffee. "And then she wasn't having any of it. Me or her."

A thin beam of sunlight broke through the trees in front of his house, stretched itself across the floor, settled on my bare feet.

"You look like her, you know," he said. He reached over, took one of my hands.

"A daughter ought to favor a mother." I still couldn't say it, not quite. Her name.

I felt the tug and pull of worry, of long days, in my gut. How do you ask someone who they are and why, or who and why you are, your own self?

"Daughters ought to favor their daddies, too." I looked straight at him. "Do you think I look like you?"

His hand tightened on mine. "What do you mean, girl?"

"I mean," I said, "I've come a long way and here you are."

His eyes were the deepest brown, almost black. They were her eyes, too.

"Just who do you think I am, Miracelle?"

13

The First, Last Place

He drove this time, all the while telling me about how they'd gutted the land. *Them with their maps and saws and chains,* he said. Backhoes and bulldozers and heavy trucks. I held on to a thermos of coffee as we drove past coal scattered from the mouths of nowhere. We took left turns and rights past the steeples of little churches and signs that prayed for kin. A wild-eyed dog came charging out from behind a hill of debris beside a house.

I was as turned inside out as a shirt. We'd spent the morning talking, but I still couldn't understand. Everything I had believed in for about a minute was nothing at all, and everything I had wanted to know sat in my mouth tasting of dust. He was my grandfather, not my father, and that was a truth. And my father? Leroy Loving had paced by the little woodstove, saying my father's real name to me like it was a sour taste. *Russell Wallen.* I couldn't yet bring myself to say the name aloud.

We drove quiet, the windows down and the before-noon air hurrying in. Neither of us had yet said her name, but he took the news clipping from the dash.

"I'd want to see the home place, if I was you. Or such as it is," he said at last.

We detoured at a tangle of trees, then parked.

"Anyone live out here now?

"Nothing but the bones of what used to be," he said. "And broke things."

Out of the car we took a way through the woods he knew, over vines and stumps leveled with the ground and hidden by leaves. Here and there, slivers of china. A toothless comb. I wanted to stop and gather things, but he hurried me along.

The trees thinned and then there was nothing at all. A scrape and tear of naked land.

In the middle of a wide, bare field there was a tree, a burly one that wouldn't have given itself up to emptiness if it had to. And on the other side of that, tucked back behind a pile of limbs, was the house.

"That's where everyone lived?" I didn't give names to us back then, neither Ruby's name nor my own, but we were there as he and I stood beside a spilled-over trash can and a fuel tank next to some steps.

The house had nigh about been a chicken coop, he said, but it was where he and my grandmother lived after they'd sold the land. After my grandmother died, he'd sold this place too so he could be closer to town. But the past was out here, and he claimed what was left.

Boards leaning up into the main door sagged with his weight. He held out a hand to help me up. "You coming or what?"

I climbed behind him through a flimsy screen in a tacked-together wooden frame. Inside was musty, dark, and he lit a cigarette and then a kerosene lamp after that. I fidgeted with the thermos and cups I was holding and took stock of what there was. Straw-colored linoleum, particle board cabinets. Boxes and stacks of paperbacks, newspapers and torn-out pages from magazines, a postcard advertising real estate in the Florida Everglades. I looked for a place to set my pack down. There wasn't a chair, or a clear space of counter, anywhere. And over top of the debris, an odor like cats.

"It's all that's left of what used to be." He moved two heavy boxes and made a seat for us.

At first, after the place was sold, he snuck back out here with a jar of liquor and a deck of cards and spent an afternoon. Then he stayed a night or two. Then he hauled in boxes of clutter he'd meant to get rid of, books and papers, clothes and cups with no handles and photographs and what not. He stayed here a week here and there, and once a whole month when it was summer and warm and there was almost no difference between sleeping out on the gnarled-up land that was no longer his and inside, with everything he couldn't stand to throw away.

A ratty blanket covered a stretch of windows across the side of the room opposite the doorway, and he held it aside like what we could see out those windows was a movie screen and, out there, everything and nothing.

Up that way, he said as he pointed, there used to be a little rise. And a path his father used to take every morning before sunrise to get to his job for the railroad, the L&N, five miles there and back, on past Radiance. And the other way, down some and across. His own father used to live there, but that place was long since gone. Loggers, first, he said, then mineral rights.

Somewhere in there he said my father's name again, and then he talked about the house and the land like they were a box made of paper, one you could fold and unfold, make smaller and smaller. The world sold for coin, he said. And the house on the land, and the land like it meant nothing at all. And the well. He pointed and I looked where he said that'd been, and on from there, a pasture where the mule used to be and a milk cow and always too many spring onions. And over there, his little mother buried a cigar box they never found later, with papers she took out of the house, deeds and maps and in there her own birth certificate and a signature for her parents' marriage. It was a mystery where that box went, and he wondered later if that had been a sign from God.

He told me stories of his daughter. When she was a girl she'd sit with him while he fiddled tunes, and she'd make him stop to listen to the call of owls.

"Ruby loved this one hymn more'n anything." He hummed a line of a song about traveling and a world of sorrow.

All the evening before, we'd danced around her name. He'd not looked at me when I tried to tell him about things she'd loved. The sound of wind chimes. Music off a radio she'd dance with me to, around and around. I meant to tell him about how we'd been happy enough, but neither of us seemed to know which words to pick for telling about before.

We were sitting now at a table piled with tools and plates and bottles, and I went to the window again, pulled the blanket back. The outside was brighter, a shape of sun from behind the rainy sky.

"I need to tell you about that night," I said.

"What night?" He was a few steps behind me.

How I held her as she died, I thought.

"What night," he said again. He laid his hand on my shoulder, and I shrugged him off like it hurt.

"She was shot," I said at last, and I told him what I knew. The sound of boots on the back steps. The way I'd run inside to her.

"And she passed like that?" His voice was so old-man sad I wanted to comfort him, but I didn't know how, and I suddenly felt as angry with him as I was with my own self. We stood at the window watching dusk settle, with the clutter of everything behind us. The shape of boxes. A dime-store picture of Jesus on a wall.

He scuffed his boot toe in the dirt and told me it wasn't safe to be out here by myself of a night. Who knew what might come out the woods, he said, but I told him I wanted to be here on my own, with the ghosts of what was. He'd be back for me by good daylight, he said at last. And there was another kerosene lamp he found for me, and the two flashlights he handed me before he drove away.

I stood looking at gashes and ruts, rocks and spots where boulders lodged. And in between those places, if I narrowed my eyes, I saw lines of earth like lines on a palm. My heart reached out for that earth-hand like I could study the past. Swirls and twists of roots, and fissures where nothing had grown back. Desolation, but the earth told lives. Faces took shape in the shadows dirt made. That face might have been the grandmother I'd never known. And over there. That flat stretch of stones. The tree or two left standing. The land looked like faces if I squinted my eyes just right. Leroy Loving's. My mother's face. *Ruby.* Her name lodged in my throat.

I had no idea what I'd find, but I looked for it. I opened kitchen drawers, pried a warm beer loose from a plastic-ringed six pack on the fridge's top shelf, sipped. I poked into cabinets and shelves, then nooks and crannies, finally the hideaway spaces beneath a bed, behind a broke-spring couch. I found papers galore, old warranties on radios and hair dryers, postcards with scrawled signatures. *Having a good old time here, sugar pie! Whooeee!!* There were ripped-out pages from magazines. Carole Lombard. Elizabeth Taylor and one of her million lover boys. Fifties movie stars with open-toed shoes and nets drawn across their smooth-bunned hair. Way back on top of the stove, folded into the shape of a sailor's hat, were pages from a magazine. A ripped-out page was part of a story that I read as I sat on the floor with a flashlight. *We wandered through streets and streets, past houses that smelled crisply of ginger. We turned and turned, through so many alleyways I could never have found my way home. And at last she led me through a doorway made of amber-colored beads.*

The First, Last Place

I opened cardboard boxes. Rooted through piles of this and that. I even bowed open the jackets of record albums I found leaning against one wall. Frank Sinatra and *Some Enchanted Evening.* Guy Lombardo and *Sounds of the Big Bands.* What I wanted but couldn't find were pictures of her. Ones back in the day, before I was born.

 I dug through a tool kit from underneath the kitchen sink. Found baby-food jars full of rusty screws and nails. Coffee tins full of snips of wire. A small metal box full of bullets, three of which I pocketed, just in case. I found an old fiddle case full of empty motel-room-size whiskey bottles underneath a wild-animal-smelling mattress and bed frame in the back room. In that same room was a closet, its sliding door off its track so that I had to finagle until the door tilted out and I could yank it aside. The closet was near empty but for a mouse trap baited with a dried-up slice of cheese. I climbed up on a milk crate to have a look on the closet shelf.

The box was cumbersome, but I lugged it down and sat on the edge of the bed beside it. On top in a scrawl I figured was Leroy Loving's, two words. *Her Things.* Her things were tossed in without rhyme or reason. A bunch of beaded bracelets held together with twine. A toy harmonica. A sheet from a diner with the daily specials. *Ham and red-eye gravy with green beans.* Underneath it all a red velvet box covered in cobwebs. I shook it, hearing what I imagined were dime-store earrings and lipsticks, Ruby-things I knew the way I knew my very own hands. As I eased the lid open, what I saw first were rose petals. Beneath them, a box of tarot cards, a woman in a robe with foxes and gryphons on the front. Beneath the deck, a pair of glossy black-and-white photos.

A tiny child stood by a tree in some yard. I turned the photo over and back, craving more. I suddenly remembered a mulberry tree. There was the one by the trailer where we'd lived when she was shot, but this one was farther back in my memory than that. Its long, seedy fruits were blackish purple and sweet. *Don't you eat them things,* some voice said inside me as I looked at the picture. *Mulberries are food for the birds.* The voice was older than Ruby's, my grandmother's maybe. I remembered hands folding the dough for biscuits, hands holding a just-washed glass up to the clear sunlight from a window. .

The other photograph made my heart do a lurch. It was Ruby, but a Ruby I'd never seen. Instead of my fortune-telling mother, this was nothing but a girl, her black hair combed and a flip of bangs across a forehead.

115

Underneath the photos, a paper tablet with a cover made of thin planes of wood decorated with glitter, the shapes of moons and stars and planets, and the cut-out faces of movie stars. Ava Gardner. Marilyn Monroe. A half sheet was glued to the front of the tablet and on it was big, clumsy handwriting. A girl's script, the near-hearts of o's and the tails of y's. Underlines beneath words she'd meant the most. *Ruby Loving. Her Property.* I remembered what my mother looked like, her jotting down spells and potions in her notebook, but this was a girl's diary, her dreams. It was full of drawings of cats made of circles and lines, drawings of big, fat moons and in between, her loopy handwriting, telling about her days.

Near the bottom of the box, beat-up pages from an old atlas. I spread them across my lap and looked at the interstate lines going west, which is where all the map pages led. The empty spaces of New Mexico. The single town leading to single town, and there in the flat nothing of it, my mother's handwriting. A circle and a heart drawn around the name of that town. *Willette.* And last of all, a couple of letters tied up with a red ribbon.

I sat with the letters and the velvet box in my lap a long while, then unfolded one more thing, a single sheet of notebook paper. Four lines only. *Come back to me,* she said. *My heart has gone out and is wandering the earth in search of you. Were you ever here, Russell Wallen? Were you some ghost-man I wanted to be real?* My fingertip circled the loops and lines of the name, the shadowy red lipstick kiss. His name.

14

Night, and Then

Outside now I shivered against the night sounds, an owl or some other critter calling out. Owls and whip-poor-wills were about the only bird names I knew. I spoke other names aloud to fend off the dark. States and their capitals. Kinds of coal. *Anthracite. Bituminous.* Slack, the coal Ruby said they'd picked up beside the road to get them through a winter. Or types of clouds—*cumulus, cirrus*—and I thought of Ruby standing and pointing at the afternoon sky. *No two clouds are alike, Miracelle,* she'd say. Above me, a full moon. So many names for the moon, too. Old man face in the sky. Rabbit, rabbit, first of every month. A sliver of moon like an earring hanging from Ruby's ear.

I raised my head to the dark of the late summer sky and screamed, loud enough my throat went raw. *Ruby Loving? Ruby? Are you here now?* No tickle in my hair, no voice in my ear. I was Ruby-empty. I took a long drink of the warm, ditch-water-tasting beer, then asked myself what I'd do next.

I reached into my pack for a cigarette and instead felt the muzzle of her gun. A lady's derringer, she'd call it, then laugh at herself, a lady and from an old western movie. I took the gun out, laid it in the lap my crossed knees made. The barrel gleamed in the moonlight. *Seashell, sea-dream, sea-once.* I could hear her, counting the ways she loved the derringer for its abalone. She'd sit with me when I was little and let me rub my hands over it like it was an Aladdin's lamp, its promises as wide as the horizon, and she'd tell me some story about a fisherman and a flounder and three wishes. What had I wished for, then? I remembered little about wishing. I remembered road signs and towns with names like Leota, Harmony, Bliss, names that could have been women, all of them hoping for as much as

Ruby had hoped, once upon a time. And for what? What had either of us hoped for, my mother and me, that had ever come true?

I felt in my pocket and took them out, the three bullets I'd pocketed in the house, and counted myself lucky they slid as easy as oil into the chambers. It was meant to be, I thought, and I spun the loaded cylinder, clicked it back in, and aimed. I aimed at nothing. I aimed at the shadows of tree branches. I aimed at what might have been tiny bats circling toward the wisps of clouds. I aimed at the moon itself, like I could explode the albumen-white of it, its moist white eye. It was almost funny, how I'd travel now with a loaded gun, but I fired it only now and only once. The shot rang in my ears, breaking the night's stillness. I didn't fire again, though it felt incomplete not to. Nothing could ever make the sound of the night my mother died. That shot rang out and boots from some man I never saw thudded out a door and I held my mother in my arms as she died.

I must have slept, because I dreamed, first of hands. Cody Black's and the tattoos on his fingers. Ruby's fortune-telling hands, and later, when she bled out in my arms, her palms as see-through as melting wax. Hands held other hands in my sleep. A shadow man's hands atop Ruby's. A father's laid atop a mother's, mine in the mix. Hand over hand over hand. A game of it for me, a little child. Hands changing to shapes on a wall. Birds and horses. Hands held out to me, their palms full of more lines than human hands should have. Then later, in between sleep and memory, I dreamed her voice. *Miracelle,* Ruby said. *Here.* She pointed to one long line across my palm's center. *Here and here.* The line broke, traveled down my wrist, across my arm, became a seam. Like that I unstitched myself and dreamed myself floating out.

I floated over this earth, before it was a flat dry place of nothing. It was a mountain, then. A dream of a mountain, dark green and ripe. I was that mountain, dark green and alive. I was that dreamed mountain when the world blew apart. Layer upon layer of mountain exploding until nothing was left but a blank earth. And beneath that, a black hole, an opening heading down. In that hole beneath the earth, there were men. All the men I had desired. All the men who had wanted me and not wanted me, all their faces one dreamed face, one dreamed hand pointing toward earth's heart, coal-black and hard, that heart, wanting and wanting. And the man she loved was there, too. The one man she wanted. That man, my father. How he must have swaggered with it, his right to walk up to a door at night. His knock, and her opening herself again and again. *That,* my mother said in my dream, *is what is at the center of everything. Wanting.* And now here I was, wanting him too.

At dawn the next morning, Leroy Loving waited as I took odds and ends—a tiny china cup I found in a drawer, a box the size of a child's fist. I took Ruby's tarot cards and the map page of New Mexico. I took her girl-diary. I took out the two letters from the velvet box, both addressed to Russell Wallen in Smyte, Kentucky. Souvenirs or proof, both.

My grandfather rode me back to his place just as the sun rose, thin and hidden by an overcast and now rainy sky. The day ahead would be muggy, but I rolled the car windows down and leaned into it, liking the way it made me come awake. We pulled over at the same edge of the road where I'd parked two nights back, and I stepped out into the Joe Pye weeds. We crossed the yard where we'd leaned into one another that first night. His house, its porch almost hidden by crates and boxes and bales of wire and straw. A yard dotted with castoffs. A boot and jars and bald-looking tires. His rangy dog sniffing.

"I got the kettle going and a pan of taters and bacon." He looked tired, his cheeks new-shaved, two cuts plastered with dabs of toilet paper.

I was hungry, but I told him no. I made up a story about Knoxville, a job I needed to get on back to. His eyes, red and hung-over looking, knew the truth of it. I would not stay in Radiance. No staying for a month or a week or even one more long morning, even if his chin had a tremble in it with the asking.

My mouth tasted of sleep and anger, and I said it to hurt. "She was family, Leroy Loving. Why didn't you help her?"

He dug the toe of his boot into the roadside gravel. "I reckon we all had a part in what happened."

A car drove past, its muffler scraping the asphalt.

"She was your daughter." I barely whispered.

"I've known that every day and night for the last hundred years."

He leaned in as if he'd hug me, but I would not.

"You'll go looking for him." It wasn't a question. He fumbled in his pockets, came up with nothing.

"I don't know what I'll do." My voice was hard and I knew it. I tried to soften myself, looked at the soft patches of skin showing through his white hair.

He looked at me. "If you do go."

"If I do?"

"There's things you ought to know."

"You reckon?"

He flinched. "Last I heard anything about Russell Wallen, he was set up good."

I rubbed my thumb and finger against the envelopes in my pocket. "In Smyte?"

He nodded, not questioning how I knew the name. "Last I heard, he owns some paper mill over that way."

I cranked my engine and watched a trail of fumes vanish behind me. He vanished too, grew smaller and smaller. Leroy Loving, grown small as a comma in a sentence, then gone into nothing as I drove fast past the heaps of coal, the houses with windows lit for dawn, past the sign I hadn't seen, before. *Radiance. Population 62.*

I wanted to disappear, leave the town and him, but memories always left a taste with me, like drinking too much and loving the wrong person the night before did, and now it was her memories in my belly, her regrets. What had I looked like to her, the first time she held me? Was she afraid of me, or had she merely wondered how much I'd interfere with loving him? I remembered the thrift-store paperweight she used to have, how I'd hold it next to my heart like it had answers, but I never got a thing back from it but glass-cold. World made of glass, full of her secrets and his. Who he was? Russell Wallen. I didn't want a thing from him, and I wanted everything.

I wanted Knoxville back, my room at the Red Sari. I wanted Cody Black, but I didn't. I wanted Miami or Cleveland or Fort Knox. I wanted cities I'd seen and ones I hadn't, ones I made up with my own name. Lovingville. Wallentown. I wanted a new name altogether, truth be told, but nothing felt right. Jane or Alice or Felicia. Or a name you couldn't make up your mind about. Sam or Charlie or Jessie. I could bleach my hair, cut it short, shave it close to the bone. What I wanted was nothing to do with anything I'd ever been, and everything to do with who I wasn't yet.

The only way I could see was forward, but not as who I was. That would never do. Loving was a name some knew. Fiddle players, fortune tellers. I'd have to let go of Miracelle Loving. If I was going to Smyte, to find my father, I'd have to go on the sly. I'd have to lie low, pretending. And I'd been good at that, most of my life. Pretend this, that, no-account fortunes, love when it wasn't. This time, I'd sit back and watch. Watch my father until I figured out who he was.

That was far from what my gut wanted. I wanted crash and burn. I wanted the car radio as high as it could go. I wanted the road to narrow into nothing. I reached in my pocket for a cigarette, felt the paper of those two envelopes. Love letters from the past. My hand burned as if I had touched fire, her ghost, hot and restless. *How do you remember me, Miracelle Loving?* Her voice was as strong as it had ever been inside my head, her memory a knife edge of pain inside my chest, and already I loved my father the very same way. Russell Wallen and her, the both of them like something inside me so sharp it cut my breath in two, cut my life into before and now, and I was smack dab in between.

"Okay, then," I said aloud. "Who will it be?" Names played on my lips. Joselle Smith. Waydean Long. I could steal a name, become Maria Murdy and pretend I was a prophetess. But before that, I had to say goodbye to who I'd always been. I drove faster, rolled the window down and hung my head out and yelled it as loud as I could. "Miracelle Loving!" I felt my name arc in the wind and slam back against the windshield, breaking into pieces as I drove on.

I took hairpin turns as fast as I could and shouted it out the window again. "Miracelle Loving, goodbye!"

I drove until the car slid off the road and I righted it, then braked to a halt in the gravel, my hands shaking. I was at a wide spot beside a road that felt like it had never seen another living soul. The day was still, not a trace of wind. I could be anyone else, as lovingless as they came. If I tried hard enough, I could even be a woman with a father.

Russell Wallen
Wellsprings
1957

15

Flights above the Earth

The first time he saw her he was in the diner and hungry. He'd been hungry ever since he set foot in that little town, the one called Radiance. It was summer, and hot, and the blue of the sky never changed, not a cloud to cover them as they took down trees and drug logs and piled them neat. They were land clearers, and that was that, but he wanted more and he knew it. He'd get his own rig, one of the boys said, but Russell wanted more than that. Wanted his own men to boss, his own company at the very least. He'd been looking at maps of out West, the possibilities for copper and the richest veins of uranium they'd ever seen. He'd looked at photos of the factories in Willette, New Mexico. Foreman, at least. That was part of what left him hungry, the next and next and next of all his plans. *And a man shall have dominion over the earth.* He woke hearing those words and he knew it was his daddy talking, after all this time. Memories made him hungry for all he still didn't want to be, all that he'd left.

When he saw her at the counter lunch place in Radiance he was not surprised, and yet he was. Her blue-black hair hung on either side of her face as she leaned in to cards spread on the table in the corner, her studying them so hard that when she did look up and meet his eyes, he almost jumped out of his skin.

When he made his way toward the booth where she was, he left his body, looking at her as she pushed her hair aside so that he saw the full of her beautiful face. No other word for it than beautiful, but it was her hands that he remembered later. Slender hands shuffling the odd cards spread in front of her, the pictures of fire and towers. Hands like wind and all things thin and fast. He just stood, wondering where he was for a little, lost somewhere between the door open onto the hot sun of the street outside and the red-and-steel of the counter. He tipped his hat to her. He didn't know what else to do, because he was lost already. Picked up and set back down inside a dream he'd long wanted to unremember.

He'd had that dream most of his life—details of it rearranged, gone—but he would never forget the first time he dreamed it. He'd grown up in a little Georgia town called Oceanus where he'd loved fighting, pocketknives, and playing in the swampy alley behind their house. A factory dumped old tires and chemicals there, and they settled on the water like green light so that at ten years old he told himself he'd seen the power of heaven. But in the dream he had later on, he wasn't in some factory-made Georgia swamp. He was in a place where the land was hard, dry. Red dust swirled up in the distance where there was a house and a woman sitting on the stoop with a cup of coffee. He tried to call out to the woman, but his mouth would not make any words. He knelt, picked up a fistful of the dry earth, tried to hold on to it as the dream changed and he was picked up, carried through the air as if he could fly. He felt weightless, capable of anything as he flew over woods spotty with bare earth and fallen trees, over dirt roads and highways. He flew through a sky lit up with hard stars and half a moon that showed low mountains jagged with tears and ruts. Smoke rose from burning black heaps of what he'd later know was coal. In this dream his heart was full and glad and he woke, breathing in the used-up cigarette smoke air of home, a voice in the wind saying, *You know how.*

By the time he was sixteen, he'd forgotten there was such a thing as a wish. Pipe dreams, his daddy called the tiny figures Russell carved from pine when he was thirteen, carting them to sell in Hack, the closest town. His daddy, Joe Wallen, was not a cruel man, but he believed in what he saw and tuned up and set right. The world made sense if you looked at it under the hood of a car. There you could fix things, tear them out and put them back, patch them up with stove cement if you had to. He preached, on streets corners or over the trading of knives and guns in town. The world, his barber shop sermons went, was the way it was and a God-fearing man kept his cards close. The world, Russell had thought, was made of tall, spindly pines, and wisteria vines that choked the air with sweetness come spring. He had tried flight, tried to make sense of a world that was brittle, grass burnt pale in summers of scorching heat, like Georgia was when he was a boy. He brought home the wisteria blossoms for his mother. He carved pine into snakes and bears, passable in their beauty. He said nothing as Joe Wallen tossed the critters fireward, watching them sizzle and rise, snapping with pine sap. A man should have bigger plans than play pretties, his daddy said.

It was 1952 and he was nearly seventeen the day he wore a brown felt hat and skinny tie to meet the recruiter in town to persuade them he was old enough for what ended up being the last year of the Korean War. It wouldn't have mattered, Joe Wallen said as he gave Russell a Bible smelling of fresh inked paper with an inscription in the front. *For Russell as he sets forth.* In Korea he'd had no need of dreams of flying. Artillery sent lightning across the sky, blinding him, pushing him outside his own body with fear and a simultaneous wish that he might somehow be a hero. He was not. He fumbled and hesitated. He trudged and found himself begging the moment before he shot a gun, begging that killing someone else would spare his own self. It did. His journey forth was for one year, and he came back to Georgia with a shot-up knee and stories of undefended hillsides drenched with blood and dead men, some of them better stories than if they'd been true. There was no celebration. You know how to make do, his daddy said to him after one night, then two, a week. Get on, boy, he said, his voice holding nothing of hot, dry winds above the earth, nor of God.

It was not God that Russell followed down the highways north, then south again, then east and west, directionless soon and not afraid at all anymore. He slept on a golf course on the edge of Atlanta. Just into Tennessee, he fetched cases of liquor in a store in a little town called Fine. In the back room at a prostitute's house in Arkansas, he let her gather him next to full breasts that he sucked on like he was a child again. He was no child. He felt neither glad nor afraid of anything at all. He never dreamed now. The world was flat miles and the rise and fall of suns. Nights with their moons and cold stars meant hunting a place to sleep and making plans for miles ahead. He was a seeker, the prostitute said, but he sought nothing yet. All he knew was that he wanted hard cash and a pretty woman to keep him company. He wanted his own two feet headed in the right direction, and that was enough for now.

He thought about God, he had to admit. God was thunder over a passing train before a storm. God was the charged air rising off wires at an electrical plant at night after pay for doubles. God was fire and water, earth and stone. He asked God for things with names. The right number for craps. A job that held on long enough to earn hard cash. Such a God was made of fulcrums and tire irons. Of iron cranes against a bright blue sky. *Lift. Hold. Push ahead.* These were the words of prayers he said into the air of any promising day. He thumbed through the no-longer-new Bible that Joe Wallen gave him once upon a time, and he found pages of angels with gold illuminated wings. He found Christ with hungry eyes and his feet crossed and nailed fast and bleeding. And who, Russell Wallen asked himself, would not prefer gold and plenty? Who would not prefer the weight of riches, and if riches came with the wings of angels, then so be it.

When he met Della Branham he knew right away she was no angel. Her eyes were the most curious color he had ever seen, a changing mix of gold and blue, and hers were hands that knew ways of doing things. Her nails were half-moons of black dirt and her middle fingers were stained yellow from cigarettes when she worked the pump at the station where he stopped for gas in Wellsprings, West Virginia. She leaned across and squeegeed the windshield, popped the hood. He followed what she did like it was a map of a place he knew but had forgotten—the way she circled his car, nodding her appreciation for a 1957 Chevy, the way she shrugged and said, "Good enough," about the extra checks she offered. Transmission fluid. Tire pressure. She'd have offered him free brake relining, she told him later on, if it meant he'd stay put. He sat on the bench by the cash register and waited until they closed, hand-rolling cigarettes and lighting them for her one by one. He found it exciting, the way she picked a thread of tobacco off her front tooth and did not smile at him at all. "Russell Wallen," she said, and it was no question, no invitation. It was as if she'd known him a good while and was reminding herself of the ins and outs of that knowing, tallying up whether to ask him to stay or go.

He stayed two weeks in Wellsprings, and he brought her gifts each day. The violets and chickweed he made into a tiny bouquet she tossed into the can behind the station that held old oil. She sniffed the Wind Song he splurged on at the five-and-dime and outright laughed at him, though she spritzed her wrists and then rubbed them hard against the legs of her overalls. One night all he brought her was an ice-cold Pepsi, and that she loved, raising the bottle to her lips and drinking it down all at once, the muscles in her throat rippling with thirst. She set the empty bottle down and put her hands on her hips. "Now what are we going to do, Russell Wallen?"

It was his third day in Radiance when he saw the beautiful girl, her slender hands shuffling cards at a table at the drugstore. After that, he stopped in mornings, lunchtime, late afternoons for cups of coffee and root beer floats, but the girl and her deck of cards were never there again. What's up with that girl with the cards? he asked the lunch counter waitress. The waitress shrugged, but then admitted that she'd had her cards read. That girl, she said, told me things about, well, things she had no business knowing.

He remembered how she'd touched the pattern of lines on his palms. Her fingers were warm, wisps of themselves as they traced his future. "You want to own the world, mister," she said. He declared that was true, and at that moment the world was her. He longed for her touch to go on and on, tracing its way past his wrist, up his arms, toward his heart, if he admitted it. He didn't admit it, the desire he felt, and yet he looked for her in the windows of the houses he drove past late in the evenings, looked for her on porches and roadsides, in the woods as they made way for their trucks and chains and saws.

You are taking the world apart, said a man whose land they'd bought for timber, looking stunned. The man's truck was stacked with chairs and a table and boxes of things spilling out into the leaves. It was as simple as showing them a deed, a part of the job. It was the way the world was, little towns like this one taken apart and put back together, changed, Russell admitted. But change was the way of it if you were ever going to, what, make anything out of anything at all, make a dollar or two, get ahead. The trees came down. The earth opened up. Inside the earth, well, that wasn't his business, the seams and guts and hard insides of the land, the coal. He was helping it along, all of it, and he couldn't help who it hurt. Things were like that. Hurting. A tree had the scent of sap, and it sighed when you took it down, and then you moved on to the next.

The night he finally saw her again, it was late, and he'd sipped too much whiskey. He stumbled along the edges of Radiance, some sound or other leading him along like it was a taste. He thought it was an open window, a radio, Hank Williams and the Drifting Cowboys. Something or other he'd like listening to as he drove the back roads. This sound was a man's voice and a fiddle tune so clear and sweet he stood still and held his head up to the night sky and just listened, breathing it in. Up ahead, a crowd outside a store, on a porch. The soft shoes of them dancing there. A fiddle cutting through the dark. Cutting through the heat of a hot summer night. The sound cut through something inside his chest he wasn't sure he wanted cutting, opened up a space that made him shiver as he saw her. She looked at him, her head tilted, a question he already knew the answer to on her lips. He drew deep on the bottle and held the whiskey in his mouth until it burned.

Della could recite the spark plug gap on most any car he could name. Could outstrip him in a mean minute when it came to changing oil, relining brakes. She was good at ways and means, borrowing, building. If he had a thought about what came next, be it bottom dollar or saving up for a rainy day, she was ahead of him, always. Before, he'd been lucky if he'd stock-piled ones and a sleeve of quarters for a poker game, but now they had, she said, a picture for the future. Saving up, buying in. They'd be someone, him and her. She was, he told himself, both sister and friend, both partner and trusted companion. Della Branham, now Della Wallen, his wife.

He felt something like love for her in spades. Tenderness maybe. Curiosity, for sure. Reams of possibility. Like that time, the ocean time. They decided on that scheme with five minutes to spare and a whole new world ahead of them. They laughed, the two of them, thinking about how they'd drive south to the Gulf with ice chests and more, drive all night and the next day too. How they'd come with a list of the best diners, the snappiest restaurants, holes in the wall, name it, and supply them with crabs and lobsters, mullet and fresh this, fresh that. Who knew? Seafood in land-locked states. What better plan? And he'd loved it, standing with Della on the edge of the great big ocean outside nowhere, miles beyond East Point, Florida. How she'd rolled her trouser legs up and waded in deep, letting the salt water drench her, kicking the wet back at him and drenching him, too. She'd waded toward him and nestled herself into his arms. How warm she'd been, the sweat and salt feel of her next to him, their wet clothes cool between them like a second skin.

He was glad to be alone in the town called Radiance. Glad that Della was back in West Virginia at her service station, laying plans ahead. He hardly thought of her, of Della in her body, her body next to his, as the riffs from a fiddle player washed over him. He danced by himself, spun some woman around and around, her flat black shoes scuffing along the boards of the porch. The song words settled inside him, so alive and full. *Desire. Regret.* As he danced and held that woman close, he looked over her shoulder and there she was, the girl. He watched her hands, how they clapped time like a song all their own, a heart song made out of the black night air.

Later, once Radiance was a dream he took out and recalled little by little, he wondered if he loved the two women as if they were one. Or did he love neither of them at all, two souls as different as the face of God? God was light and dark, sorrow and joy, a God both real and full of a dream he'd long let go. He loved Della. He said that to himself again and again. Said it like a prayer you recited word for word each night. Said it into Della's back as he held her close, breathed the same breath as her as they fell asleep. Love was love, and it was just part of the things you did and made. After Radiance they'd head west, make their biggest plans yet come true. That was how he loved her, his wife. Loved her as strong and true as the factories in Willette, New Mexico. *Copper. Uranium.* Things strong and sure, dredged up from the earth and made into something. Themselves, made into something. He'd be a foreman there in no time flat and soon they'd head back east. Their own business. His own business. The both of them, working hard and making the world take shape. And love? Wasn't that it, when you came right down to it? Wasn't love the making and doing and seeing it come alive, the work of their hands?

How they had loved that first time in a Radiance motel room with a sway-backed bed and a sink the color of rust. The pale skin of her unveiled, the rose of her nipples, the curves and hollows of her chest, her belly. How she held her hands above her head like she was pulling light and song right out of the air. Her fingers slid down his bare skin like he was a song too, a song he'd never heard, never felt, never believed possible. How he flew again at long last, hovered above her, believing again in more than all the earth he'd ever traveled. All those towns and roads. All the plans he'd made rose too, a mist, a fog, an after-the-rain. He felt washed clean by her.

New again. Like dreaming was as real as anything else, more real. Real as unfamiliar skies and stars, stars no longer cold and hard but a melting sweetness he took into his mouth again and again.

All those afternoons with Ruby, he told himself he was working at getting her out of his blood, getting her out of the very air he took inside his body. Her hands reached for him again and again. Hold me, she said, her eyes as sad as leaves beginning to fall, sad as summer passing. One more afternoon, stolen from the rest. His body all along hers, his body inside hers, making one body, one heart. But he could not let himself say that word. *Love. Heart.* There were places he could not go. There had to be rules, after all. Had to be limits to what he let himself want. There was that much, at least. An endpoint. A boundary. The edge of the cliff you did not cross. He wrote that to Della. *Four more weeks here. Two more weeks there. One.* All our plans, she wrote back, coming true.

Miracelle Loving
Smyte
1993

16

Rooms to Let

By the outskirts of Smyte, I'd settled on who I'd be. *Waydean Long.* I'd known a woman named Waydean, a red-headed girl I'd danced with for two weeks in a bar down in Florida. I liked the name well enough as I passed fast food joints and shopping centers that sold saw sharpeners and beauty supplies. Then the fast food joints gave way to a two-lane with a cleaned-out row of empty storefronts. A little farther along the river I came to the place that was his. There were two good-sized buildings, one a squat warehouse, the other a larger building with a smokestack. *I studied the two buildings, their darkened windows, behind them a muddy brown river.* What had Leroy Loving said? "Your father tried to own anything he could get his hands on." A sign like a fist hovered above the building with the smokestack. *Wallen Industries.* Both buildings looked like nothing had ever owned them before and like nothing would ever own them now.

I pulled over, getting my calm back, but not for long. Right across the road sat a beat-up little restaurant called the Black Cat with a sign that featured a cat curling up around itself. Exactly what Maria Murdy, the seer I'd called for Willy's, had described. *A sign with lights, and a purple cat.*

All of the nervous I'd held inside—the past hundred-odd miles, Radiance and Leroy Loving, that wild-animal-smelling house—welled up inside me. "You're like a word left out of some sentence," Cody had said about me, and that was a fact. Me, a woman alone in a car beside a diner full of strangers, waiting to see if the father I'd never met was one of them.

Inside, a bunch of old men were playing cards at some pushed-together tables while what seemed to be the rest of Smyte, all its children and great-grandmothers and everybody else, sat at the rest of the tables and booths. A waitress with hennaed hair came toward me, one arm with a tray of dishes and the other hand toting a lit cigarette. She looked fit to drop.

"If you want a stool at the counter, it's yours, sweetie. I'll fix you up a booth when one's ready."

The bell on the diner door jangled hard. More customers. I could hardly see for the bodies that stood or sat or crossed each other. Plates fell. Glasses broke and someone fell.

A huddle formed in the center of the room.

"It's Lacy May," someone said.

The huddle broke and I could see scrawny legs wearing a pair of scuffed-up penny loafers. It looked like a woman had fainted, but she soon sat up, her arms flailing. "Y'all get your hands off me."

Another woman wearing coveralls pushed her way out from the kitchen and stood surveying the mess.

"I can't raise that doctor she likes," someone said.

Lacy May was standing now. "I don't know when ever I asked for a doctor."

"Some of you just head on home, now." The woman tucked soft-looking hair, carbon-colored and threaded with white, behind an ear. Her coveralls had a name sewn on them. *Della.*

I stayed up most of that first night in a Motel 6 on the outskirts of Smyte, reading pages of Ruby's girlhood diary, that world-before-me in her round girl-handwriting. There were stories about head-of-a-holler ghosts. There was a story about riding to the city with her mother, a woman named Esther who was my own grandmother. She was sick, it seemed, and they'd stayed for some days in a motel and eaten blue plate specials from the motel restaurant. Inside the diary were pasted cutouts from the menu. A cabin with smoke coming out of its chimney. A dancing pig. My mother before she'd even known I would exist.

I laid Ruby's diary aside and took out her tarot deck. These weren't discount-store entertainment like the tarot deck I whipped out, late nights, at some bar. These cards had the scent of magic, like the books I'd spend afternoons reading at the public library in this town or that one where Ruby and I were living, then. Books like *The Golden Bough.* Biographies of Marie Laveau and Harry Houdini. I wanted magic back then, enough to set the sheer force of my own will free. It took me a few years to figure out what I wanted to be free from, but I willed it, again and again, and when no one was looking, I slipped pages from those books in my pockets, or a whole book if it was small enough. Supernatural tales, ghosts and voo-doo priestesses. Or something with a cleaner edge. Mysteries about lost treasures, missing children. My own life a mystery I had not been able to solve. Who was I? In my farthest-back memory, Ruby, her long black hair, me reaching up like she might disappear down some loverless street. My father's whereabouts a mystery to us both.

I shuffled, cut, drew three cards, relying on memory for what each card meant. My past, the Tower, showed a castle going up in flames, min-iature women jumping from windows, the mountains in behind criss-crossed with roads in no particular direction. No surprise there. My pres-ent card was more interesting. Priestess of disks. A cross-legged woman beside a tree with a parrot in it and a bare-butt kid and a hand with the Third Eye. *Through the gift of loving touch, you stay in contact with life.* I'd called Cody Black for three days running with no answer at all. And the streets out there in this place? I knew not a soul. It was my future card that sent me chills. Priestess again, of swords, a woman in a place of stripped-down mountains and owls. A woman with a coat made of snow. *A journey to a cold realm. A separation.*

Behind me in this strange room, white sheets on a bed and an open window and a little air coming in through a screen. *Wait,* Ruby, said to me. *Just wait and see.* Along a few of the highways I'd driven, I'd sketched out any number of scenes in my head, and none of them involved much patience. In some scenarios I rushed up onto porches, pounded on doors, punched a fist or two into a wall in a dining room where some man who might or might not look a bit like me was playing board games with a family I'd never met. Or I'd more often seen myself giving up altogether, wasting away in a hospital ward when a man in a father-looking getup poked his head in at the last minute, his arms full of roses, just as I was despairing of ever knowing my own name.

Fathers were as much ghosts to me as Ruby's holler haints. They were magazine advertisements, clean-cut men with polo shirts and shiny ladders to climb to fix the roofs of houses where I'd never lived. They were movie-star men. Heroes and bad boys. They rode off into sunsets and nev-er came back. Leroy Loving had been a miscalculation, a granddaddy in-stead of a father. Ride into Radiance and hug a father's neck or slap him across the face, my choice. But I was no closer to knowing my own father than ever. All I had was a name. *Russell Wallen.* I flipped open Ruby's diary to the last page and wrote the name down. Wrote it again, with my left hand. The name itself seemed to have nothing at all to do with me, when you came right down to it. Miracelle Loving. Waydean Long. My own names were just fine without adding his to the mix. I scooped up the tarot cards and slid them into their box. I still wasn't banking on cards telling me much truth, but I supposed waiting would have to do. Russell Wallen, mystery man, unknown father, was out there somewhere. *A journey to a cold realm.* Outside in Smyte right this minute a late summer night was letting go of its heat, and I told myself some weeks here would do.

When I asked about rentals by the week at the Motel 6 and a couple other Smyte motels, it was no dice. I sat outside a convenience store with a cup of coffee and a newspaper. In the *For Rent* section, I found a listing for a room upstairs in a house. The last time I'd thought about a room for rent was about a million years ago, and that one had involved some once-upon-a-time place where Ruby and I had shared a sofa bed. Did anyone even rent a room anymore? This ad came from none other than Lacy May, the woman who'd fallen in the Black Cat Diner. She offered the room and supper which, that first night I found myself a brand-spanking-new boarder, was a big bowl of red potatoes and a plate of fish sticks.

"We have to wait." A teenage girl took a seat beside me.

"Why's that?"

"You'll see." She smiled at me, her mouth full of large, gnarly-looking teeth.

A man in a turquoise leisure suit was on the other side of the table. "She offers a hearty appetizer before the meal."

Another guy in a sweatshirt with a fish and *One Way!!* on it came in from the living room. "Appetizer? That what you call it?" He glanced around the table, took the seat on my other side. "Can't eat prayers."

"Both of you." The girl patted her hair. "Would you just quit it?"

Lacy May kicked the kitchen door open and made her way toward the table, two hands full. She set down a plate piled with slices of white bread and beside it a beat-up Bible with a tiny cross hanging from its spine. "Always polite to ask the new guest first."

No one said anything.

The girl nudged me. "We do this every night. I tell myself it's mystical."

"Oh, for pity's sake," the leisure suit said. "We pass the Bible to someone new each night and that person opens it and points and reads a verse." He pointed with a thumb at Lacy. "And she tells us what we need to know about it."

Lacy handed the Bible to me and I held it awkwardly. "It speaks," she said. "Not me."

"Just open it." The girl looked hungrily at the sliced bread and at a jar of red jam.

I flipped through and let my fingers land at the Old Testament. Book of Psalms. *Out of Zion, the perfection of beauty, God hath shined.* I read it aloud, then again. *Out of Zion, the perfection of beauty, God hath shined.*

She went around the table, starting with the big-toothed girl who would, Lacy said, learn how to understand her own sense of beauty, how to unloosen her heart. And the turquoise-suited man. Heaven, she said, was within him, in the palm of his own hand. He needed to learn how to be gentle.

Lacy looked at me last of all. "The verse tells what you could find right in front of you if you waited. What you've forgotten."

I looked at her and nodded and said nothing, thinking that I could have been over at the Motel 6 with the Gideon Bible, but this place? *What you've forgotten.* There was a reason, I told myself, that I was here.

"What did you think?" the girl whispered to me.

"Fortunes," I whispered back as we began to eat. "There are worse things."

17

At the Black Cat

The next morning the Black Cat was nearly empty. The same henna-haired waitress was there that I'd seen the other day. *Ona Short,* her name tag said.

"Get you something?" she asked.

"Coffee," I said. "And I'll take some wheat toast."

"Make that another toast, Della," she yelled toward the swinging doors. She set down a tray of sugars and salt and pepper shakers and brought my coffee.

"Things are a lot quieter in here than last time I saw this place."

Ona looked me over, trying to place me. "It's so empty in here you can hear your shoes squeak. But come in here on a weekend and whoo-wee."

The only other customer was the leisure suit guy from the boarding-house. "You folks do a refill?" he called.

"Humph." She headed for the suit's table and topped up his cup.

I'd taken out my cards, my poker deck.

"Solitaire?" Ona asked, pausing on her way back. She leaned in and studied the spread I'd laid down.

"Fortunes."

I shuffled the deck, cut it, held it out. "I'll do you a three-card spread."

Ona drew an ace. That was easy enough. "Strength and courage," I said. "The universe, giving you what you needed most." Ona smiled and drew a new card.

"This a diner or a poker party?" The woman called Della made her way toward the leisure suit's table, set down a plate of toast, and brought another to my booth. "Ona, you planning on helping out with the house salads before or after?"

"Just finishing up my break." Ona fussed with her apron, scooped up a napkin dispenser from the table beside my booth, and headed for the kitchen.

"Finish what you were doing." Della reached for a card off the top of my deck, flipped it onto her open palm, and studied it. "I heard you say you read fortunes."

"They read you," I said.

She took a seat in front of me. "Try me."

I shuffled the deck, cut it again the three ways, left to right, while Ona hurried some coffee out to Della.

"Cut them," I said.

She shuffled them again her own self. Shuffled like I'd seen good poker players do, a stream of cards up, down between her two quick palms, the cards winging into each other. She laid them down with a swipe of her strong hand.

I turned over her first card. A two of diamonds. I made up the meaning right on the spot. "Love and loyalty gone."

"You reckon?" She laughed a little.

The next card out was the queen of spades. "Take charge and name yourself," I said.

"My mother named me Delilah." She looked down in her lap at her big hands. "But everyone calls me Della."

Her third card was a king. I told her something about false hopes and dreams.

"The truth is," she said, "I don't much believe in fortunes."

"You don't?"

"I don't trust things that know you better than you know your own self." She folded her arms across her chest. "What's your name anyway, girl?"

"Waydean." The name came easy. "Waydean Long."

"You said your piece, Waydean?"

I scooped up the cards, stacked them neat. "Just about," I said. "Except maybe for that job over there." I pointed at a sign I'd noticed earlier. *Waitress and Part-Time Cook Needed.* Mysteries took gas money and spare change.

The other renters said my room was haunted, and by the time I'd stayed awake in there a few nights, hearing every creaking board and rattling window, I believed it. The room was on the topmost floor of what had once been a swanky Victorian hotel. The first afternoon I had followed Lacy May to see the room, we'd gone up two flights of steps, then through a door at the end of the main hallway. We traveled more small and winding steps to an attic, then under an archway into the room and all its things to be mine for a time—the worn-out braided rug, the low-watt bulbs and the nightstand with its broke-off corner. The walls were a dark tongue-and-groove, and there were so many pictures of fierce-looking women in starched shirtwaists and wild-mustached men with undertaker jackets, I didn't know where to start looking. Ancestors, Lacy said.

We stood looking at another frame, this one thick and heavy and full of mounted pictures and postcards and photos.

"Her, now." Lacy pointed at a framed picture. "Name's Tince May. My great aunt."

"This was her house?"

Lacy May nodded. "She signed it over to me so the state couldn't get their hands on it."

"Who was she?"

"Tince May, honey? A healer, I guess you could say." She dusted the glass in the frame with a tissue. "Study this awhile and you'll know right smart about her. She touched a few souls, anyway."

"How's that?"

"Ever hear about the laying on of hands?" A ceramic heater was lit on the one wall, its blue flames dancing, but the room was chilly and Lacy rubbed her arms.

"They say all you have to do is touch a picture of her," Lacy said. "Touch it soft-like and anything you need will be answered."

Branches scratched against the windows and small clawed feet moved inside the walls as we stood looking at Tince May. The photo showed a woman of what must have been three hundred pounds lying on two shoved-together beds. I reached, traced her eyes in the photo. They were surprisingly light, for an old photo, pale eyes, with shadows. I put my hands against the glass and could somehow feel my own self inside Tince's chest.

My second or third night at Lacy's, with the rest of the house asleep and the streets below so quiet I could hear wind chimes from a porch some-where, I made my way downstairs. In the kitchen I found a package of saltines and a jar of peanut butter and stood eating, then opened a few more cabinets, found the last of some red wine I poured into an empty jar. It was vinegary, but I sipped at it as I tiptoed into the sitting room, then sat on the scratchiness of the horsehair sofa where a rotary phone on an end table looked way too tempting not to risk a call. I dialed, sat on the floor by the wall, counted Mississippi's, and was ready to hang up when he answered.

There were other voices and television applause.

"Someone there?"

"Yeah," I said at last. "Someone."

Cody sighed and I felt it in my gut. "Miracelle."

"It is."

"I expected you'd call."

On the end table above me was a Jehovah's Witness pamphlet. I took it down and spread it across my lap. "I've called right many times."

"They sent me and a couple others over to Chattanooga, to get some new displays." The television sounds shut off.

Now that I had him, I wasn't sure what I'd meant to say, but I told him I had a job at a diner, a place to stay.

"That's good, Miracelle," he said. We both were quiet. "And what's working like?"

"It's not like anything."

"Well, tell me about nothing, then. What's nothing like?"

I thought about the empty streets of Smyte, the big-fisted sign at the deserted buildings of Wallen Industries.

"Where you calling from?"

"A rooming house place."

"And it's where?"

"A town called Smyte."

"And the diner?"

"The Black Cat," I said.

He laughed. "You would pick a place with a name like that."

I sipped at the last of the wine.

"And the street where you're at right this minute?"

"So far, it's like all the other ones, I guess."

"Tell me one thing you see that's different," he said. "Just one."

"The paper mill here's been shut down a long time but I swear the air still smells like old soup." My chest was tight with all I wanted to tell him, but I fell silent.

"Any sign of him yet?"

"Him," I said, though I knew who he meant and couldn't say it out loud.

"Your father. Any clues at all?"

I told him about the velvet box I'd found, about Ruby's diary and her tarot cards. The letters. But then it came to those two words. *Russell Wallen.* The name caught in my throat.

"I can't talk about it more than that," I said. "Not just yet."

We were quiet again.

"You called me, Miracelle." His voice was tired. "Why is that?"

I remembered how he looked as lights from the parking lot swept across his face. "I guess I called to say I'm not sorry, Cody."

He laughed. "What does that mean?"

"I mean"—I took a breath—"I have to be here and I don't know why yet."

"Then you shouldn't call me."

"I just wanted you to know I think about you."

"Sounds like you shouldn't do that much, either."

Upstairs somewhere a door opened, slammed shut.

"Just remember, Miracelle," he said. "You're a reader of fortunes."

"Yes?"

"Read the signs. Look for clues about your own life for a change."

Footsteps sounded on the stairs. "Someone down there?"

"Your ghosts have to come to rest."

"Every day haunts the next." I wasn't sure at all what I meant by that, but I said it, then more than I meant to say after that. "You haunt me, Cody Black."

And then I wished that I'd not called him at all, or that I could call him again and could start the conversation over, with better words or fewer. Ones that left my heart feeling less empty.

18

End of the Season

I was lucky. Della heard me when I said I was down and out, and when I hinted that it would be easier that way since I lived here and yon and had no permanent address, hired me under the table. Customers knew me by name in a week. *Waydean Long,* they'd say as I served their pie and ice cream, *settle yourself down here a minute and tell us what it's like burning up the highway for a livin'.* Seems I had a certain reputation, without even trying much. Gossip traveled, and the diner was a hub of it.

The Black Cat was a diner with a fix-it garage in back. Della was out there by six a.m., already telling the boys she'd hired to do this, do that, get her done. I'd slip an apron off a wall and see Ona waking herself up over the coffee pot, her red hair still shower-damp. We'd set to, making lunch salads.

We had our regulars, Smyte lawyers and card players from the local Kiwanis Club who owned a coffee cup to hang on the rack behind the cash register. We all eyed the chain-brand drive-through coffee shop that had gone up near the shopping center they called the small. Della scurried from garage to pumps to fill up tanks and make a pass at cleaning car windows and, afternoons, she sat going over the books and adding and subtracting figures, her eyes a deep, sad blue.

Some days Della's eyes were cool and gray. No color, really. They were goldish when the sun was looking at her a certain way and she thought no one was noticing. With autumn not far off and cool coming in early, her eyes turned a washed-out blue. A cold winter lay ahead, no winter at all compared to the ones I'd sampled up north, but they said diner traffic would dwindle.

Nights, I didn't go anywhere. I sat outside the diner as cars trailed music and beer bottles shattered along the asphalt. Semis loaded with everything from chickens to lumber hauled through in those hours, taking a short-cut around the bypass. I counted trucks and coal rigs with their windows rolled down and voices hollering out at no one in particular. The Black Cat sign stayed on all night, its half-burned-out neon a light I grew to trust. Across the road, the sky was nigh about hidden by the smokestacks of the factory. The Wallen Industries sign over there became my reference point for why I was in Smyte.

I saw plenty of men at the Black Cat who could have been my father in some other life. A mill worker with his big hands wrapped around a coffee cup on his late-night break. A salesman with a briefcase in conversation with Della by the cash register, early of a morning. But I didn't ask Ona Short or Lacy May or anyone else about Russell Wallen just yet. Cody had said finding my father would shake me up more than I could imagine. *He's here already, girl,* Ruby said to me, late at night as I lay watching streetlight shine into my room at Lacy May's. *And here, and here, and here,* Ruby said. And that was true enough. As I walked to work near sunrise and stopped to buy a pack of cigarettes, I seemed to see him in the muggy late summer air of Smyte. It could have been his hand pulling a blind down on a window as I passed some house. The folded-up love note I found on a sidewalk—*I told you I'd meet you, and where were you, mister*—that could have been what my mother wrote to him in another time and place. That woman at her mailbox on Smith Street with the shadowy skin beneath her eyes and how she said, "Morning, this morning. Fine morning, this morning," could have known him better than I ever would. That couple quarreling on their front porch? There was something of my father in that, too. There was something of my father every night as I sat outside in the parking lot at the Black Cat, looking at the dark windows of the shut-down factory buildings called Wallen Industries. I'd so far held my cards close to my chest in asking about my father of anyone here, but sleuthing had to start somewhere.

On my day off, I visited the Smyte Public Library, a one-story brick building behind an out-of-business women's clothing store. I made myself at home in the library's underworld—the basement microfiche and film room. I found out all I could about Wallen Industries. Old microfiche issues of the local paper described hard work in a paper mill. Twelve-hour days, heat, asbestos burns in lungs. And all alongside the mill, the river:

One summer—in a drought year—the water level of the river dropped and the concentration of sulphur solvents became sufficiently intense that it began to blacken and then peel the paint off houses. It has been rumored that the river actually caught on fire, although this has not been documented.

I found stories about the founding of the mill, the first warehouse built along the river road, the first paper machine that made its way to Smyte from up north. One machine became two, became three. Wood stock came from western Kentucky. From the east. From up north and as far south as Mississippi. I read about papermaking until I could about taste it. *Slurry. Nip. Slice.* Then the articles gave way to ones about Wallen Industries, and three machines became four, five, a dozen.

In the midst of all those articles I scrolled through, there were pictures of my father. Russell in a white T-shirt, a cigarette pack stuck inside a rolled-up sleeve, him looking down into a big chest full of wet white pulp like it was gold in the making. Him in a three-piece suit, black, with a skinny striped tie. My heart nearly quit as I looked at his photo and the column that went with it.

Now that Wallen Industries is falling on hard times, it seems fitting to turn our attention to history. The paper mill is the history of Smyte, in some ways, so they say. It is certainly the history of one man in our town, Russell Wallen, co-owner with Della Wallen of an eatery that is nearly a town legend.

It was her. Della from the Black Cat. My mouth went dry. Della was his wife? Only this Della was a whole other woman. I traced my finger along an outline of a white dress, along the arm she had draped around Russell's waist. Della Wallen was my stepmother, or some other name akin to that. Wife, lover, another woman from a life Ruby never knew about, or had. I held my hand against the glass of the microfiche screen, blanking out the both of them, my father and this Della from another time. My forefinger traced the shape of my father's face, the spread of his fingers on Della's shoulder, his half-smile. *Russell Wallen.* I said his name again and again, good as a nighttime prayer, but what they said about hard times? When I looked at his face, I felt nothing at all.

The days grew shorter, cool air from the river drifted over the streets, and the library microfiche room became my second rented room, that and the library break room. When I'd had enough microfiche for one night, I'd make my way to the break room, where three vending machines and four long metal tables about filled the place. An old woman with rolled down stockings and a bad perm was eating cheese crackers. There was hardly a chair but the one back in the corner near the Coke machine.

Weaving in and around were four or five others that belonged on a night with Cody and me in Knoxville. One of them, a skinny girl, had strange large eyes and shiny gold threads in her hip-length hair. With her was a fat boy covered with tattoos and baggy pants hanging low from his hips. I scanned the room and just like that, there was Russell Wallen, the very man all the news clippings had shown.

I want to say the world stopped right then and there. That a spotlight came down out of nowhere or that it was all like a scene in an old movie with a backdrop of mountains and snow, heartfelt music. It is true that a kind of music came from him, a low-down blues from the very pores of his skin. Beneath a slouchy felt hat, he had gray and black hair and a full mouth. I picked up the trail of his music and followed it over to him where, under the dim lights of the break room, his eyes looked me up and down so my cheeks felt hot.

Spread out on the table in front of him were documents. Letters with handwriting so old the ink was brown. Maps. Some signed forms that looked like deeds. *Property,* I read. *In the ownership of.* I couldn't read a name.

"You're Waydean Long, I hear."

I stood, looking at my hands.

"You that new girl over to the diner?"

"Word gets around fast, it seems." I kept standing.

"I hear you read a card or two." He laid his hand down in front of me, palm up, waited to see what I would say. "What's the story on this palm, now?" He stretched his fingers and waited for me to take a look.

I hesitated, then reached across and traced my finger along his life-line. The line was clean and neat, one part steady until it broke, disap-peared into the wide cuff of his sleeve.

When I got back to the boardinghouse it was late, and I sat a spell on the porch swing. Across from me was some other porch, and its light was on too, and three houses down, an upstairs window was lit behind a shade. *Russell Wallen.* I want to tell you I stopped breathing, knowing I'd seen him, that a hand gathered around my heart and massaged away at some ache I'd always had, and that the world picked me up and shook me and said, *You, Miracelle Loving.* That should have been true and it was not.

I had been carrying Ruby's fancy tarot cards with me the last couple of days, and I took them out of my shoulder bag. I held the box against my chest like I was expecting it to breathe, then took out a card, studying the picture in the low light. A woman, caught in a tangle of dreams and swords. Another card. A woman with long black hair, a rose in her hand. "Ruby Loving," I said aloud. "Are you there?"

The front door creaked open. "Somebody out here?" It was Lacy May in her housecoat and slippers. "Waydean?"

"That's me," I said, and scooted over to make room for her.

We kicked the swing forward and back and she picked up one of the tarot cards from my lap.

"What's this here?" She held the long-haired woman's card under-neath her eyeglasses.

"Just a little reality check for tonight," I said.

She picked up a second card, the tangled dreams one.

"I always see you and them cards out here and you waiting like they have something to tell you."

"I keep waiting for the right card to fall, I reckon."

"That room I rented you, now." Lacy stood and looked down at the spread I'd laid. "I will say that room has seen some folks over time."

"Enough pictures up there to prove that."

"I won't say it's haunted." she said. "But maybe Tince's still up there somehow. Maybe healing's up there, too, if you believe it's so."

Up in my room I paced, knowing I needed no cards nor the lines on my own palm to tell the kind of man Russell Wallen was. I'd already memorized details of him. A deep scar began at his wrist, wound its way across his knuckles. He wore his hat tilted just enough to make it hard to read his face, but in that face I already saw myself. When I smiled, my mouth also held teeth crooked as a dog's hind leg. His eyes were red-rimmed, tired as I myself could be with nights awake or nights needing some back road to drive with a bottle of whiskey and radio songs. His hands knew as much hard work as I'd known, and I imagined that when he stood, we'd match one another for lean and tall. If Russell Wallen had been a word, I'd have rinsed him through my teeth and spat him out, neat.

I stood in front of the frame that held Tince May's photo. So she'd been a faith healer. As far as I was concerned, faith was maybe a tiny shake in your bones that came and left right quick. I wanted to believe, but what I'd always trusted most was the road out, the next town ahead, with strangers making a lot more sense than kin. Still, it was worth a try. I closed my eyes and laid my hands against the glass over Tince's photograph and waited.

I could hear the least thing. A dog howled at something and the something yipped back. Down in the street, people walked by and I could hear them talking. "Just go on then," the man said. "I will," the woman said, her voice high-pitched and sad. "And just see how much you like it." After that, not a sound from anything, and I waited, my hands against the cool picture-frame glass that shook a little as a train whistled and the cars hustled by on the far-off tracks.

I guess wishing hard enough means I had to see a few things, and I did. I saw my car, headed west, cigarettes scattering sparks along a highway. I saw Cody's face when I told him not to love me. I saw the color of Della Wallen's eyes, a cool blue as she carried trays of burgers in from the kitchen and smiled at me like she'd known me all her life. I saw my mother, her scared face as I ran through a trailer door and found her lying in her own blood. Here I was standing in a rented room with my hands against a picture frame, waiting on the voice of God. What had Lacy said? *Healing's up there, if you believe it's so.* Belief had always been a day late and a dollar short in my life, and now here I was waiting on the ghost of a fat lady to tell me some answers, and I wasn't even sure what my questions were in the first place.

I stretched my hands against Tince's framed picture, dug my fingers next to the glass like it was skin. What had I expected I'd see when I saw my father's face for the first time? Kindness, maybe? Had I expected he'd stand beside me and whisper in my ear like he was some preacher man ready to bless me from here on out, forever and ever, amen? What I wanted and what I got were two different worlds. I had wanted to know my father, and now here he was. *Hurt.* Maybe that's what I wanted most of all.

Della Wallen
Wellsprings
1944–1968

19

The Sheer Weight of the World

She was twelve that day in Wellsprings, West Virginia, a day she remembered so vividly she could feel the heat at noon in the one-car garage belonging to that man her daddy knew. She spent her days that summer slipping out of the house at the crack of dawn to avoid the list her mother had for her. Sifting flour for biscuits every morning, whether or not any of them wanted such a thing as breakfast at the crack of dawn. Hearth shoveled out, a thin layer of ash left for the next fire. It was no less a chore, the things her daddy and the men did that day. Remove the hood, disconnect the battery. Unbolt the transmission, the engine mounts. Disconnect hoses. Hook chain to engine. Hoist and swing aside. Replacing the engine took the best part of a day.

Ever since, she'd loved the feel of a good day's work. The warm feel of oil when she changed a filter. How sharp kerosene smelled when you soaked a carburetor, or the way something like sugar could clean grease from her own two hands. She loved a phrase like *thirty degrees of dwell.* The burnt smell of dragging brakes. That was an ordinary sign in this world, a sign she could understand and fix. There were things about Russell she could never name, as hard as she tried, things inside him she could never reach, let alone repair, as hard as she loved him and as long. "What do you want from me, woman?" he'd say again and again as they moved, east to west, west back east. What she wanted was a world that made sense.

Before she met Russell, she ran her daddy's gas station, a place she'd been left after both her parents passed. She was an only child, and odd-turned. When she was little her mother ironed the bows on her dresses of a Sunday, but by mid-afternoon she'd be out in the garage, helping her daddy strew sawdust across the floor to soak up oil from changing. "Remember," he'd say, "never use sandpaper to clean a plug gap unless you're in a pinch." Her mother herded her back inside to knead dough and learn the ways and means of tiny stitches, but it was her daddy she learned to love. How he'd take her with him to test out the truck he was fixing up, show her how to turn the distributor and adjust the timing get to rid of a ping.

"Listen up, girl," he'd say. "The biggest problem's not over-greasing the cam and the spark." And he'd show her the intricacies of advance plates, teach her more about how to listen to what an engine said.

Engines, she learned young, had a heart and a soul bigger than any person she'd ever meet. They were a thing you could count on, nothing like the Good Book or sermons about end times, or any old movie with moony-eyed girls who sang about love. Engines were a love story. A good light to set an ignition timing beat any boy she knew. Drive-in movie of a Saturday night or hair in pin curls and a high school dance. She liked the taste of tobacco in the mouth of some boy, but she liked it better when they let her roll her own cigarettes or when they realized that she could hold her head better than them any day after enough neat shots of whiskey as they sat looking out at the quarry by moonlight. It wasn't that she didn't like their lips, their hands, where those hands went, and how it made her feel inside. But it made her impatient, too, made her want them to get on with it, the unzipping and unbuttoning, the quick intake of breath, the pleasure that never seemed to be her own.

When she met Russell Wallen, she was twenty-three going on twenty-four, and most of her days were spent cleaning up, setting up, sweeping up. By then she'd owned the station for some time, and she'd expanded it too, opening up a little coffee and breakfast place in what had been a storehouse beside the garage, and she was working double time, serving up doughnuts and doing tune-ups near about in the dark. She hired helpers, one for the breakfast shift and another for bigger repairs in the garage, but she was running daylight to evenings, seeing to it all, and missed pleasures she couldn't even name. She laid her hands against the warm hood of a car as she waited for a tank to fill up with gas and she felt that warmth travel up her arms, down her spine. She lay on her back under a car and the warm spill of oil from an engine ran over her hands, her wrists, the warmth making its way into her belly.

Russell Wallen was different. He seemed to get her right away, his black eyes moving along her body as she stood fiddling with his side mir-

ror, cleaning the windshields more than they needed, taking time to ad-
mire the fanciness that was his car, a red Chevy with fins and whitewall
tires. He needed new wiper blades, she said, though he didn't and they
both knew that.

"Don't want to get caught out there in the rain," she said as he stood
too close behind her while she slid the old blades out.

"Some days are made for rain," he said as he reached over to help
her tighten the new blades on the arm. "Some days are for listening to it
falling."

She didn't need, had never needed, help exactly. What she needed
was his particular warmth, how it had already traveled from his body next
to hers, but how it hesitated, just at the surface of the skin beneath her coveralls, waiting for her to invite it in. He took her riding that very next day,
out to the quarry at night. She shouldn't have gone, she told herself, but
that shouldn't dissolved like moonlight on water. Shouldn't have reached
for the hand that lay atop the steering wheel, tapping time to some radio
song. She laid that hand on her chest, her fingers nearly spelling out the
words for him, like it was Braille in the dark. *Unbutton me.*

They swam in the cool water, and they became for one night like
the sleek silver scales of fish. They became the wings of night birds. They
became all things that flew, raced along the wind, all things that picked
up the two of them, guided them along a road, then many roads, roads
neither of them especially wanted nor understood. It was simple enough.
His body entered her body and her body answered. That was the way of
it, and only as time passed did she realize neither of them should have
called it love.

At the garage she was known for being able to put her hands on the hood
of a running car and know what was wrong. Laying on of hands, her daddy
called it, and he was good at knowing just like she was what was wrong
with an engine by sitting quiet and listening, fiddling around in the mess
of wires and caps and belts. She'd even seen him dip his finger in an oil
pan and put the finger to his mouth, swearing he could diagnose what
ailed a car from the taste. At night she lay beside Russell, taking in his
scent, a salty sweat. She put her hand against her mouth and memorized,
again and again, the musk of his taste. She put her hand atop Russell's
chest and held it there as lightly as she could, feeling the least beat and

skip. There's a miss when it's running, a customer would say, and she'd be able to diagnose pistons or rods, valves, head gaskets. She was more and more sure that with Russell's heart there was a missing beat, but she had no notion what caused it.

He was a strange one, the way he talked in his sleep. The way he'd say a name or two of other women he'd known, and God-words too. Women were the way of it for some men, those who loved running the roads to get a wildness out of their systems. God was another thing, and one she'd never questioned like he did. Dominion, he'd say when she asked him about speaking the Lord's name in his sleep—ain't nobody got that. She curled herself next to him, her knees to the backs of his, and she'd hold on for the ride that was a night spent through and through with him, his tossing and turning, his fits of waking and pushing her away. She held on and rolled with it, the waves and waves of his sleep with dreams she would never know. Hush now, she said, as if she were soothing a child. She put her hand against his chest and knew there was a miss there, a secret, an enormous misfire that might someday cause this thing that was them to crash and burn, but she had no exact remedies. Surely, she told herself, the weight of the world would be enough.

In Florida they dreamed big. They hooked up with a fisherman who showed them crabbing. They traded in the Chevy for a truck, that time, and she went along with it, telling herself she knew the ins and outs of some Dodge pickup good as you please. It would be easy, he said, to slap a camper on the back of the truck, load it up with chests of ice, how they'd make time back north, fresh seafood for folks who knew nothing about it and, why, that breakfast place would be packed to the nines with customers ready to kill for a blue plate special. She kept good memories of that time, how he took her out on the beach late at night and showed her the rough barnacles and shells on the backs of turtles and deadwood, how you could trail your fingers to make a shine in the dark like pale green neon. She rolled her pants legs up and waded far out, feeling the live things shift and scuttle between her toes.

She'd begun to build a clientele at the garage and at the little breakfast place beside it, and she kept a room for herself upstairs. She sat by the window smoking cigarette after cigarette and keeping watch at night, for what she wasn't exactly sure. Russell was away for weeks at a time, working for a company that bought up land to clear-cut and make way, he told her, for the booming business that would be coal. Radiance was the name of that place, and she imagined it as a world that smoldered, ready to explode with the way of it, the big trees pulled down, the trucks loaded and heading out. No one loves us here, Russell said in the postcards he sent, and yet at night when she sat by the window she knew better.

She'd hear the stamp of feet on the road outside, voices, the rev and tearing off of cars into the dark. She lit matches and smoked until a cigarette burned down to the quick of her fingers. She'd raise the screenless windows and touch the cool air, bringing her hand back to her mouth to taste it. Her daddy had said you could diagnose trouble in an engine like that. The distance between herself and Russell Wallen was like that. The night tasted of a body not her own. It tasted of his sweat and heat, of nights she'd held him so tight she could feel the sharp bones of his shoulders and back next to her breasts. Another woman was holding him now, she knew, but her only proof was the taste of all the long nights he was gone. Like that, she followed him and his dreams of heading west.

In the deserts of New Mexico, he told her, he would make their fortunes clean and clear. They'd make money aplenty—enough to make their own way in this world, own the world even, enough for sure to make that world shine with their own two names. She counted herself lucky as they broke down here, needed a patched radiator there, in the miles of heat and distance. Deserts. She had never seen the like, how nothing led to nothing and on from there, to motel after motel and finally to Willette, where the factories that processed uranium and copper gleamed.

She took a job in Willette her own self, one that pleased her enough, factory work at an auto parts assembly line. She needed the work, the dullness of it, and she lulled herself at night by counting down the screws and bolts she'd gathered, hour after hour. He sat up laying out cards for solitaire and only came to bed to wake and sleep and wake. *Where were you?* She whispered in his ear, hummed anger to him until his breathing grew deep and smooth. *Where are you now?* More and more it set her teeth on edge, the way she put her hands next to his heart, waiting for the signs she already had. He was gone, then back again, half of him at most.

She saw the two of them, Russell and a woman, as she walked back from work of a late afternoon. After that, she looked for the woman everywhere. She noted the way a wisp of black hair blurred around a corner in the waves of heat off the streets. A particular shadow behind the plate glass window of a store. She followed her a few times, the pale-skinned woman. One day she walked behind the woman to an office building, waited outside a movie theater for her for two long hours as she sat in a slice of shade, mouth dry and breath coming hard. The glimpse she had that day was of the woman's fingers, her red nails in the white-hot heat.

The red settled inside Della's body over time. Russell was gone more and more, the sheet tossed back, the bed empty. Surely, she told herself, she should have sensed it. Should have known, all those nights she lay beside him, holding on to him, turning with him like they were one self. Should have known as he came home smelling of that black-haired woman's sweat, his mouth tasting of her most secret spots, but that wasn't the thing either. *Should have known, should have known, should have known.* What difference did knowing make? Other women were other women, and she had lived with them, one by one. *Why don't you love me?* Della said this aloud, testing the air. The question tasted stale, used up, and it was. Russell wanted a place, a woman, a lover, work, a tract of land, some deep heart of the earth he could never, never find.

Miracelle Loving
Smyte
1993

20

Moon over the Black Cat

Tree frogs foretold autumn, but I was restless, and night became my time-out-of-times. By ten-thirty the diner floors were mopped, and by eleven Ona Short had taken her turn at carrying the trash to the Dumpster and had headed to her apartment in the outskirts of Smyte. I'd stay by my lonesome and finish up the last slice of banana cream pie and feel some near-midnight regret settle in my chest. At night my fingers itched to pick up a phone and call Cody, but I'd not forgotten the wary in his voice that last time.

I sat in front of a fast food joint for two hours one night with my radio jacked up to Nirvana. Girls cruised the parking lot looking for boys to take them out on back roads for a big time and a bunch of party favors I couldn't have named these days. Words from Ruby's girl-diary haunted me. *I am hungry, but nothing fills me up.* If I took a good hard look at myself in my side-view mirror, I knew that truth well enough. *Waydean Long.* I'd hidden behind a name here in Smyte, but surely, I told myself, if Russell Wallen knew who I was—and he should have by now, if he'd looked at me good and hard—wouldn't he have claimed me? Or maybe not. I was a roadie who'd lived a million places and wanted a million lives not her own, and now here I was wanting the father I'd never known to tell me he loved me. I ached with lonely and I wanted to be alone and I wanted nothing at all to do with my own self.

After I closed up one night, I walked a little along the highway and then back into the wide parking area for the mill. The steps of one building had become a spot I liked to go to sit and smoke a cigarette, come the end of a long day. It was the squat warehouse building, and it had a sign teetering over a wooden door. *Wallen Industries.* I figured if there was an office to his place of business, it was in this building, and apparently I was right. About then a truck pulled in, its windows down, a radio blaring rockabilly. *Well, that's all right, mama. That's all right for you. That's all right, mama, just any way you do.* A truck door slammed shut. Russell Wallen himself stumbled out of his truck and then stood, mumbling to himself. I could smell the whiskey from where I sat.

He'd left the truck lights on and taken a seat on its bumper when he saw me on the steps. "You a night owl too?"

"Seems like you are."

He fumbled in his pockets. "You got another one of them cigarettes?" His voice was thick as honey.

"You're lucky." I walked over and held out my pack.

There was enough truck light so I could see his face.

"I've seen you around a time or two." He smiled in my direction, slung one leg over the other. "I know who you are."

"What's the word on me these days?" I crouched on my heels by the truck's headlights.

"Woman traveling here and there, ending up in Smyte, for all the likely that is."

"Something the matter with a woman traveling alone?"

He shrugged. "You never said what you saw on my palm the other night at the library."

I thought about standing in my room, how I'd wanted, bad, to crash my fists into the glass of Tince May's photos. "I haven't got that figured out yet, mister," I said.

"I've got two or three futures." He flicked his cigarette butt onto the asphalt. "Two or three pasts, for that matter."

Back in my room I said his name aloud. "Russell Wallen." It was a name full of l's. A name full of lulls and spaces and times I didn't know. I paced, holding his name inside me, then I pushed the window up and said the name again out into the cool night air. I tuned the name inside myself, like it was the fiddle my grandfather had played back in Radiance. I changed the name as I said it to myself, trying variations on for size. *Father. Not-father. The-man-who-made-me.* I spoke the name again, again. "Russell Wallen." And then I repeated the sentence from Ruby's diary aloud, like it was a mantra. *"I am hungry, but nothing fills me up."* What had my mother desired when she met Russell Wallen? I said his name again, letting the letters linger over the hardness of his face in the dark near the mill. Had his face looked like that as she tried to love him, all those years and years ago? I remembered Cody Black, the way his eyes went blank with hurt. *"Don't love me,"* I'd said.

I was Ruby Loving's daughter, Russell Wallen's too. Daughter of a woman who wanted the love she never seemed to find. Daughter of a man who had no idea how I'd lived my life. His name settled inside my chest, took hold of my heart and held on, hard. He had never loved either of us enough to live our lives. He'd never loved me. Never loved the woman who told fortunes and made potions and wished for him, town to town to town.

21

Make the World Go Away

By late October customers had dwindled, but Ona and I found ways to use our time. Afternoons, I scrubbed the walls alongside the booths, washed the front window with vinegar and newspapers. I picked country, blues, any old song on the jukebox to play along while I cleaned. I danced the mop, swung it around the floor between the tables and dipped it under the booths.

One morning rain was falling against the kitchen windows and there wasn't a customer in sight, so I set about making myself some breakfast. I stood at the stove—a skillet of eggs, sunny side up, and bacon sizzling in a pan—when Della pushed through the swinging doors from out front. She looked like she'd been awake all night.

I added a couple eggs for her and then made us each a plate. We sat near the open oven door for warmth.

"You seem right to home," she said.

"I guess the backseat of a car is about as close to home as I've come sometimes, and this is nice."

Della stretched her legs. "There was a time when Russell and I about lived in his truck."

"When was that, Della?"

"Too many years back." She tapped ash onto the knee of her coveralls. "That time we went as far as Miami."

She told me about the grit of sand between your teeth. About the way shadows of little things, light and ghost crabs, moved so quick you'd almost have not believed that much quickness was possible. About the way a sunrise looked as it stretched from sky to the middle of an ocean. She'd only seen those things those times, three at most, when she and Russell Wallen had driven right along the beach for miles.

"We were going to ride down twice a month and head back to Kentucky with the freshest seafood this side of anywhere." She'd taken off her work boots and socks, and rubbed the soles of her bare feet. "Fisherman just shy of the ocean."

In the kitchen's half-light, her nails were blunt and chipped. "It could have worked," she said.

"Some things work and some don't." I reached for her cigarettes, lit one more. "I always wanted that. A life that worked."

When she'd gone back outside, I sat a long while, picturing Della's hand held out an open window on a drive down a long stretch of beach.

A muffler-less car raced off into the distance, and not too far away someone howled like a dog, the sound circling back from the dark. I walked a ways, but the cold rain had formed puddles along the edges of the road, and I found myself heading to the spot I'd come to claim—the steps of the warehouse.

A voice came from out of the shadows of the parking lot. Russell Wallen, his black felt hat dripping. "You always seem like a bird, times I've seen you." He sat beside me on the step.

"How's that?"

I held my umbrella over the both of us.

"You seem like I feel, nights like this one." Sitting that close to me, he smelled like smoke and wool and the rain. "A bird with its head under its wing."

"I feel like it should be two months from now, and winter's just started." I huddled inside my coat.

"That's no good," he said at last. "Let's ride somewhere, what do you say?"

I hesitated, then followed him to his truck, which was a world of its own. Enough empties to fill up the branches of a bottle tree. I reached down and picked up the water-swollen pages of a Kentucky map as I made room for my feet.

We rode to the outskirts of town, then beyond that to back roads, then gravel. We kept on from there to roads that grew darker, the houses with fewer lights. He pointed out a place he'd once played poker all night and about lost his shirt. Past that, a flimsy bridge spanned the distance between roadside and a far bank where he said a community called Dwale used to be. "Used to walk that swinging bridge just to see if I could," he said. A bit farther on, we parked at the edge of what he said was a quarry.

We sat in the truck and looked at how the water stretched black like cotton cloth as far as the headlights reached. I pulled my uniform skirt over my cold knees.

"I used to fish this spot." I heard him rub his hands together, blow against them. "Crappie and bluegill, mostly."

"You ever cook those up at the diner?"

"Nah." He struck a match and the sulphur smelled good. "Just for my own self."

"I've never fished much," I said. "Just a stick and a piece of string and make believe off the steps of a trailer when I was little."

"Where you been besides Smyte?" He took out a silver flask, sipped, and handed it on.

"Here, there, everywhere."

"Not much of an answer."

I named some places. Philadelphia. Fort Wayne. The desert. Naming sounded strange and hollow, the places drifting out of my mouth and over the water.

"You make it sound easy." He flicked his cigarette out, and it trailed a quick streak of red.

I told him about jobs I'd worked. Hotels. Bars. Willy's. I sipped, and blessed the fire going down. "Tell me a story about you, Russell."

I drew my coat closer around me, rubbed my elbows as he talked about being everything from a radio disc jockey to a full-time poker player.

"Tell me a story about something amazing you've seen." I sipped from the flask again. "Something that takes your breath and makes you hold it in."

He didn't say anything, but I could feel him thinking. Thinking about Della, maybe, whether she was awake, like us. Or thinking about a woman in a tiny-waisted dress the color of smoke, her dancing with a cup, a lip-sticked kiss on its rim. This was the man Ruby had loved. I sat inches away from the man who was my father. How big the sky was and the strongest light from a planet I thought might be Mars. How far away the planets were.

"The only wonder I can think about right now is how lonely everything gets," Russell said at last.

22

Night Adventures

Sometimes when I closed the place down for the night, the lights were on in Della's rooms above the Black Cat and Russell's truck was there. The next morning her eyes were bright. She curled her hair and wore a rhinestone pin on the front of her coveralls. Then he'd be nowhere in sight for days. I came upon her once at the back of the kitchen by a window wide open to the icy air. "A little spell of gone doesn't mean a thing," she said without turning around.

As the cold came on, Della and Ona cooked army-sized pots of chili that we all grew sick of. Bowls of banana pudding that went to syrup before we could spoon them up. Pans of sweet cornbread that ended up as crumbs for the crows and cardinals out back. As much as she cooked, Della seemed to grow thinner by the day, her coveralls held up by the sharp angles of bones. All of us seemed hungry as snow covered the roads and fewer and fewer customers came in past dusk. I slept through free afternoons in my room at Lacy May's like I'd wake up and winter would be over and done.

The room spooked me into thinking about Miami nights and hot lights along a strip of bars I'd haunted once. Knoxville and the basement of Willy's Wonderama. I remembered electric lines stretched across long highways to cities where I'd once lived, and my dreams were the lines snapping and sparking so I could see their faces by dream light. Russell Wallen telling me one more tale about drinking and card playing. Della, beautiful and dancing in a dress so blue. Cody Black, the tangle of us in the blankets at the Red Sari. But more than anything I dreamed again and again of that night Ruby was shot. Me out in the yard. Music from Ruby's record player. *Hold me in the morning, hold me at night.* Curtains blowing back and down and a shadow at the table. Glass breaking. Voices. Shadow-chair crashing against the floor. A voice so angry it broke open the air. The sound of a gun firing.

Cold set in, but we took to the roads, Russell Wallen and me. I often met him at the warehouse steps after I'd closed the diner, and we traveled country lanes to hole-in-the-road places with names like Filligree or Janes. We ended up at dive bars where you hauled in your own bottle in a brown bag for poker games that lasted till dawn. As he rolled his sleeves up to deal, I saw that Russell had a tattoo on his forearm. It was different than the one I had and all of Cody's. It was rough-drawn, a sketch of a \ bird that made me want to fly off to nowhere and stay put all at once. The wings stirred words at the back of my throat, but I held them there. *Tell me you're my father. You say it, not me.* If Russell Wallen said the words all on his own, a spell would break. The past would be real, once and for all.

It was almost snowing, little whispers against the tree branches by the time I got off work. I held on to the slick ground with my toes inside my shoes. He was sitting in his truck in the diner parking lot and I stood by the window he rolled down. Music spilled from the truck radio, country with a hard-edged guitar. The dark thinned out as I stood, letting me make out what he was doing. He was scraping a length of wood with a blade. Whittling.

"You the last one here?"

"Just closing up shop," I said.

He held out the whittled piece and I took it. It was cedar, and the thicker end of the piece had been carved, as fine as he could get it, into a face. I could make out a thin nose and left-on bark for hair. In a pinch, it could have been me.

The beam of light swept from my feet to my face and back down the front of my waitress uniform and my winter coat. "Get on in here, then."

His passenger door was nearly frozen shut, but I yanked until it gave and pulled myself up into the cab, careful with the thermos of coffee I'd brought from the diner. I kicked aside bottles and bags and fast food boxes to make room for my feet. The two of us stared off at the road. The glowing eyes of a critter disappeared into the tall weeds.

He took a mouthful of the hot coffee, then rolled the window down, spat. "You boil this stuff all night long?"

We sat, not talking for a little. "Where do you go when we don't see you, Russell?"

"You could probably figure it out."

"Church retreat?"

He laughed. "Church of five-card draw, maybe."

"Lose your skin and have to stay gone till you got it back?" Weak light shone from the Black Cat sign and I studied his face. Two long scratches, red and scabbed over, marked his cheek. He was unshaven, tired. "I can understand how it feels to want to win, Russell."

He lit a cigarette off the last one, handed it to me. "How's that?"

I told him about a job I'd had once as janitor for a community center in Tallahassee, how some nights there were prayer circles and AA groups and how, other nights, when I was ready to lock up and head on, I'd let a few of them in to sleep on the couches—homeless men who'd take out their cards and spare change. "I'd sit there all night just to feel it, them playing like winning change was the only thing that mattered."

"Winning's part of it." He rolled the window down again, held his hand out. It was snowing a little and ice sat in his palm.

"What's the rest of it?" The application form at Willy's came to me all of a sudden, those question about true visions, and Russell spoke to that so neatly now it startled me.

"It's part fire and part dark." He paused. "Part something without a name at all."

I remembered how black the basement was at Willy's, the way ghosts had traveled up from the boxes full of lost towns. Ruby's voice, how it had come to me for weeks and weeks, and now did not. "Tell me about that something else, Russell."

He told me about sitting up till good daylight dealing seven-card stud with a guy named Red. The parts of that story he liked best were about the taste of good whiskey and how he didn't lose the Pontiac he owned then on the last hand of the night.

"Nights like that are close to being saved," he said.

I tried to imagine what he meant. The way cards slapped down, one and two, but more than that, the way one card flew out from someone's hand, sailed through the air and held there, just a second or two before it landed on that table full of wet-glass rings and cigarette ash. Those seconds were what counted, he said. They were almost holy. Of course, Russell Wallen never used a word like holy for any of it, but I knew what he meant—that space between. Between now and then, between wanting and having, between what you got and what you wanted so much it tasted bittersweet. What I wanted, I told him, was something that caught hold of me, went inside me, into my bones and blood and breathing. Maybe I was talking about the spirit, but I hadn't seen that yet inside the four walls of any church.

"I always subscribe to the moon and stars as the name of the good Lord, myself," Russell said. We were driving by that time and he looped one hand over the steering wheel and reached for the glove box with the other. "Might surprise you some," he said, and it did. Along with maps and wadded-up papers and half a carton of cigarettes was a Bible. A beat-up brown-covered thing with a zipper. "Had that book since I was sixteen years old."

"I somehow never pictured you with the Good Book."

Many of the Bible's pages were ripped out and many of the colored drawings—Jesus on the Cross, Jesus in the Garden—were torn out and stuck back in at odd places. Jesus up front in the book of Genesis. Lazarus rising from the dead back in the book of Revelations. Where the family tree usually was, there was a taped-in piece of notebook paper with a big scrawl that must have been Russell's. *Here I am! I stand at the door and knock. You bet I do.*

"All those missing pages?"

"On the walls one place or another, hoping somebody else would understand what it was I didn't."

In the back of the Bible, in the inside cover, was a taped-on square of thick paper with the same loopy handwriting. *For a time that hasn't come,* Russell had written, like a boy writing his Keep Out sign for the door of a room.

"Did you grow up believing?" I asked.

"I grew up with enough of them that did," he said, and we got quiet again. He turned the engine on, found a radio station, and turned it low.

I fell to thinking about the times Ruby had taken me to a church or two. Once we'd sat in the car at night outside a little white building with windows about bigger than it was, and light poured through every pane of glass, sending out light that was red and green and blue as singing voices carried out to us in the parking lot.

"My daddy would preach now and again, but never to a crowd." He lit a cigarette with one hand and flipped the match out the window. "And the intentions he showed me and my mother? Everything from love to enough mad to light a fire in any heart."

I looked him. "What was it could set him going?"

"I could, if I tried, or even if I didn't." Russell wiped the sweat from the inside windshield, looked out. "But most times he was just angry at nothing at all and everything."

We drove with Russell not saying where, took a sharp curve off the highway, then turned onto a gravel road at a mailbox. He handed me that little flask he carried and I paced his sips as he told some story. How the desert looked at night, or the ocean or a stretch of mountains at night or the way the moon came up and reached across a highway at the edge of a town, even if it wasn't Smyte. His stories were so alive I could almost wrap them around me to keep me warm.

I closed my eyes and made myself see it. The question I carried inside me like handwriting on a page. The night she died. If I tried, I could see it easy enough. The derringer would have been so small in his hands, rendering it useless, almost. A bullet flying straight for my mother's chest. Was it him who killed her? Or was I wrong?

"I can't say I know there's a God," he said as we drove. "I can't say there's anything bigger than what you can hold on to in your very own hands."

I listened to him talk as we rode, and his voice was almost a comfort.

We slowed down at a field and bumped along over its ruts amid all the cars. "Where are we going, Russell?" I asked about a dozen times as we got out of the truck and stumbled across the frozen earth, but he didn't answer all the way until we were at the steps of a wooden building with a cross lit up by a moon that had begun to shine. In a big room people were kneeling, about a million of them. Heads bowed and praying, all of them at once and all of them aloud, a mighty but soft collision of voices whispering and waving of hands and fingers pointing toward heaven. I wished for Sunday-go-to meeting shoes at least as we took a pew in the back. Good pine, like the walls and the far-up-there pulpit with a piano and seats for a choir and red silk roses in abundance.

I mouthed a question at Russell. "What place is this?"

Beads of sweat clung to his upper lip. "Something about belief, I reckon."

Bare bulbs hung from the ceiling and candles were lit on every window ledge below the faces of Jesus and Mary. And the whispered words—"deliver . . . forgive . . . grievous sin"—were like tiny white doves, hundreds of words circling and tickling one another, vying for space in the dim church light. All over the place hands waved, and then there was shouting. "Jesus! Jesus!"

At the keyboard was a young man with a Nehru jacket and pomaded hair who was doing a light riff. A spotlight shone down on a dozen other young people, their choir robes a motley mix of blue and green and purple. Moses parting a human sea was a preacher like no one I'd ever seen except on the backs of romance novels. She had bleach-blond hair teased into a beehive, and she held her hands out as mouths moved in song. "There is pow'r, pow'r, wonder-working pow'r." She spun, hands guiding this song from its makers, left, right, higher in the back, please. A high-heeled foot turned and she held her arms out to us. "There is pow'r, pow'r, wonder-working pow'r in the precious blood of the Lamb."

Her sparkly skirt and sequined jacket set the pulpit afire. Whispered words circled into the hymn. "Pow'r. Pow'r."

Russell was staring at the pulpit, his eyes wide.

"We want to be here?" I said, but the main event was starting and a woman in front of me turned and made a shushing gesture.

"Blessed children, I bring you joy." The preacher's hand waved at us, a kind of parade wave from the back of a float. "Blessed ones, all of you."

Need floated over the crowd, deciding where it would land. It snuggled up at my side like a little cat. "Listen," the preacher-woman said. The sermon commenced.

"Ruth was a traveler. Naomi said, 'Return home, my daughters. Why would you come with me?' And Orpah, she turned back on the road and left them there, children. Left Naomi and Ruth, but Ruth was the one who wasn't a bit afraid. She planted her feet in the dust and went out into a strange land to find her truth. And she, my children, she was only one of those who were not afraid."

The preacher did a little rat-a-tat-tat with her silver pumps. She paced.

"And I'll tell you, Ruth wasn't the only one who was a traveler. Not the

174

only woman who went forth. There were women who took to the streets," she said. "Women who traveled to foreign countries. Women who had no families but made them. Women who stood up or sat down, who planted their feet, made themselves heard. Esther, taken to the king's palace and made part of a harem but become queen over Vashti and become the king's savior.

"Oh, my sweet ones," she said, and she pranced and turned and raised her ringed hands to us. "Even them, the women of no names. Even them, the women who are lost and countryless. Even them.

"Abishag, who kept King David warm in the night and became the voice of songs. Hagar, who fled into the desert but gave an old man a first-born son named Ishmael. Zipporah, who followed Moses on the road back to Egypt and said unto him, 'You are a husband of blood.'"

The names of women who had traveled wound their way down my throat, settled in my gut. She was looking at me, this preacher-woman, her sparkles, her rings and her mascaraed eyes.

"I call upon you," she said. "Jesus himself calls upon you, my dear hearts."

She'd picked me out of all of them in these pews. She pointed no finger, said no name that was mine, but she knew me. My belly felt it and my bones did. I tucked my head, stared at my lap.

"Come forward and receive the gift of healing, all ye who hear the words of Christ Jesus. Come."

The whispers crescendoed and hymn words joined in. The crowd was a tight fist of excitement and fear and wondering. My feet itched, urging me up, but I held on tight to the edge of the pew.

"Look." Russell laid his hand on my arm.

A girl. Longish hair of no color in the beam of light and the candles. Head held down to her chest, a baggy dress long enough to reach her ankles.

"Welcome, dear heart." The preacher touched the girl's shoulder. "Welcome."

The girl was one of those Willy's Wonderama faces. Eyes and mouth like a tangle in a jar of formaldehyde, a face wanting out. A melted face. A face like wax dripping down lit candles. A wrinkled flow-down of a face. Face made of waves and rivulets of skin that flowed down, a river of face.

"Pray, brothers," the preacher-woman said, her voice rising. "Pray," she said, and her words touched us all like a sweet balm that stung and woke us too.

"Love?" she asked, and we answered her, like we knew, "Amen!"

"Love?" she said. "You think you know the question and the answer, children? You think you know the why and the wherefore. You think love is easy as a brand-new car. Easy as a check, first of the month. You think love is a person, a place. You think love is a fifteen-ninety-nine jacket you dress up. You think love is that sweetheart on your arm of a Saturday night. You think love comes to you for free, and I'm here to tell you the truth of it, the truth and the light."

"Amen!" we said.

Prayers and words rose as we looked at the girl's face with the light shining down on it, a face naked and so true it hurt to look at her. Wax and hurt flesh and behind it a brightness she'd swallowed, the light of her own suffering, the roads she'd been down. Roads past houses with their shut doors and their secrets. Back-of-a-hand roads. Kick-you-out-and-don't-come-back roads, roads away from here and toward there. Houses that would never be her own, arms that had not held her at night.

"I'm here to tell you the truth, children," the preacher said. "To tell you about love."

"Amen!" we said.

"Love is a ghost that settles inside us. A ghost made of blue fire. The light of apple wood burning. A holy spirit made of our own selves. Call it in, brothers!" she said. "Call it to you, sisters! Oh," she said, "bathe your-selves in it. Drink it deep, children. The spirit of love."

"Amen!"

"Oh, the sweetness of it. Love, oh, it blossoms in the heart of winter. Breath as warm as your own heart's blood. Oh, and the sweetness of sum-mer. Love like cool waters of everything. Love will comfort you, fill you, bless you, make you tremble. Love, oh my sweet lambs. Love is a ghost of all things we have feared and left behind. All things we have cast aside and could not bear."

"Amen!"

"Raise it up inside you, sisters! Raise it up inside you, brothers! Love is what we most want and what we most cast out. Oh, love. Listen! Sisters, pray. Pray for the grace of precious Jesus to fall upon us. Upon this one who needs you most."

Around me people stood, shouted.

"Yes, brothers! Yes, sisters!"

The hurt-faced girl in her big, baggy dress was dancing. I could feel her feet like they were my own, her pointy-toed boots scuffing rhythms on the platform where the shiny preacher took her hand. I could see her eyes now. Oh, her eyes. They were the wanting in that face melted down to its own pain. Oh, love me, her eyes said, and I wanted to cry as I looked at her, but instead I looked at my own hands, my own lap.

"Sing praises, brothers and sisters," the preacher said. Full-throated and off-key, she raised her hands, leading all our voices on.

Russell shifted his leg against mine, like we could keep each other safe from this thing called healing.

And then the girl sang, a sweetness you could taste. Her voice tugged at our coats, begged us to listen.

The preacher lifted her hands, her nails a shiny red. "Heal her, heal her," the preacher said. "Listen."

More dove-whispers from those kneeling prayers. Words farther down, inside me, underneath us. Far down in the church floor, beneath stone and solid ground, down in the earth's pure heart, a place neither hot nor cold, in which I saw my own self, begging for mercy.

What power lies in hands folded in prayer? Russell's hands gripping a spoon and stirring soup. Cody's hands, stroking the long stretch of my arm and down. And Della too. Oil-black nails and strong. Her too. Ruby. Her nails painted red. And another hand, one I didn't know. That girl's up there? Not hers, but a vision-hand in my mind and a palm I studied behind my closed eyes. What future had I made? A lie-future, a made-up road ahead. A woman traveling nowhere.

Neither power nor glory but some other feeling lay bare on the truck's dash where both of us could study it while we lingered outside the Black Cat.

Russell rolled the window down and cold spilled in. "I don't believe. Don't disbelieve."

Who were we? Backsliders who'd gone there to rack up a point or two toward salvation? Probably. Thrill seekers after all the oddities that Smyte had to offer the lost? That too. What I'd come away with shook me and I wanted to hide. I felt around under the seat for the bottle I knew he kept there. Whiskey trailed down my throat, warm and musky. "What did you want healed?"

"I don't know how to say." He shook his head. "Maybe not healing. What did they used to call it when you went out with a stick looking for water when there wasn't none?"

"Divining?"

He took his own sip, wiped his mouth on his sleeve. "Looking for what isn't there." He laughed.

We were quiet and looked at the dash some more.

"All those futures I've told," I said. "Cards and palms. All our truths, written on our own skin."

He held his hand out, palm up. "What do you see there tonight?"

There was just enough moonlight that I could see the wiry fingers, the tough worked skin. "Your lifeline." I traced it. "It heads on around the side of your hand."

"Does it?"

"And it forks off." I traced the line from the point where it broke.

"And?"

The forks met, disappeared.

"I think what I wanted," he said, "was to make a future no one could argue with."

"Did you get what you wanted?"

"Sometimes." He stared into the dark.

Russell Wallen
Oceanus
1970

23

Till Nothing at All

He'd never much believed in fortune, and he could name the times and places he'd been truly lucky. A royal flush once when he was a kid and it was winter. He'd holed up with a bunch of them making home brew and he'd bet everything he owned down to his good pair of boots. And before Della, the times he'd been down to his last fifty bucks and they'd picked him for the job because they liked the way he walked or talked or the way his hat was broke in good from use. Fortune was two ways off a stop sign in the middle of nowhere or the way a phone could ring at night when you were lonely and the voice was one you didn't mind too much, that time.

Fortune was Ruby Loving, how she shuffled and spread those fancy cards on top of the sheets, a spread on his lap as they lay in bed of an afternoon. Your fortune, mister, she'd say. Two steps forward, another step back, and you always waiting, never sure which way you should go next. She was right, and he knew it. Until he met Ruby, love was a question he left aside.

Della brought him a way of things he had never had, a steadiness, and she knew things, that was certain. She knew the ins and outs of an engine to beat anything, and he'd never get over the way it felt to drive some highway and her calling out the make and model of any ride they saw from a 1963 Plymouth Valiant to the 1955 Chrysler Imperial they saw one time in Florida on A1A. It wasn't just that she was a woman who knew how to fix things, though that surprised him again and again. It was that she didn't see things that were unseeable, neither God nor angels nor spirits. Della saw the here and now, the right-in-front-of-you, and she made him feel about as safe as a straight run, ace high—but that was putting it in a way he didn't like. He honored Della more than that, to put her in a list of things that included nights of poker or how a man held his liquor. He honored Della for being of this world when his bringing up had been about so much that was not.

His father was all not. The fruits of the Lord are not of this world, he'd say as he brought home glassy-eyed squirrels, laying them out on the metal kitchen table and showing how to divest them of their skin and bones. The fruits of the Lord. He rode Russell around a pasture to show him how to drive a four-on-the-floor when he was no more than nine. The day was stormy and the land soaked. He drove circle after circle, the back tires digging in, the clutch dragging and that scent of burning. His father watched from inside the truck as the rain fell and as Russell knelt, scooping handfuls of mud, patting down the wet earth and trying, trying to clear the way. He failed again and again. Failed at man-things. Gun oil and the sharpening of knives. The mornings at the hillside junkyard and a .22 at his shoulder, drawing a bead on the side of a rusted-out washer or the back of a gutted couch. You miss it every time, boy, his father said. He meant how many hours he could hold up with a pickax, just how long he could not hurt when his hands blistered and healed over and broke open. And far down inside, all that hurt, he meant God, too. He meant the true name of the Lord that Russell could never, never say.

That day at the Hack River, a place known for its stink of cast-off oil and things long dead. That day his father was once again a part-time preacher. Part-time man of the Word, and the few that listened to him. Always after in his head he'd hear that song they sang as they gathered to hear his father preach, knowing that afterwards they'd raise a bottle to the sky while they prayed beside the beautiful river. The river had nothing of beauty about it, the way it snaked around the town and could not wash away the refuse of the brittle Georgia land. A merciful God was not even a memory for him there. He remembered nothing of God long after that day, but only how his father's hard hands pushed at the back of his neck, shoving him under the brown waters all the time he prayed. For long there had been such prayers. Prayers about holding on. About waiting until the spirit came forth. Waiting until the bright, shining light of heaven cracked open the gray sky.

Expecting nothing holy, he was lowered into the dank water and was surprised in that near-minute of his baptism to see something after all.

It was the same place he'd dreamed before, and he recognized it immediately. The same dust swirled up behind a caved-in house where some skinny woman sat on a stoop with a cup of coffee. She was crying, an angry sound that came from her gut. The sound shook him, and he began to flail, kicking his legs and pushing hard against his father's hands. The hands held him down, and he heard distant praying and the hymn still being sung. *Gather at the river.* He couldn't breathe, and he struggled hard as the hurt sound changed, became a shape. All the sounds of praying and hurt gathered and transformed into a pocket of air, a hole inside the muddy waters. Later on, he would remember the hole as a mouth and he would call it the mouth of God. The hole led down or up, he could not tell which, but he dove there, feeling himself being sucked inside eternity, a place where he floated, terrified, until his father's arms pulled him back up into the world.

When Ruby strewed her fortune-teller's cards across his chest, he was as afraid as he had been in years, floating in the memory of a holiness he had never quite reached. He had never quite reached many things in his life, he knew. The shake and shine, not just of money in his pocket, but of whatever it was that men did to have dominion, to own, not just the world, but that drunk thing called power. Jobs of work, work that was glory, they were one thing. She too was a precipice of power. Her sweat's scent, the power of her fingers tracing the skin of his back. Her hands scared him more and more. The way they wrapped themselves around a secret inside him and shook him until he shivered with the want of her. And still, how often had he said it? "Tell me my future, Ruby Loving." He felt himself falling inside that future again and again. Felt himself terrified once again beneath the dark waters of what he could not quite be.

She knew his fortune all along, she said. Knew it already the first time she looked into his palm. Knew it the first time she drew a card. This, she said. Long stretches of desert. Heat rising off highways headed west. How steam would rise from the factories where he would make bitter things with his very own hands. Don't tell me, he said. Don't tell me any more. But she did. Told of afternoons of wanting, afternoons of secrets and sex. Told of their child, even, a child with her eyes, his hands. Child half of fortunes, half of restless plan after plan after plan. No more, he said, and yet she went on, went on into all they were and would be and would not be. Envelopes full of love letters sent out and back. Love sent out into the air over and over and over. Love felt and not returned. Love and love and love. Don't you love me? she asked, and wrapped her arms around his waist like ties he could not unbind.

Miracelle Loving
Smyte
1993

24

The Stories Our Bodies Tell

Ghosts and spirits, haints and traces of before. On the drive back from the church service, Russell and I had talked about whether or not we believed in such things. Looking for what isn't there. I'd been doing just that all these weeks in Smyte. Waiting for Russell Wallen to appear at my door, his black hat tilted over an eye, a bouquet with a note wired to it. Welcome home, my own baby girl. I wanted my mother so bad right then, I nearly cried. I wanted to be a girl again, wanted Ruby telling me to do and fetch. Me fetching her tarot deck with the first card on top always the same. The Lovers, holding hands. But I wasn't a good daughter. I never had been.

I couldn't have slept more than a few minutes when knocking woke me. I pulled the pillow over my head, but the knocking continued.

I was cold in my nightgown as I padded over to the door, held it open a few inches.

Della stood there, her winter coat half unbuttoned. She put her hand against the door, nudged it open a few more inches. Her nails were as clean as they got from the engines she'd worked on.

I sat on the edge of the bed and folded my arms across my chest, bringing myself awake, feeling her there.

She moved around the room, looking at my few things. A paperweight. An empty wine bottle with a candle in it. A postcard from Miami. She picked up the box of tarot cards, looked at a photo I'd taped to the dresser mirror. Ruby, her back turned to the camera, the long shadows of afternoon behind her.

"Where were you tonight?"

"Church, if you believe it."

"Russell's been taking you a lot of places."

"We're friends, Della."

"There's friends and then there's night after night." She looked at the floor. "You and him."

I set the kettle on the hotplate going while Della walked past the framed photographs on my walls, stopping at a photo of a little baby in its coffin. She shook her head. "Ellen Johnson's great-grandbaby," she said. "She still talks about laying her out her own self."

At Tince May's photo she put her hands against the glass like I had done often enough. "I haven't seen a picture of her in forever," she said. "You can almost think you're touching her."

"I touch that picture most every night," I said. "I'm not sure what wants healing most."

"I used to come to see her. It was a sight, her in those beds against that wall." She pointed. "And her a lake of skin. A river you could touch, all warm. And you stood there and asked your question."

"Like what?" I put spoons of coffee and lots of sugar in two cups.

"Just about anything, from a heart that hurt to a lost soul."

"Which one were you?"

We sat side by side on the edge of my bed.

"I was there the day she passed." Della sipped her coffee, stared at the picture and told me about that day.

"Folks think this house is haunted." She clicked her lighter, inhaled deep.

I shivered and drew the edges of my nightgown close.

"What's this?" Della reached over, touched my upper arm where it was bared.

"A little body art reminder of Knoxville," I said.

I drew the cap sleeve back off the shoulder, let her see the road, the woman standing at the crest of the mountain.

"A road and a mountain," she said as she leaned in, studied the tattoo.

"If you follow that road to its end, there's a town," I said. "You have to imagine that. The road's end."

"What town would there be?"

"A town called Radiance," I said. "Have you ever heard of it?"

She was so quiet I could hear her breathing. "I hear tell that in some towns," she said after what seemed a long while. "In some towns you wake up in the mornings and your heart could almost break for wishing."

"I think Radiance could have been a town like that once."

"And who would she be?" Della ran her forefinger along the outline of the woman, the long strands of her hair.

"I think that might be a woman who wished just like you say, Della. And I think maybe you knew her."

"A road and a mountain and a woman," she said. "What would I know about that?"

"I think you might even have known her name, Della."

"What name would a tattooed woman have that I'd know?" she said.

"It's a name I believe you've known a good while."

She reached again, touched the lines of the tattoo, but I pulled away, pulled the gown around me.

"Your name, girl," she said at last.

"My name?"

She laid her hands on my shoulders, looked at me straight on. "Your name's one I knew the minute I saw you."

"You've known my name all along. Waydean Long."

"That's not your name. We both know that."

"We do?"

"I knew the minute I saw you that you're her daughter, that you had to be."

"Her?"

"You look like her, every bit of you in every part of her I knew."

I shivered as much as I had every time I'd heard my mother's voice inside me, though there was no word from her now.

"Your name's not Long," Della said. "It's longer than Long. It's Loving."

I tried not to sound like I could cry. "Tell me what you know about my mother."

At the window Della lit a cigarette, and smoke left her nose, traveled against the cold glass. "Your mother? The only thing I can tell you about her is how a body can be a stranger to love, as much as they want it."

"Say what you mean."

"Hearts don't always hold love," she said. "As much as you try to make them."

"Whose heart?" I asked, and took a deep breath. "Ruby's? Is she who you mean?" The name was there, said and done.

Snow was falling, and under the streetlights we could see the streets, covered already. "You've known all along who I am? And you never said?" I stood beside her, close enough to touch her but not. "He's never said a word."

"I can't speak for him," she said. "For what his heart knows. Maybe I never could."

"Why now, Della?" I clenched my hands, felt my nails digging into my palms. "Why are you here *now* telling me anything at all?"

She touched the window with one finger and drew a square in the frost. "Had a ghost of a song in my head all day, so maybe that was the sign I needed."

"What song was that, Della?"

"One from a long time ago." She hummed it a little, and I thought it was a hymn we'd heard, him and me, then she added the words. *Love me in the morning, love me at night. Love me, Radiance, honey, till long past midnight.*

"Radiance," she said as the square in the frost became a house. Thin lines of smoke trailed from a chimney. "That's where your mother came from, and where your father never really left, the minute he saw her."

I thought I'd fall into it, the words. Mother. Father. But the world was spinning and I fixed on it, the tiny patterns of falling snow outside.

"Miracelle," I said. "My name is Miracelle Loving."

Ruby Loving
Fortune Teller's Daughter
1967–1972

25

A Taste like Steel

Where did she come from? they asked her. They asked in bus stations, at middle-of-the-night diners, at rest areas, in the lobbies of cheap and good motels. Her hair was grown near waist length and her eyes were outlined with kohl. The truck driver who rode them for most of a day along Highway 40 East said Ruby seemed like a beautiful ghost from an old movie. She'd seen her share of haints, she said as she held his hand on her lap and traced his lifeline, a stunted thing, though she didn't tell him so. She told him he'd end up in Ousley, North Carolina, with a house and a pit bull and four rigs all his own. He gave her a derringer with a handle covered in abalone. Won it in a card game, he said, and looked at Ruby like he'd loved her all his life. What's abalone? she asked, and he said it came from the sea. And you ought to think more about staying safe, he said. You with that girl and all alone.

As if Miracelle wasn't already learning to hold her cards close. She'd sit close enough to see every spread Ruby laid out. Ruby let her shuffle the cards, hand them over to the truck drivers who thought she was the queen of the world. They bought her grilled cheese and milk. They slipped dollars and spare change into Miracelle's pockets, and they looked at Ruby like she was less than a mother ought to be. But Miracelle brought them in by the dozens. Hard-eyed men went kind when the fortune teller's daughter was there. Men who'd laugh most times to think a line on a palm might mean good luck laid down their fives and tens when Miracelle smiled just right.

It wasn't that safe didn't matter. Ruby wanted a house and a fence and a little dog and her sweet girl. Down in Georgia, Miracelle shone in school. Gold stars and ribbons, and once she wrote a story about clouds. But Ruby wanted him more. Wanted Russell Wallen to hold on tight to at

193

night and how she could reach up and touch his face. Ruby couldn't help herself, the way she'd stop at a phone booth and call, just to hear his voice. He had that place by then. A diner they called the Black Cat, and he said it was okay, calling late at night when it was just him closing up. When she'd hear the clink of ice in a glass or a voice that must have been his wife's, she felt a white hotness inside.

Look, Miracelle said, a town called Neon, but even with a name like light they were stuck there for weeks, waiting to see if they could turn enough fortunes or clean rooms if they had to. Make enough money to take them somewhere. Where? her daughter would ask, her eyes so pitiful. She was eight, nine, ten, just a girl still, but already she wanted the whole world. She wanted a house with a door that shut. A kitchen with sunlight through windows vinegar clear. All Ruby wanted was him, one more time. Her lips along his skin like she would know at last how to draw it out of him like breath or heat. The heart he'd never given her.

By the time Miracelle was fourteen, she left her safe, with neighbors if not friends. Left her once to her own self, in an apartment behind a store. She almost changed her plans that time, stayed put just to fill up the hurt she felt when she saw the joy in her daughter's face at Ruby being gone a few days. She knew Miracelle well enough to know there'd be no boys, no partiers. The joy was for something else, for her mother being gone, for the world being all her own. Already Miracelle wanted every-thing, doors that locked behind her, drawers no one opened but herself. Already she wanted the whole world. And Ruby swore, by God, the world would be a better one soon, for one of them at least.

He finally rented himself a getaway room in a boardinghouse, and it got so she'd meet him now and again. The landlady hid a key behind a picture of Jesus nailed beside the door. Up the two flights, then the winding steps after that. She turned the doorknob to the attic room inch by inch so she wouldn't make a sound and wake any of them, the house or the pictures and all the ghosts asleep in that room. How she'd lie there, the quilts pulled over her head, waiting, that half-sleep of waiting. One time she dreamed the ghost of her own self she was becoming. A thin ghost, a shadow light as air. Who did she belong to? Surely not to those tobacco farmers and bank tellers and auto mechanics who came to hear the stories of their lives. To

Russell Wallen. How he'd throw the covers back and stand there looking down on her in the fancy night things she wore to make him love her. This place, he said, used to belong to a healer woman. She'd lay hands on you and bring you back to your own self. What self would that be? she asked him.

She brought presents when she came back home. A keychain like an "M" from a rest area gift shop. Dollar bills from Russell's pockets. More and more Miracelle wanted nothing from anybody, and why should she have? Gifts from a ghost daddy, ghost mama, from ghosts of places she'd never seen, places that left her mother with the scent of sex. She was older than her years, old enough for sleights of hand that made customers turn their heads at the right minute so money could disappear. Fourteen years old, going on a twenty, going on forever. Gone already, in some ways, Ruby thought.

She'd see Miracelle standing at the doorway of a dive bar where they'd gone to read palms and cards, and she could feel how the distance between them had stretched, taut and ready to snap. Already Miracelle was dreaming highways of her own, dreaming byways and backways and lovers. Lovers? How a girl could dream such a thing as desire? Surely it was not too late to keep her safe. Don't do this, don't do that, she told her daughter again and again. Don't look at boys like that. Don't wear your shirt unbuttoned from the top. Don't and don't and don't. Don't disappear. Some days she'd swear her daughter had vanished already into bar light full of smoke and the face after face of strangers.

She wanted to tell Miracelle it was easy to find, what saves us from ourselves. Good strong coffee and a shot or two in a favorite cup. A stranger offering a hand up on a street where the rains fell hard and standing still was cold. Or the Holy Spirit. Maybe it wasn't even too late for that one for Miracelle, for faith or prayers or fire.

When Ruby was four years old, she believed in Jesus. Jesus on the Cross, Jesus in a garden, Jesus kneeling in prayer. She believed in the slick patent leather of her shoes tapping against the back of a pew. She lay on a rug by the stove and listened to the tumble of wood and that hiss and sigh as the fire took hold and sent its heat and she guessed that was God, too. But she'd never been a book-learned woman. Couldn't say all the names of God if she had to, those thousand names or more for the power that made everything. And what did she really believe, if it came down to it? Spirits sang in the trees and wind carried the name of God and she could almost hear it if she listened.

And fire? Out there somewhere there were fires so big she could only imagine. She sat in roadside motels and watched television news about it, the faces of children running, the bombs in the trees behind villages across the world. Fire was war and glory. It lit the heavens to crimson come a summer night. It roiled in the center of the earth and made promises of hell and hereafter. All those tales of those who'd gone blind with love, from Samson and Delilah to Judah, blinded by Tamar's beauty. Ruby was heavy with blindness and longing.

When she lay with him, she loved him more than God. Every time she saw him, the world got made and remade. Fire stirred one more time under her skin, and her belly was rich and full of love. His touch was as close as she ever really got to holy. He could pick up the world and hold it in the palm of his hand, he could make her think love tasted of ash and sweet. She laid her hand against the warm skin of his chest and felt his beating heart and wished for it. The world exploding, made new just for him and her.

Tell me who he is, Miracelle said, again and again. How could Ruby tell about a man who ran through your fingers like water? He was Russell Wallen, and the name was a fact, but what else could she offer up like it was proof? He was maybe a preacher's son, though he'd never tell about it. He was brought up to believe the world had margins. Right. Wrong. Hallelujah and amen. He knew better. Poker and shine and never let anyone steal your heart. How he'd lie beside her and meet her eyes and say, *We can be anything if we believe hard enough.*

She'd lay her hand on his chest alongside a scar, not one made by knives. A hurt scar only a fortune teller could see. A heart scar he would not name, but she saw how it had been. Him nothing but a small shape in a bed at night. Him a boy. The hard words of some father-man. The cold of an open window and how it began. How he climbed out and down to start his life. Child become man. Fist fights and knives to steal your heart. Man as hurt as a boy left behind so long ago.

He was made of liquor and bets and riding with the windows down in a thunderstorm. Bottles of vodka. The women he'd had. In that boardinghouse attic room, she read his body, just as he read hers. She followed the long scar on the inside of his leg that a fine-honed razor had made. When she touched him, she saw the world gone so big she couldn't take it in. Like standing on a bridge and the L&N passing by underneath, rich and full of coal. Like the first time she saw the desert at night and the moon huge and white and lonely. That was a world, he said, that truly made a man. She was just glad, she told herself, that it was her that had given him a child, not that other woman, his wife.

The world, she told Miracelle, couldn't be counted on much. You couldn't find safe, like it was a stray sock or the chew of some rat inside a wall. She'd look inside her daughter's eyes, read her eyes, looking for answers to how her life might go. She'd reach for Miracelle's hands and lay them palm-up in her lap, looking at the lines. Your heart line, she'd say, is deeper than deep. And see that, right there? A split end to the heartline. *You will always be of two minds.*

In the diners where they sat of an afternoon for card readings, Miracelle sat by herself and looked as hungry as she could until some man in a business suit bought her a slice of coconut cream pie. She sat in a bar and slid coins meant for tips into her lap and dropped them into the jukebox for song after song, dance after dance, her girl hips swaying, her neck musky with cologne that said, *Taste me.* Miracelle, her skirts slinky, her wraparound shirts tight over her small breasts. Love me, love me, her body said as she danced with long-haired golden boys, their hands lingering along the small of her back. Miracelle, Ruby said, over and over. Watch yourself. Be safe. Safe? Miracelle said, her laughter like the rim of a glass rubbed with one wet finger. Seems like you're the one who should have watched yourself a long while ago, she said to Ruby. If my daddy didn't love you, then who did he love? she said as she plunked another quarter down for one more song. Who do you love, the song asked, and Miracelle played it over and over.

Ruby imagined a hundred million stories about how Russell and Della met. Her hand reaching into a cooler at the back of a store and his hand too, the ice-cold bottle, and how the two of them touched the first time. Or a job Della might have had. Desk clerk at a motel off Interstate 40. Working retail at some auto parts store. Or done up pretty and selling lingerie behind a counter. Her heart burned as she imagined Russell's hand at Della's waist and how the two of them spun around the dance floor at an Albuquerque bar at midnight.

Some nights as she lay there waiting for him, she let herself become his wife. She moved her hands and felt Della's. Stretched her legs along the bed and felt Della's. Cupped her hands at her ears and heard the words Della and Russell must have last said. *Love me love me love me.* It was the only thing that stilled her heart some nights. Becoming Della Wallen. And surely, she told herself, if the heat inside her chest grew strong enough, one night it would happen. Della would vanish, melt clean away, and nothing would be left but her own self. Her and him, at last, and that would be the truth of it.

She knew Russell, that was sure. He wanted love more than most and didn't want it at all, and when he got it? He sent it hurtling over the steep sides of roads, under bridges, into trash cans at rest stops. He let it slip through his fingers like the wailing voices of women at the funerals of men they'd loved and couldn't have. Love was the ice-cold voice of a creek at night, him lying with his ear pressed to the boards of a bridge where he'd laid down at last, tired and too drunk to care.

He'd learned love from the hands that touched him way back. When he was little and they taught him fear and not to want too much. Prayer and songs and hellfire. Words from the mouth of God that taught him to be afraid. Sent him south. West. The desert and the ocean and everywhere in between. The world taught him that love was what he could own, what he could be. After that, love got smaller. It became like parts of people left behind. An ear. An arm blown off in an explosion at a mine. Love was an eye, shut, refusing to see. A heart grown hard as a lump of coal. A heart that wanted nothing better than owning the earth and her and Della Wallen, both of them.

Why, watch her, Miracelle Loving, dancing by herself on an empty floor by midnight bar light. Watch her stand by the speakers turned as loud as they could go. Watch her putting her arms around her own self. See it around her, an invisible box. A glass case that no one could open. Tell me who I am, she said again and again. Who she was? A girl dancing alone and already loving no one. Girl keeping her self, far away from everyone and any chance of hurt. Does life make hardness a thing we are?

Do wounds grow inside us from so far back we can never know the beginning of that hurt?

She wanted to think of Miracelle those times—think how her daughter's hair caught the sun as they waited beside their broken-down car for someone, anyone to stop, and she would say, *Miracelle. Hold out your hand and smile. They'll stop for you*—but she was hardly there. Ruby was nothing but a bubble riding along the surface of a river. A trick of light. Touch her too quick and she would turn to shadows. She had no name when she was with him. Neither bones nor blood nor skin without his name written there.

Night upon night. Winter and cold. Dead of a summer night and bats touching the screens of open windows. As the hours passed in that room, she could hear the least thing. Downstairs a clock chiming midnight. Outside, the streets of Smyte. She could walk there and smell the paper scent, the smoke, the slow river. She'd seen the purple neon shine of that place he owned with Della. A diner where jukebox tunes spilled out along the highway.

She lay alone in the dark and imagined the night with a taste coal black and steel. A taste like the metal of that gun the truck driver gave her that time. If a gun had a taste, it could have a sound, too. What held the world in place was thin as soap and air. Sound could tear open the skin of the world, rend all things, even herself. She imagined that, an open seam running from her mouth, across her chest, her belly. It could be that easy. Him torn apart from her and one of them disappearing forever, free. Who am I? Miracelle asked. Tell me where I came from. Tell me my father's name.

Miracelle Loving
Smyte
1993

26

Last Call

I *can't speak for what his heart knows.*

I carried Della's words with me to the diner the next day for an early breakfast shift. Ona Short was baking biscuits and frying potatoes and the kitchen was warm with it. I stood in the dining room with a box of straws and packets of sugar and I imagined what he'd known. My mother wearing shiny red slippers from the Dollar Store, a cinched-waist dress with a belt. I imagined us in a roadside dive, the jukebox playing all the songs she loved. *Dance with me, mister. Dance me to one of them old songs.* Ruby, smiling at my father her last night on earth. Why, I asked myself, but I no longer had any idea what I wanted to know. What did it mean that he was my father?

After work, I rode the highways Russell and I had taken together, sat in the parking lot of the church where the blonde preacher had blessed the freak-girl and her sadness. I sat in my car beside the slate-gray waters of the quarry waiting for him. Smyte seemed like a huge winter coat that could not keep me warm. He was out there, on the way to nowhere good. Juke joints and preachers. County lines and ways to stay alive that nobody questioned. My belly roiled with anger and grief.

He was gone a week, and when he showed up again his truck had a missing bumper and a dangling headlight. Della traveled from garage to kitchen and then upstairs with a cloth-covered tray. Their voices rose. "What do you want from me, woman?" She hardly looked me in the eye before I headed home. "You're his daughter," she said as I zipped my coat. "Let him tell his part."

It was before sunset when I reached the warehouse. The sky was bruised-looking with a winter storm they said was ahead of us—ice and who knew how much snow. I lit a cigarette and kept the match flame going until it almost burned my fingers. I studied the upstairs of the factory building. A few panes on the far corner of the upper floor showed thin light. I could feel him up there.

The place inside wasn't the pitch black I expected. The tall windows were painted haphazardly and broken light filtered in, leaving the big room full of shadows. My eyes adjusted. Machines crouched along each side of the long concrete floor. Gears and chains. Rust and dials. And back in the corners, towers of gray-white. Reams of paper. I bent and picked up a piece and it felt like skin. My boots skidded and stuck on concrete that felt like oil and sawdust, but I took some stairs up to a hall and followed that to a doorway. The room was what must have been his office once, and it was half warm with a kerosene heater that tinged the place with light. I stood a minute by a desk heaped with ledgers and a rotary phone half-buried with papers. The room was touched by what looked like black snow from the heater that had shed its fumes and soot.

On the far side of the room was a mattress and he sitting there, his face buried in his arms, the tail end of a lit cigarette still going in an ashtray near his elbow.

"Russell," I said.

The office had that scent of paper pulp, but his smell too. Whiskey and sweat, and from the corner the wavery lines of fumes from the kerosene heater.

I knelt and took a seat beside him on the mattress. "Tell me a story, Russell Wallen," I said.

Like he always did, he reached me the flask, but I shook my head.

"Tell me a story about you."

"Nothing I haven't already told you'd want to hear twice." He laughed, but I didn't.

"Then let me tell you the story," I said, and the sentences and words had the hard edges of y's and t's in my mouth. "It's a story that starts with mountains and a road."

I slipped my coat off, let it fall around my hips. "At the end of the road there's a woman."

I unbuttoned my uniform at the top and slid its shoulder down. I could have been anything but a daughter with her father as I sat beside him on the mattress. I touched parts of the tattoo, one by one.

"And there's a town, Russell." I told him about the empty streets of Radiance, the boarded-up storefronts. I told him about the mountains and the heaps of coal where houses once had been. And I told him about the woman, her dark hair and eyes, how the road over the mountain was the first distance she'd ever traveled away from home.

"Then the woman had a daughter, Russell. A daughter named Miracelle."

"You're her daughter." His hand was rough with winter as he touched the tattooed woman's hair.

"I'm Miracelle Loving, and I want you to tell me what road I should take now."

Her name hung in the air between us, unsaid as his fingertip traced the inked outline of my mother.

"Tell me about her," I said, but he pulled back from me, buried his face in his hands.

"You should head out and never come back, Miracelle."

"You traveled this very road, Russell." I could hear my own voice, the plead in it, a sad child sound I didn't want, but it was there. "You went to a town called Radiance, and after that nothing was ever the same, least of all her."

"Yes," he said, then yes again. "I did know a place called Radiance."

"How about music on a porch at night? People dancing and fiddling a love song?"

"That I don't recall."

"Did you used to believe in love songs?" I hummed it a little that song about Radiance and love long past daylight.

"I used to believe in Della and me," he said like he hadn't heard me. He shook his head.

"And her?" I still didn't say her name, but it was smoke in the cold.

"I've never known any woman that could equal a love song."

I couldn't stop my questions, though I was begging now. "Did you love her?"

"You don't have the least notion."

"She's on my skin. She's inside my blood as much as she's inside yours." I wanted him to say it aloud. A charm. A potion. Here and now. "Say her name, Russell Wallen. Just say it."

"Why did you come here?" He leaned against the wall.

The taste of the story I wanted told was dark and I bit my tongue, holding it back, waiting for him to speak. "You know why. You know her name as well as I do."

"Do I?"

"Della said—" I began, but he hushed me.

"Della says a lot she doesn't understand."

"She said you knew things I'd come to find out."

"Did she."

"She said houses don't always hold love, even if you want them to."

He struck a match against the concrete of the floor, held it up to his face. He looked hollow, a skull of a face in the shadows.

"She said that hearts could break if you let them."

"She think she knows that?

"Tell me the story I need to hear, Russell Wallen."

"I told you all the ones I know." He reached over, touched my shoulder. "I've shown you water and preachers."

"I want another story," I said. "I want one with me and her in it. Tell me that one."

"I swear," he said, and he didn't finish the sentence.

"What do you swear?"

"I swear that I'm made of lonely. And you are too."

He could have been humming that song. Radiance. *Love me in the morning, love me at night. Hold me, Radiance, honey, till long past midnight.* A remembered song like winter nights, like sipping honey and lemon and drops of moonshine in a cup.

The room was dark. Dark as a half-closed closet door, clothes hanging inside like haints. One night. A storm and the covers pulled high above my head. How afraid I'd been those nights, and how afraid I'd been half my own life since. Anger prickled inside me as I turned and looked at him.

"Holding on to someone," I said aloud. "What does that mean to you?"

I'd let holding on work before, time upon time upon time, when words did not. Cody Black. And before him. Boy after boy, men and more, and me a woman wanting. What had one of them said? Cody or the one before him or even Russell some night as we drank cheap whiskey in a truck by a quarry. Girl, all you want is love, and you'll never find enough. I remembered shapes Ruby's hands made on the wall beside my bed. I'd had enough of shadows and half-knowing.

"Do you even know what lonely means, Russell Wallen?" The words came out with an edge and I was glad of it, how they sounded. Mean and fed up. Full of all these weeks of cat-and-mouse. These weeks of a daughter with a man who was her father and was no father at all.

"Russell," I said, and held his name in my mouth, tasting it, making sure of what I meant to say and do. "I have something for you I should have given you before."

I reached for my pack, unzipped it, reached inside, feeling the metal like I had a hundred times, what she'd called a sea-dream. How I could hear her, even now. *It looks like we're safe, even if we're not.* I took the gun from my pack and held it out to him on my palm. "This look like anything you might remember?"

I studied his face, looking for signs. His eyes changing with memory. The raise of his brows with the surprise. He reached out, and at first I thought he'd take the gun from me, but he didn't. He reached past my open hand, laid his fingers against my cheek, an awkward touch. Wisps of hair from my winter hat trailed against his rough skin. "You're just a girl," he said. "A girl wanting something she can't name."

I hated him then, and the hating was in that one word. *Girl.* What did he know about girlness or about being a woman or being anything at all? I was no girl, but he was right. I wanted to be ten again. Five. Never born at all. I wanted cards spread across a table, telling me my future, telling me my past. I wanted something so bad my mouth felt dry with its lack.

I leaned in close, like I was really looking at him for the first time, the veins in his no-sleep eyes, the shadows and planes of his face. I want to say that what I felt for him right then was akin to dregs in the bottom of a glass, akin to all things left, things left behind without regret. What I felt wasn't even hate. It was less than that. It was a blank space where love had tried and failed, failed and nearly given up.

"This is for Ruby. For my mother."

I stood and I spun around as graceful as some dancer and the gun spun with me, fit into my hand like I'd known the use of it all my life. Thumb and palm against the slick abalone of the grip. It was easy, how my forefinger hooked like it knew how against the trigger, and the rest of it could have been almost nothing. Me taking aim, not at him exactly, but at all the wishing and not, the years of no one to fill up the space where there should have been a father. I stood sighting down the barrel, finding his forehead, his shoulder, his heart. And then—there's no other way to describe it—I couldn't. What was he but a sad excuse for love, after all?

I aimed at the window, the one up high that let a little light into the room. There were, if I remembered, two bullets left from that night at the middle-of-nowhere house with Leroy Loving's things. With her things, girl-things from long before, love letters and fortune-telling cards and the slipshod debris of lives I'd never known. The anger I felt burned in my chest, and the bullet sped along that anger, crashed into the window glass, the room echoing with the sound. It was a clean sound. "It was you all along, Russell Wallen," I said. "You shot my mother. You killed Ruby Loving."

He'd jumped as the glass exploded, falling in flakes and jagged cuts of itself that sparkled and settled like they knew exactly how to hurt. I'd made an opening and both of us knew it.

It was an opening made of this cold winter. It was made of run-down, of towns left behind worse than when they started, of two lanes gone to one and gravel, of sad lovers and lonely girls. It was an opening made of my own self, too, my heart. And I looked through that opening and saw him for what he was. There was one bullet left and I thought about it. Him and his empty body where high and mighty used to live. A man sitting alone in a run-down paper factory he'd wanted as an empire. I flung the gun away against the wall and I knelt beside him again. Pushed against his shoulders so hard he fell back on the mattress.

"Tell me about that night," I said.

I looked into his face and it was just as sad as my own.

"What is it you think I did, Miracelle? What is it you think I know?"

Della Wallen
Smyte
1993

27

What It Takes to Replace a Heart

All that long evening as it snowed, the diner was empty and she sat by the window out front thinking about things she had no business remembering. How she'd followed him south to the ocean, west to the factories in Willette, then back east again to Smyte. All the places in between. Russell Wallen's heart ate up her life, year by year. How to love a man who did not love himself? A man who loved power but watched what he had sift through his fingers. A man who loved the buying up of land, timber, coal, paper, but ended up owning next to nothing. What had she told Miracelle? *Some people are like cold houses in winter, houses that can't stay warm.*

She wandered back to the kitchen, spooned coffee, knelt to light the stove. She could hear the storm more back here, and far streetlights showed how the snow was piling up on the roof of the garage. She peered out, wondering if Miracelle had gone to see him at the factory, wondering what they'd said. Wondering, like she always did, whether he'd show up here before dawn, his boots making time up to her room. His fingertips in her mouth, how they tasted sweet. The taste of a cigarette he'd light and put between her lips and now and then a jar of shine, red cherries floating inside. "Come on, Della, I know you love how wild it makes you feel."

She had loved so much. How young the two of them were at a drive-in with a marathon of old westerns, everything from John Wayne to Gene Autry. He unfastened the speakers from the windows, tossed them far out in the dark and pushed her down on the car's seat, laid his ear next to her heart. Shh, sweet pea, he said. The weight of his body moved into her as she listened to his breath in time with hers. Those nights were joy, and she shivered with the memory of them.

It wasn't patience all these years. It was teetering on the edge of a deep place she saw when she shut her eyes when she was alone at night. And when he slipped away and didn't come home until dawn, his fingers smelling of the fortune-telling woman. Ruby Loving. When had she first known her name? She saw herself at the foot of the stairs in Willette, New Mexico, stairs she'd seen her own husband climb too many times. "Who is that woman who lives up there?" she saw herself asking when a man came out a door in the downstairs. "You mean that card dealer?" The man's teeth were dark and he spat in the dust beside the steps. "Rose or Ruby," he said. "Yeah, that's right. Ruby. Ruby Loving." She was ashamed of it, the ways and means she found to follow her. Study her face, the curves of her cheeks, the lines of her eyebrows, the fancy trail of her scarves.

She remembered a day she watched as Russell met Ruby, her arms full of paper bags brimming with bread loaves and strings of peppers, the kind so hot they burned the tongue. Russell took the bags and followed up the steps as Della sat on the curb, feeling sweat course down between her breasts. Later she walked the distance across town back to the house. A rancher on a street beside the open doors of clubs and the cha-cha of feet dancing all night long. She liked it, the rooms where she never turned on a fan, how the heat kept her hungry.

Russell Wallen's heart was not that easy, and it never had been. Wandering heart. Lost heart. Heart that missed and beat and missed. Heart with hurting she knew nothing about at all. Some days she stood outside the Black Cat staring across the highway and watching the river, and she had no explanation for any of it, how her life had gone. He was the mountain that could not be moved, he'd said once, and she'd nearly split a side laughing at him. He was the mountain that had been moved, over and over again. He was the tunnel cracking the mountain open from sky to eternity, and she might as well have been perched at the top of that mountain, watching him fall, end over end over end. How she'd watched, job after job. Woman after woman. Bad poker hands where he'd lost his shirt. And his soul? She told herself some days she'd seen that one too. Seen him standing in the parking lot of the Black Cat in the middle of the night. She'd long been firm about him having no claim to them, these rooms she called her own, but often she'd hide him a key, leave him a door to open. Or she'd look down at him from her window, his sorry face, him begging until she gave in. How he'd tried, tried to shift the core of the earth with his own two hands, again and again.

The wind rose from a place far beyond the parking lot. It saddened her, thinking of how the coldness came from the sky or the mountains or from some land beyond all of it she'd maybe seen once but would likely never see again. She remembered her daddy's face that long-ago day in West Virginia. How he and the men pushed a cart outside and loaded a no-good engine in the back of a pickup truck to take to the junkyard later on. She remembered how they hoisted the new engine, loaded it on the cart, and wheeled it into the garage. That final moment where they used the hoist and how they whooped and hollered, their voices rising in sheer jubilation. The engine dangling bright and clean, ready to be lowered. The final give and settle of a car's new heart.

She sat in the dark of the dining room, watching the snowy ribbon of highway out there like she could grab hold of it, reel it in, pull him back to her. There was no such a thing as fixing what could not be fixed, what had been hurt beyond fixing all these years and years now. "The thing is, Miracelle," she'd said at the end of those long hours of talking at the boardinghouse. Those long hours of at last telling the truth. "The thing is, nobody has ever known what Russell Wallen really wanted." And here she was, all over again, expecting that what he'd want was more from her. It was the more she'd lived with all these years. The more was a truth she'd folded smaller and smaller, tucked away in the hidey-hole that had become her heart.

She put her hand against the diner's window, then cracked the front door, letting in the freezing air. She felt the cold of it in her heart as she cupped her hands around a cigarette and lit it. She had come this far, and there was nothing to do but remember it now. All these years later she saw Ruby's face, the half-smile and shrug as she said, "He's mine, always has been." Then they were struggling, first for that notebook Ruby had been writing in, then reaching for the gun, for each other's hands and shoulders. Behind them a record played, and Della could hear that song still. *Hold me, Radiance, honey, till long past daylight.* Below the music their breath worked hard, and one of them was saying and saying, anger a force their hands pulled at as they fought. How had she gotten there, after all? That trailer in that no-place town called Dauncy. She'd found its name on matchbooks and slips of paper she'd hoarded from Russell's pockets. Their arms circled and held on and it was almost, for a minute there, like they were themselves lovers in the heat of it, the trying to get hold of what neither of them had ever had. *Russell.* For years she wondered if that was really what Ruby Loving said as the gun went off. *He's not yours either.* The explosion deafened her, but it was like there was no sound at all as the bullet slipped into Ruby's body, leaving the look on her face changed hardly at all. There had been surprise, surely, but also a kind of release, a kind of *well, now, there it is,* as if she'd been waiting for her own death all along.

It was late as Della stepped outside the diner into the parking lot. She folded her arms around herself, rubbed the chill inside her coverall's sleeves, glad of the clean of the cold. What in God's name had she wanted that night Ruby Loving died?

She raised her hand to her mouth, breathed cold steam between her fingers. What she'd wanted, she'd told herself then, was to finally, finally fix the miss and beat and miss of him. She could see herself out in the yard as her daddy loaded the hoist in the back of his truck, hear herself, her girl's voice gone begging: "Let me help this once and I'll never ever ask again." How she'd wanted to see it, the car's engine taken out, made new. She'd thought it would be just as easy, to fix his heart. To talk Ruby Loving out of his life. His heart set free at last. Then they'd fought, the gun firing like it still did in her memory, and now here she was, alone on a winter night as bitter as any she could remember.

She stood a long while in the Black Cat parking lot, studying the highway east until it disappeared over a rise. This day ahead there were two cars waiting for tune-ups. Transmissions checked.There were hours to go before dawn, but she'd like as not stay up, wait on the day. She was always waiting. Waiting for when he'd leave. Waiting to see if he'd tell her where he'd gone, this time. Him with his hangdog looks, him with his wallet empty of his last red cent, and how she opened her arms and held him, one more time. She stamped her feet, bringing warmth to them before she let herself back inside the Black Cat and bolted the door. In the kitchen she fastened the storm door and locked the inner door once and for all against the cold night before she made her way upstairs.

Russell Wallen
Smyte
1993

28

Hold Me until Morning

He stood beneath the shattered window and picked up the gun. Looked at its fancy handle, the abalone cracked. He held it like it was a wounded thing and went back and lay with it on the floor. Once holding on to anything had seemed so easy. He'd come out of the service with enough cash to buy just what he wanted. That Chevy with its whitewalls and its slick red seats and life had seemed as sweet as cream. Fine as three fingers of good whiskey in a glass. Fists full of this, that, coal, land, truckloads of paper to sell, the bodies of beautiful women to love, this one and this one and then. And then what happened? That, too, was a tale told and done. Everything he'd tried from digging deep to driving steady, mile upon mile vanishing like smoke with the sour smell of paper being made.

He slept awhile. Dreamed snow, dry and so cold his hand ached. Dreamed he was afloat and could look down, not at woods and bare earth and fallen trees, but at a town he knew as his own. Smyte. He hovered in a sky full of cold stars, and as he looked down at the highway beside the Big Draw, the moon was a cat made of neon. The flicker and quit of the purple light held him up in the icy air. He did not wake from the dream like he had those many years ago when he was a boy, his heart full of possibilities, nor did some God speak to him in sleep. *You know how*, a voice said, and he lay still, listening to the timber of it.

A woman's voice, neither soft nor kind, a voice rough around the edges, full of as much liquor as he himself liked to drink, a voice full of giving in to want upon want and, like him, never much finding satisfaction in the end. Was it his daughter's voice? Miracelle. He had known who she was the minute he laid eyes on her. Ruby Loving all over again except for how she held her cards close to her chest and sat back, watching and waiting for him to own up about his life and hers too. Better, he told himself from the minute Miracelle set foot in Smyte, to let it all play out on its own. Better to wait for her to figure out who and what he was and ride off in the same direction she came from, but maybe not. Maybe, once she'd seen him for who he was, she'd just disappear.

Miracelle had stood with the gun, leveling it at nothing. Pointing it at him, he'd thought for a minute, and right then he'd wanted her to hurt him. When she aimed without care at the high-up office window and the glass shattered, he'd held his breath, wishing for more. She'd knelt and pushed against him as hard as she could and that still wasn't the more he wished for. *More.* Her father? Was that what he was? In that minute of meeting her eyes he'd reached inside himself, feeling around amid bone and blood and breath, and he'd found love, love too late and nothing more, not an ounce of fathering that would help her. He remembered that look of wanting more in the eyes of women he'd loved. *Love me more. Stay longer. Touch me here, not there.* They all wanted more, Ruby Loving most of all. He couldn't bear it, remembering the more he'd seen in Ruby Loving's eyes.

You know how, the voice said, and he got up, found his jacket and his silver flask and drained it, wishing hard he didn't know the voice, but he did. Ruby Loving. Her voice had haunted him forever and a day, and he'd done everything to purge himself of it. He'd drunk hard, bet harder, quit everything he could and sold the rest, disappearing down numbered highways and no-name roads. He'd held on to his wife night after night, hiding his face in Della's hair, hoping against hope that he'd wake up and Ruby Loving would be gone from his heart for good or, better yet, that she'd have been only his imagination in the first place from a too-drunk night where he'd said too much, a tale told into the wind, there and gone. *You know how*, she said again as he pulled his fist back and slammed it against the wall, enjoying the way his knuckles smarted and burned. This he knew how to do.

He clicked open the cylinder of the derringer, rolled it. One bullet. Almost empty matched the hollow he felt in his belly, and he breathed in the cold air from the shattered window. It was late, late, and the office was full of shadows. Shadows from the still-lit kerosene heater, and his own shadow, tall and thin and following him step for step. *You know what to do.* And what exactly was that? Nothing. That was about the size of it, after all these years. The years he'd known her, driven to see her, held her, raged at her, wishing, wishing she'd vanish into the smoke and mirrors of her two-bit fortune teller's life. And she had vanished, but not the way he'd ever planned.

At the office desk, he pulled the top drawer all the way out, turned it over, the things it held scattering at his feet. Old news fliers and envelopes from bills he'd never paid. He knew the hidden place on the underside of the drawer like he was touching her again after all these years. *You got no better place to hide my treasures, Russell Wallen?* The voice was tipsy, playing him, but she knew well enough. He'd made a pouch, choosing a thrift-store square of cloth he knew she'd have loved, rose colored and threaded with silver, like the scarves she draped over lamps for her nights of telling futures. Her notebook. He stood holding it in his arms, then gathered his things quickly, jacket and empty silver flask, the gun in his jacket pocket.

He made his way downstairs, across the floor and past the abandoned presses. He leaned into the door, bracing for the cold and the winter storm, but once he was outside he enjoyed the biting wind of the drift of falling snow. Snow settled in his hair and he raked that back with his fingers as he stood in the parking lot. Behind the factory was the winter-white of the river. He looked across at the Black Cat Diner, glad he'd parked his truck over there with the snow how it was. There'd been hard winters in Smyte. Barren times. This snow topped his boots as he crossed the asphalt, stepped in, stepped back into the tracks his feet made. He kept his eyes on the diner. The place was shut down, dark and deserted looking, and that was a comfort to him. He imagined the steps leading up to Della's room.

Across the highway, he kicked hard at the door of his truck as the inches of snow fell away, then kicked again and again as he yanked against ice until the door gave at last with a stiff sound. He reached under the seat, feeling for the bottle he kept there, but there was none and he cursed that, knowing he'd have to face Della half sober. He'd long ago learned the way of that, quiet, stealth, the slip and slide of middle of the night. How many times he had come to her like that, half lit and half sorry, but she always hid a key by the kitchen door or left it open, let him in. Turned the covers back and made room for him. Tonight wasn't about that. Tonight they'd talk about Ruby.

He tugged hard at the storm door of the Black Cat's kitchen, telling himself it was icebound like his truck had been. He yanked again, but the door didn't budge, not even when he rattled at it. He felt irritation rising in his throat. This night of all nights, a door that wouldn't give. He stepped back and peered at the upstairs windows, imagining that he saw a light on up there. Just a shade of a light, a candle or one of those oil lamps Della favored, but he was sure of it, the pale cast of light and her up there, as awake as he was.

He yanked at the storm door once more, called up to her, his voice loud enough to startle him. The night had no other sound except for the hush of the falling storm and, far off, tires spinning against snow. He felt the shape of the notebook inside his jacket and shouted again. "You there, Della Wallen?" How, he asked himself, had they not talked about Ruby again after that night? Ruby, hidden. Ruby, never spoken. Ruby, gone as gone could get. And not. He kicked at the storm door and waited. The air was still with cold.

You know how. He had no question at all that it was Ruby Loving this time. The voice had honey in it. It had sweet wine, and it had records with low-down blues and the slick wet of her tongue in his mouth. Her voice entered his ears, traveled slow and not unkind down his throat, settled in his lungs and inside the clouds of breath that came out and hovered in the cold. He laid his bare hands against his ears, feeling their cold. He pressed hard, muffling the roar of quiet that was this night, muffling the sound of her voice. She was laughing now, and that made him shiver, the laugh that was at once delighted and head-shaking. He could almost see her, her black hair falling over the one eye, the other winking at him, her finger reaching out like a comma, a curve, the hook on a dancer's cane to draw him onstage, onto the stage of his own life. *You know what to do, Russell Wallen,* she said, her voice so clear he saw her there in front of him, her and her fortune teller's cards. The snow scattered as wind blew against the roof of the diner, sheets of snow, snow in reams like paper, neat cards of snow that shuffled and settled at his feet. *Pick a card,* she said, *and I'll promise to tell it right.* He remembered all the times she'd held those cards in her lap and made him reach for them. Three cards. Past. Present. Future. His whole life.

He gathered the sound of her voice next to him, holding the sound close inside the folds of his too-thin jacket, willed the voice to settle inside the pages of the notebook. *You never did know how to take care of your own silly self,* she said now. *But this. This you know how to do.* And he did. He knew how to retrace his steps. How to find the right foot-sized places, the quick track back across the road. He almost imagined the river over there had a sound, a sound like black ice thawing come some far-off spring. Or different than that. The sound of the long sigh of ice touching ice, of the moan of the river settling down, waiting out the bitterness of cold. She was humming now, a song he remembered all too well. *Hold me in the morning, hold me at night. Hold me, Radiance, honey.* Radiance. The snow was like that, the night and its whiteness, its gathering cold.

He almost passed the truck, almost went back across the road back up the steps to the still-burning heater in his office, the lull of kerosene fumes. Surely up there was a bottle he'd forgotten about and enough whiskey to get him through to morning. But the cold was a blanket of itself and she was inside him now, nudging him where she wanted him to go. Her voice, its long, warm dream. *You know how.* She said it again, twice, a third time, a once-and-for-all charm against time and all wrong fortunes ever told. Her voice was coy. It was love and it was not. It was holding and it was letting go. It was a song on a record long spun down, a song caught in the grooves of its own self forever and forever. *You know how,* she said again and again and again and her voice was warm, heavy as love. He counted himself lucky that the truck door opened easy as pie this time. *You know how,* she said, and he did.

Inside the truck, he cranked the engine and turned on the heater, the dome light. Flipped through the pages of the notebook. Photographs. Paragraphs from stories, news clippings. Rose petals taped onto pages. Other pages scrawled with her handwriting. Recipes. Potions for sickness. Potions against fear. To bring on dreams or to take them away. Potions to make you remember what you'd tried to forget. Ones for love. "Why, Russell Wallen? Why her all these years and not me?" He remembered Della's wild eyes and he remembered how he hadn't had to ask where she'd been. He'd sunk to his knees, laid his hands against the bloodstains on her coveralls. Past grief, past anger, past understanding any of it, what he knew right then with more clarity than he'd ever felt was that love in its all and all had never been a possibility in his heart for either of them. When Della laid this book in his lap, it was as nigh as he'd ever get to holding Ruby in his arms again, and he had never known if that was a kindness or a curse.

When he came close to thinking about that night, he put the memory as far away from himself as he could. He left the memory outside doors shut fast. He tossed it from the windows of his truck as he took the curves on back roads too fast. He'd wadded up that memory and thrown it away again and again, and still. The memory of both of them washed into his chest, his mouth. His wife's face as she told him about the trailer, the gun, the wound in Ruby's chest she'd tried to staunch with her bare hands. "And then she said your name, Russell." He tasted it, the sourness of his past. Outside the truck, the snow was heavy and he concentrated on its blankness. Snow as blank as paper.

You know what to do, Ruby said. At the back of her notebook he found blank pages, a pencil nub from amid the floorboard's debris. He balanced the book against the steering wheel, began to write. *Dear Miracelle.* She wanted the truth, and what was that in the end? The last time he saw Ruby, here in that rented room, here in Smyte. He remembered how their voices rose, the tired anger of Ruby's eyes. "She's your daughter, Russell Wallen, and I am the woman you love. Me. Say it." Love, a word dry as sand, pushed inside his chest. "I'm tired," she said. "Tired of town after town and loving you and never, never." And after Della came home, this book in her arms, there'd never been a night when there wasn't a ghost in their bed, the warm iron scent of Ruby's blood between them in the dark.

He wrote knowing there was so much to say that he had not. *And the world shall know the ways of the Lord my God.* His daddy's long-ago words. As the truck's heat held him steady, he wondered what the ways of the Lord had been in his life. He lay down, back against the seat, the book in his arms. He'd been a boy once, and he remembered that boy, the comfort of lying with his knees in his arms, the house still and dark. As a man he'd sought comfort, wanted it and turned it away like a cup of kindness he did not know how to receive. He took the gun from his jacket pocket, steady with the feel of it, glad of how it felt next to his belly. It wasn't empty, the gun, no emptier than this long night of snow and silence. There was one bullet there, and the thought of that bullet took shape for him, its slight weight and shape and how easy it would be, a small movement of his finger against the trigger. But that was way too easy. What he wanted was to speak to Miracelle one more time, to tell her it wasn't too late to forgive. It was late, late, and the snow was falling less now, halos of light from far down the road.

The motor hummed and he drifted, hearing her voice again, as clear as if she were with him again after all this time. *You know how*, Ruby said, and her voice was a soft whiteness. He gathered that too, wrapped it around the both of them once and for all.

Ruby Loving
Dauncy
1973

29

That Night

Russell Wallen, I will be nothing but a ghost come tomorrow, but once I knew things. Knew that cancer in my mother's breast was a sign of heaven. Knew my daddy was a man of songs who somehow forgot the name for love until it was too late.

I knew you, Russell, right away. Knew what you had to give and what you did not. You believed love was glory and owning. And I knew this, too. A heart gone to nothing, one gone sad and sour and empty, is worse than owning nothing at all. And still I went there.

Ruby Loving, if you're a fortune teller, you once said. Tell your own life for awhile instead of mine. You said that to me, Russell Wallen, and I say this.

Once I believed in cards and crystals. Believed in lifelines and morning's red skies. I believed in prophecy straight from the spirit. But I gave my life away a long time ago. I've given myself away, again and again, some of that self to you. How I have waited for you, Russell Wallen. Waited and waited to be loved, like loving will be a final thing to reach, a holy truth between you and me rather than between me and any God at all.

Every night, like I still believe in it, I open the windows and turn the fan down low. I circle my eyes with kohl and pour a second glass of red wine. I drape scarves over the lamps and set the record playing again. Love me in the morning, love me at night. Love me, Radiance, honey, till long past midnight. And Miracelle says, When will they come? She means the men with their hungry faces. She means the women come to have their palms read. Here, I tell them as I put a tiny bottle in their hands. Put two drops on the center of your tongue, I say. Wait.

Today, I tell myself, will be different. It is you I will cast out, oh lover of mine. It is you I will discover, my own dark heart, the same song. Love me, love me. My heart is not my own. It is small as a bird's. Hard as a pebble in the mouth of the dead.

This is the thing, Russell Wallen.

I have loved you and that love has eaten me alive.

Today all day, Russell Wallen, I've written it down. Our futures, yours and mine.

I've known all along how I'll be sitting here in the kitchen shuffling my cards and hoping it's you when some truck slides to a stop in the gravel out by the highway. I've drawn a card, one to hand you right when you walk in the door. The Lovers, or the Fool. Miracelle's radio music ripples the window screen, rock 'n' roll drowning out that song I've played all the livelong day. Love me, Radiance, honey.

I know how boots will thud up our back steps and the trailer door creak open. Tonight there will be thunder and shots from a sweet little gun, one and two and three. I will lie in my daughter's arms as I die. This I know.

Like this, Russell Wallen, I have sat all afternoon writing my own death down.

But that won't be the end of it. The end of the story is out there, ahead of us both.

All afternoon Ruby Loving, Fortune Teller, has been writing down her own future, and here is yours, too. You with snow dancing outside your truck windows. By then I will have been dead for years and you will be thinking of wind in the skeletons of trees.

You will be thinking of houses and rooms and the women you have loved.

Women like me who smelled of wine and sweetness. Ones who knew what holding means and when to let you be. One, oh, she had hair the color of corn silk. Another who tasted moist as rain. How you drank and the world got less pretty, when you liked to think beauty was true as it got. You, drinking and hearing my voice drifting over the ice-cold world.

Someday, you will light the last cigarette you'll ever have and pitch the lit match out the window into the snow. How you will wish it were easy to say who you have always been, you and your preacher daddy. You with a mother who loved you once or twice and then not at all. You will want nothing at all the last night of your life and you will want everything.

You will be alone in your truck thinking how what you want this last time is aces. Thinking you want a penknife with a little diamond on the handle. *Thinking maybe you want a prayer or another bottle of whiskey, but all you have is the memory of a song. Hold me, Radiance, honey. Hold me all night long. You will be sitting alone in the dead cold of winter, remembering the night I died and how you wanted never to think of me again.*

The truth is you hated me and you loved me. You left me and you came back to me. You have said it, over and over. You want me, woman? This is what you get. This is what love is in the end and nothing, nothing more.

The truth is my own future and yours have been inside me all along like my own mama once carried a cancer in her breast.

The last night of your own life, Russell Wallen, the only truth that will count is a heater running to keep you warm. A snow-white world and the ghost arms of memory reaching out for a man who could never love. You. A blank slate.

Hurt will be fire and it will burn up inside you. Loneliness, dry as kindling. Dry as paper where are written words you will try to read one more time. These pages, these words, written ahead of time.

You will think of all you could have had. Della. Me. And her. Your daughter.

By then you will have known her for weeks and weeks. You'll have driven her down back roads, shown her a fine old time, shown her little parts of yourself, but never the part, never the one part she wants the most. You. Who you really are.

The truth is this, Russell Wallen. You'll lie down in the cold and dark, lie down alone, lie down thinking it's never too late to tell her the truth. Here I am, Miracelle Loving. For better or worse, I've been your daddy all along. We'll be father and daughter, happy as clams.

But it will be too late.

Right over there, the lights of the Black Cat are shining lavender, your last known radiance. The heater hums a song to lull you. The night tastes like soot, sounds like the last hush of snow.

Are women always ghosts? Our bodies empty after we send our hearts out again and again, hearts made of waiting for love. I've held on to love, water draining between my fingers. Wanted you to fill me up like light from fireflies in a jar. Ruby Loving, Fortune Teller, dreaming how she wants you beyond death, us meeting each other's eyes, hungry to see each other, seeing each other like it is for the last time.

Ice will cover a windshield. Snow will fall and fall.

Miracelle Loving
Smyte
1993

30

The Sound of Glass Breaking

I hardly slept the rest of that night after leaving the warehouse, with their names and my own inside me. *Russell. Ruby. Miracelle Loving.* And her. *Della Wallen.* The minute I closed my eyes, I heard the voices from that night, heard the sound of gunshots, saw the shadow behind the curtains in the trailer where my mother died. *Della.* She was the shadow at the window, the sound that boots made as they ran away in the dark. It was Della who had taken my mother's life. *Della.* Unanswered past answered at last, and now the shadow had a face and a body. When I closed my eyes, I saw Della with a cigarette cupped in her hand at the Black Cat. She looked at me as I brought her strong coffee in the mug with a chip on the rim. *Good morning, this morning,* she said as if nothing had ever, ever happened.

When I finally slept, I dreamed I was driving drunk, snow falling straight down and then rising up, a white veil that hid the world. In my sleep, I skidded. I swerved. I fishtailed and set myself right. I floated across a plain of ice and back out the other side onto a sheet of snow that went on and on. I dreamed that snow was a warm wool blanket that pulled itself down from the sky. The snow was made of haints. Tince May, light as a cloud, a dream floating past, she singing a torch song. Ruby lit incense and draped scarves over a lamp on a kitchen table while a record played a love song. *Love me in the morning, love me at night.* I was there, too. I was swaying and toe-tapping and swinging, slow-dancing with someone who could have been my father. Russell Wallen took hold of my hands, and we swung each other round and round. It could have been.

By late morning the world was after-snow hushed. From downstairs, not a sound. I'd missed the meal Lacy May had laid but I wanted no food, no sounds, nothing but the streets below so quiet wind chimes sounded from a porch far off. Bare branches scratched against the windows. Smyte was holding its breath while the snow finished and the world cleared away the storm. I heated leftover coffee in the microwave on my little table and studied the room where I'd spent these months, the things I'd accumulated. An alarm clock. Waitress shoes. A thrift store sweater set with rhinestones. I'd left towns before with a lot less than I had now.

I paced past table, chair, thinking of Russell Wallen the night before. Him sitting on the floor, his head in his hands, and me wanting him to say anything, any one word I could accept. The words we'd sent back and forth, each of us waiting for the other one to say any word that counted. *Lonely. Hearts that could break.* The sour taste of anger, how I'd swallowed it back as I took the gun out, held it out to him. *This look like anything you might remember?* I remembered saying that, my chest hot with wanting him to say what I needed most. *You're my daughter.* Or a simpler thing than that. Asking my forgiveness, begging me for it. As if he would. As if he ever, ever would. I could hardly breathe by then, the kerosene scent burning in my throat, and all I wanted was nothing, clean and pure. The window shattered, letting in the cold and the start of the snow. It haunted me, the way his eyes showed not a sign as I knelt in front of him, full of anger.

I lingered like I did at the photos on my room's walls, the haints I'd come to know. Thirties, forties, fifties. The photo of that woman in her tight-throated striped dress, her eyes as sad as they came. And that photo that always gave me chills. A tiny little baby in a coffin, its waxy hands holding white roses. And Tince May. I looked at her photos every night before bed, wondering. Had Tince been young once? She seemed to breathe in her photograph, to sigh from the folds and valleys of her skin. She was nothing but a ghost now, and I was nothing but a haint my own self.

A ghost of roads and times, of lovers and hands. A girl wanting her mother, Russell Wallen said. Woman wanting her father. Wanting lover after lover, none of them ones that lasted. I'd always liked it before, the ease with which I'd left love behind. A night here, a night there, strangers the best part of loving. Lovers were strangers, when you came right down to it, and I'd always liked that just fine. I sat, trying to remember the exact color of Cody Black's eyes. *You're like a sentence with a word left out, Miracelle.* I'd yet to find that word.

Through window glass laced with ice, I peered down into the streets. What did I know about any of it? Where did memory even begin to matter? Was it that night? Lightning and behind it thunder and the record, still playing. *Hold me, hold me.* Glass breaking. Voices. *Russell, I had always believed.* Chair crashing against the floor. *I know what I know.* Angry voices. *Della. Ruby.* My own name. I ran through the yard, up the trailer steps, pushed through a door a million miles from myself. Thunder become gunshot. Boots crashing down out the back way and tires spinning gravel as I reached her. My mother lay dead in my arms, her blood sweet-salty and real.

I made my way to the Black Cat at the edges of the partly plowed streets, taking in the snow world like it was new. The inches of snow on roofs, the unbroken snow in yards. Color broke the blankness of it first, purple neon from the diner's sign across whiteness. And at a distance, there was Russell's truck. Red broke against blank white slate of snow, and I later swore I could hear her even before I saw her.

Della was kneeling beside the open truck door, her wail floating out. Her voice cut into the cold air and I ran along the sound like it was an electric line I had to cross to reach her. She looked so small reaching for him, his body half out of the truck, her arms tight around him. I looked down into the lonely face of a dead man I didn't recognize at first. He just was any other sorry-looking man right then, his mouth gone slack inside dying. And then I saw him for who he was. All those times along roads and in juke joints and in that wayside church reaching out for some blessing. He was my father after all.

It was truer than any fortune I'd ever told, how I knelt there beside her. "Russell," she said as she nudged him. Russell Wallen, this father I'd never known, lost inside a sound sleep we couldn't wake, his face turned to the back of the truck's seat. The truth is neither of us would ever know the last thing on earth Russell Wallen saw. The lights of a radio on his dashboard. Ghosts in the snow. His own two hands.

She saw me but didn't. "Won't nobody have him now," she said, looking beyond me at no one.

There were lines below her eyes, beside her mouth, and I wanted to touch a hurt place I couldn't see. Her hand stroked his forehead and she held her fingers next to her face.

31

Wake

The afternoon of his wake there were stories. They said an idling motor and carbon monoxide had killed him when he'd curled up in his truck those hours before dawn. He'd knocked and Della, that last time, would not let him back in. Dozens gathered to say goodbye to Russell Wallen, as if seeing him would answer everything.

We followed behind the casket up the steps into the diner. There were tambourines and fiddles and guitars. Blues and bluegrass echoed through the Black Cat. The place was packed from the front window back to the kitchen with everyone from the strange to the merely odd to the downright ornery—people he'd known from years to a day at every joint from here to there and back. They were everywhere, holding on to steaming cups of coffee and jars of shine, the air around us thick with cigarette smoke and warm with bodies.

A man slapped spoons on his knee near the open casket, which was beside the kitchen doors. *Won't come around my kitchen, oh, won't come around my door.* The song words slid out between his little yellow teeth and a woman with a thin braid wound more than once around her head tapped her black shoe against the tile. *Won't come around here again, come around here again no more.* A party, and he'd have liked that, but the music was flat and there was talk and talk. *He was a good 'un. A fine man, most of the time.* In one corner of the room, I could have heard tales of what they said were prison days. In another, army tales. More gossip about him and Della. A thick-necked woman in a gray dress strapped a washboard around her middle and set to strumming. Sounds drowned out sounds.

"A regular take on peculiar, that Russell Wallen was," a woman near me said.

Wake

From where I stood I could see the plain pine box, which would have pleased him, and an open lid, which would have not. I couldn't help looking at his face. His mouth, as sealed shut as a pouch. *Him. His. His.* He lay dead in a box, and neither Russell nor father nor any name at all suited him now. Old tales said that when someone died, there'd be an owl hovering near the house, but it was the questions I'd had for years that circled the room and came back to curl up inside my empty chest as I looked at him and at this roomful of people he'd known. I watched Della where she sat in a chair near the cash register, shaking hands as people came in. We'd closed the Black Cat right after he passed, and we'd spent some of these last two days, Della and me, sitting at a booth circling one another with half-talk and no talk at all. It was you, I'd said, but I hadn't been able to head beyond the beginning of a question.

"Don't ask me about it." Della shook her head. "Not now."

A hard-looking boy with a bowler hat took out a harmonica now and his feet tapped time. *Won't come around my heart again, come around no more.* I stood near the kitchen and spread my arms against the plaster wall, feeling the dryness against my palms as if it were a comfort.

When I finally couldn't stand any of it, I grabbed my pack and headed out to drive. I drove along the river, up the main street in Smyte, around the corner where the public library was, past the dime store and back around, where a pizza parlor had gone in a few weeks back. I drove to the outskirts of Smyte, as far as the plowed roads would take me, took a left-hand turn at a field covered in snow where I saw the shadow of some critter slinking into the trees. I found a new way back into town, past houses with lights on and televisions going and children already tucked in for the long winter night. I ended up parking in the lot at the warehouse.

I climbed the steps of the factory building to Russell's office. I tried to light the kerosene heater, but it seemed to be out of fuel, so I sat shivering. I opened drawers, found a bottle with an inch of whiskey. A blanket lay on the mattress where I had sat with Russell, and I huddled myself beneath it, the office phone down there with me. I drew my knees into my arms and breathed inside the tent I'd made until I felt warmer.

The phone rang and rang until he picked up. He seemed to know it was me before I said a word. "I somehow thought you'd call."

"Why's that?" I asked.

"Been awhile, I guess." His voice shrugged. "And, okay," he said. "I admit it."

"What's that?"

"I laid out three cards last night, right here on the kitchen table."

"You laid out a fortune, Cody?"

"Let's just say I made up a story with cards," he said. "And you might have been in it."

The phone was warm against my ear. "Everything's changed," I said at last.

"What's everything, Miracelle?"

I thought about the roomful of strangers. The sound of fiddles and the burnt taste of the coffee and neat whiskey I'd drunk. "Russell's gone."

"Russell?"

I held the phone with my shoulder and pulled my sleeves over my hands. I told about the Black Cat, getting to know Della, then Russell. And how the diner was to be closed for two weeks, a mourning banner strung across the Black Cat neon sign.

"For Russell?"

"He was my father, Cody." Tears edged into my voice. "And he's dead."

I laid the phone in my lap, held my hands over it, like it was small fire to warm my cold fingers. But I could hear him.

"Miracelle," he said, like calling up from the bottom of some well.

"Yes," I whispered into the air.

He said my name again, then once more before I held the phone to my ear again.

"Tell me," he said.

I cried, a few slow moments of it with no sound, and I told him about how small Russell had looked in Della's arms, about the wake. "It's finished."

"What is?"

"This place."

I heard a chair shift. Imagined the sounds his footsteps made across a floor. "What's your future now, Miracelle?"

I held the phone and neither of us spoke. Far away there was a train, and a hint of snow, its almost invisible flakes, fell through the shattered office window.

I cleared off his desk and took out Ruby's tarot, looked at the cards with their fancy women in silk dresses. Black-robed men, looking wise. All cards, she said, could open up the world for you if you looked inside yourself for the answers. *You know what to do,* she said to me now, and I jumped, her voice so clean and clear I could see her handing me the cards one more time. I shuffled, remembering what Ruby always told me. *Keep your mind on the question. See all the possible outcomes.*

My past, the Shaman of Disks. A woman on a horse, riding through a desert. That was true enough. My past was an empty place I couldn't re-call. It was potato slices fried in an iron skillet and tossed into a backyard. Come-and-go light from a kerosene lamp on a table down a hall. Scraps of soap, spoonfuls of lard. And Ruby. Her candlelight and her visions. The women who came seeking spells and charms and remedies. Men ready to take whatever she had. My past had been no more my own than hers had been. World without love and a woman riding through. Della sending me to Russell, Russell sending me back to the Black Cat, and there I was, waiting for the whole bunch of them to tell me my own name.

The Crone was my future. An old woman in a black dress. Ruby, if she'd lived long enough, or Della maybe, her hair swept up and pinned in place. Two women, mourning, the both of them, hearts full of love and nowhere to give it. How many nights did Della lie awake listening for Rus-sell's truck, after all those years, his body part of her bones and blood. Della. Her changing-color eyes no color at all this day.

And me, longing for Cody Black to hold me tight, wanting Russell Wallen, a daddy-shoulder where I could lay my head.

I was no fortune teller. All I did was give false hopes, put stars in the eyes of lost souls. I thought of that woman named Beatrice, the one with the kitten sweatshirt back at Dill's, her wanting nothing but someone to send her back to Mr. No Good and his cheap bottle of red wine and a promise. It'll be all right, sweetheart, I'd said when I'd no idea what was right or not for anyone, least of all myself. I'd heard Ruby tell it again and again, how fortune could come so quick, could change you forever. Who had I ever loved for longer than a few weeks before I wanted to shed them the way a snake sheds its skin? I was a motherless child trying to remember who cut her loose in the first place.

After midnight I let myself in the back door of the diner and prowled the kitchen. What was mine in this place? A second pair of waitressing shoes. A pair of pants I could have left behind. I left the lights off, glad for the dark, the line of light under the doors to the dining room. I sat on a chair near the stove, the same old plans in my head. Highway out, road atlas and putting my finger down on a spot. But I was tired before I even began. I needed to say goodbye to something, but I hadn't yet figured out my hellos. I sat warming my hands by the oven, dreading the road and longing for it and wishing he were here. Russell Wallen. The slouch of his black felt hat in the rain, the scratched metal flask he'd send my way as we slid into the curves of roads and parked ourselves outside juke joints whose names I couldn't remember.

The kitchen doors swung open and Della flicked the overhead light on. She set a kettle on the stove and got the instant coffee out. She didn't speak, but pulled up a chair of her own, sat astride it. We both stared into the stove's open door. When the water boiled, she filled two cups.

"What do we do now?" I asked her as I poured sugar into my coffee and stirred.

"Work's always kept me who I am," she said.

The coffee kept my words coming. "It was you, Della. You that night she died."

She didn't look at me. "I've known it every hour since."

"It took the both of you, you and Russell, to keep the past in a drawer," I said.

"It took me, and her, and him. It took all of us to make the past what it was." She raised the cup to her lips and flinched with the heat.

"And what would the world have looked like if that night hadn't happened?" I said. "What'll it look like now?"

How much time there'd already been, but we sat, listening to the quiet. The kitchen. The diner out there, the crowd that had come for the wake now long gone.

"Right from the very first minute you saw me," I began, but we'd been down that road and I got quiet, watched the end of my cigarette smolder.

"God, girl." The stove clicked as it cooled down, and she laid her hand on my bare arm. Her voice was soft. "We think it's easier to forget than to remember. To not speak rather than say what we know."

We sat saying nothing at all until she got up, fetched a bag from the storeroom, reached it to me. She stood with her hands in the pockets of her coveralls. "The things he died with, Miracelle."

Inside the bag was the gun I'd left in Russell's office. And a thing I hadn't seen in more than twenty years. A notebook, across its cover a taped-on piece of paper. My mother's handwriting.

Della and I didn't talk as we headed out into the cold night. We crossed the highway, passed the steps of the warehouse where I'd often sat for cigarettes, rounded the building and made our way to the river. She shone a flashlight at our feet as we made tracks in the snow, then as we stood on the steep riverbank looking down into snow there, too, and patches of ice. The river had frozen over, its muddy waters still alive. We could hear them seething underneath winter and ready, already, for spring and whatever came after that.

We stood saying nothing, though we were both full to the brim with the world. World full of a river at night and my father's memory. Full of times before and times that might or might not come again for both of us. Times free of what had been. Times untangled, free and clear, as free as anybody could be of whiskey and grieving, love and wanting. I watched the smoke from our cigarettes rise and disappear, little trails of gray in the frozen air, and I thought of all the roads the both of us had taken and all the ones we might still travel.

I'd sat with her in the kitchen with my mother's book for almost an hour, then made my way to the empty dining room, where I sat with coffee, reading. I read the recipes for love potions. Ones to ignite passion. *Red coxcomb and gold from desert's dust.* To make a soul remember. *Lavender and calendula in equal parts.* I read about what she'd wanted and not had. Head of a holler and loneliness as her daddy fiddled love songs to the wife who'd closed her heart away. Cards, charts that showed the alignment of planets, lifelines and the color of someone's eyes after a full moon. These were the arts my mother tried to believe in, the magic at which she failed again and again as we took to the highways and set up shop in one more town. And then that night, the truest fortune she ever told. *Snow will fall and fall,* she said. Pages were torn away, some of them streaked with what could only have been her blood the night she died. And at the end of the journal my father's words, his last night on earth.

"I guess this is as good a time as any," Della said as we moved close to each other, shielding the fire from her lighter in the space between us.

She'd come out to the dining room after I'd read from the book, sat across from me and held her hands out to me like she was begging. I saw the lifeline on her palm and I want to tell how it ended. No fork in the road, no paths over the side of her hand. I want to tell how I hated her. To tell how I found one thing to take from her that she could never have back again, like she had taken Ruby from me. That wouldn't be the truth, in the end. All I felt was a hollow place inside me where the questions had lain for so many years. All there was as we sat there was mourning. The hating I wanted became another thing, and then another until I finally reached a place inside I could live with. If that place wasn't forgiveness, it was a place almost as necessary.

Now we stood in the cold by the river, flipping through the pages of the journal, tearing out a recipe here, a love charm there. We took a whole page from that time in the desert, how Ruby had walked the sidewalks of Willette, New Mexico, in the pitched heat of summer. Those afternoons of waiting for Russell Wallen's love. Between us we knew there was no such thing, really, as forgiving or forgetting, but she held the lighter against the bundle of words. That moment would become in my memory a kind of spell. A spell made of fire, Della's and mine.

The words caught and flamed up, an easy and quick brilliance that lasted only a minute. It lit up the planes and lines of Della's face. How beautiful she was, I realized, and I met her eyes. We both looked, up and up and up. The flames made ashes and those rose too, up into the bare branches of trees. Della let go of the burning sheets but I held on, thinking on the words I'd read.. *Are women always ghosts? Our bodies empty after we send our hearts out again and again, hearts made of waiting for love.* Wind moved along the river, a low howl of cold and snow's drift.

There was no final truth in that spell. Maybe I laughed or cried or recited some kid-prayer about souls before morning. Maybe, at that very last second, I hummed, even. Hummed the song from that record Ruby loved, the song she was playing over and over on the night she died. *Love me in the morning, love me at night. Love me, Radiance, honey, till long past midnight.* Were the souls of lovers there, weaving their way above waters of all the past? *Ghosts settled at last and ready to wake us.* I thought I heard Della say that. Or maybe there was nothing but silence as I let go of fire and watched the ashes catch the air, traveling past both of us toward the river, unsure of where this night would take them.

Miracelle Loving
Knoxville
1994

32

The Wonder in Wonderama

I'd like to say I found just the right potion made of lavender and thyme and mystery, one to make all the world right. Nothing had ever been that easy, and it wasn't after my father passed. I wandered for a time, just as much as I had in all the times before. I drove over the mountains, through the flatlands. I kept my mother's gun as a warning on the dashboard of my car when I slept there some nights, telling myself I had the one bullet, just in case. I circled west, east, west. I even found myself at last back in Radiance, at his door. My grandfather's. It makes a fine story, how he came with me and we found our way to Smyte, found ourselves across the road from the Black Cat Diner the same way I had, all those months back.

Looking over there shocked me. They'd hauled out the tables and booths, even the kitchen sink, which lay upended near the gas pumps, its pipes reaching skyward. The diner sign leaned upside down against the side of the building, pitiful looking without its neon. We could have come upon the aftermath of Armageddon. *Here, Precious Seekers. Here is the Hand of the Lord.* The Good Lord had yanked out a clothesline full of winter duds, stick-legged nightstands, and a big fold-out table laden with everything from bobby pins to the lard can from the stove.

"I don't know if you'll need that fiddle right off." I nodded in his direction.

"I need it," he said as he shifted the case higher in his arms.

The dining room was bare, linoleum rolled up and set on end in a corner. "Della?" I called in the general direction of the kitchen, but got an echo and then finally a voice.

"She's over at the warehouse." Ona Short had her shirt sleeves rolled to the elbow and rubber gloves. "Look who showed up and when most of the work's done, too. How are you, Miracelle?"

"What in the world's going on around here, Ona?"

"World's shifted, Miracelle." She pushed straggles of hair out of her face. "I reckon you knew that, if you've kept up much." She studied Leroy Loving out the corner of an eye.

I sighed. "I'm bad that way."

"Well," she said. "Della's cleaning house."

"I'd say."

"Bound to leave Smyte, she says."

"Headed where?"

The kitchen looked like even more of a disaster had made its way through. The door of the fridge hung open, with freezer water pooled in the bottom.

"She's not sure." Ona gestured at open boxes. "She's a whirlwind of a cleaner, that Della."

We crossed the road, headed toward the building that had held his office. Russell's. My father's. *Father.* The shadow of that word made my heart lurch and fall. I thought of his black eyes, the slouch of his hat. His silver flask and his tattoo of a bird. I wanted wings to pick me up now.

"We didn't bring a thing for her," Leroy said. "Not a thing." He looked nervous, like he needed a package with a bow to hide behind.

"It'll be all right." I hooked my arm in his.

In the construction lot in Radiance, I'd picked up the most beautiful piece of coal I could find. A shiny, cobalt-black piece, rubbed slick and round with its own history. He was the other gift. Leroy Loving. A man as grieved by the past as she herself was. The two of them were the only ones left who really knew that time before.

A light was on in the office, and I almost expected to see him in there, his feet propped up on the desk. "Sit yourself down, Miracelle," he'd have said, and I'd have pushed aside papers and ledgers.

"Well," Della said. She looked at me and not at him. Leroy stood off to the side, his booted foot testing the waters of the place. "Had a dream about you the other night." Her eyes were light today. "You were driving someplace with mountains so steep you could go way up on top of them and see forever if you wanted to."

The top of the desk was cleared of everything but a coffee thermos and a few framed photographs turned in her direction. We were as shy of one another as new lovers or children, and all those feelings that were ashamed of themselves hung in the air.

"You still play that fiddle?" She finally looked at my grandfather.

"Now and again," he said.

"I always liked that one song you used to play back in the day. What was it?"

"I don't know if I recollect." He laid the fiddle case across his knees.

"You know." She laughed. "That song about winter come and gone." She laid a hand on her knee. "You used to play so fine, you just about took off flying from the earth. I swear you did."

"Maybe it was so," Leroy said, and we got quiet.

"Don't you see them still, when you close your eyes?" She looked at both of us, at last. "I see them even without my eyes shut." She shook her head and held her hands up.

"I do," I said. "I see their spirits, if I try."

She looked at him now, and it made my heart hurt, the way he looked back.

"They follow me right close," he said. "They always have."

He held his hand out to her and she studied it for a bit.

"Maybe they're here for a reason. Ghosts settled at last," she said as she reached out, "and ready to wake us."

It was late summer, August, when I ended up in Knoxville again and stashed my things at the Red Sari. I looked up Willy's, and the biggest news I could find was a year-old ad for their Grand Re-Opening. *View the Wonders of the World, Ladies and Gentlemen, and Don't Travel Far! See the Two-Tailed Mermaid! The Pencil Headed Woman! The Hits and Misses of Life on Earth!* When I actually turned up in the street outside the museum, I found shiny stone lions out front and took the granite steps leading inside.

I bought my ticket for $14.95 without letting anyone at the sales office know I'd been a Willy's recruiter, and inside I stayed that way, drifting from exhibit to exhibit. In the center of the main foyer was a giant replica of a Neanderthal man made entirely of electrical tape. I studied a map to the newest exhibits. *Blind fish from the heart of Mammoth Cave! Girl with Wings!!* The boxes and crates and cardboard were gone, and instead there were lit display cases and a crowd of summer tourists. I spent a long while in a room full of photographs and framed newspaper clippings I recognized. *Abandoned Ghost Towns of North America.* San Toy. Fayette. Prince. Mining towns, all, ones left behind by railway development and the Great Depression. I studied photos of closed-down hotels, empty tipples and water tanks. A headline below a tintype of railroad tracks leading between mountains and a gray sky. *Unremembered.*

And the shark tank exhibit—a length of blue carpeted hall, quiet and cool and with almost no tourists. I sat on the floor at one end of the hall and wondered if a shark could remember a person.

"Miracelle Loving?"

I'd dozed, lulled by the swish and sway of the shark tails.

Reading glasses perched on the top of her tied-back hair and a gold chain that shone against her skin, it was Marvis Temple. I stood and shook her hand. "It's me."

"Back from the grave, from the looks of it," Marvis said. "Honey, you've lost about a stone and look like you've seen a highway out of the underworld. What're you doing here?"

"Couldn't miss seeing Willy's," I said. "What's with the pants suit?"

Marvis spread her arms and turned around and back "They downsized," she said. "Got this place up and running, and then they gave the ones of us they didn't lay off two jobs in one. I run tours, now."

"You could be running this whole place, Marvis." I shook my own head.

"I shouldn't even be here, sister, but you know. There's something about it." She looked up at the tank light. "Brought you back, didn't it?"

I drug the toe of my shoe against the carpet. "I'm between worlds."

"Come back here to work, girl." Marvis reached in her pocket, handed me a Willy's Wonderama card. *Best Show This Side of the Mississippi! Wonders Aplenty and Curiosities Galore!!*

"Oh, I just wanted to visit some old haunts." I paused. "Cody. You seen him?"

"Cody." She tapped the side of her head. "Let me see now. Cody," she said and winked at me. "Oh! That buddy of yours. Your sweetheart?"

"I wouldn't go that far." I shrugged. "He been around lately?"

"He was one of the demoted ones."

"Took off for better parts, I guess?"

"Took off for south Knoxville." She tapped her chin. "Opened his own place. Just about as full of freaks as this one."

"What kind of place?" I asked, knowing already what she'd say.

"Tattoos and such." She took out another card and a pen, and scribbled. "I think that's its name." She folded her arms and looked at me again. "You eaten yet? They got a great café in here and I'm buying."

"I need to get on, Marvis," I said, but found myself following her along the shark hall and back out into the marbled foyer.

As we walked toward the café, I thought about the name of Cody's shop. *Cody's Visionary Body Art. Tattoos and News of the Spirit.* I pictured the tattoos, the inked swirls and brushstrokes and the empty planes between on Cody's skin. I pictured his clear, amber eyes and I wondered if he would ever look at me again, much less welcome me in.

I was staying at the Red Sari, doing what I always did. Watching late night television and studying doodads on the shopping network for some home I'd never had. Between, I counted things until I could sleep. Exits signs out of Knoxville. Right-hand turns and left-hand turns by the river in Smyte. The number of salt and pepper shakers at all the booths at the Black Cat Diner. I ran my memory fingers over the keys at the register. Wandered, remembering us sitting outside and neon light inside his truck and us turning the volume up on his tape deck. *Mama she done told me, Papa done told me too, 'Son, that gal you're foolin' with, She ain't no good for you.'* Nothing could make me sleep, and I wanted her ghost voice telling me what to do next, but Ruby was gone, for good it seemed.

I sat by the window and pulled back the drapes. Out beyond the Red Sari were streets I'd ridden with Cody Black to bars and coffee shops, to late night diners for plates of hash and eggs. Beyond that, Highway 40, exits I could take, just for fun. If I wanted to, I could even head to Florida and sign on to some high-falutin' cruise ship to Key West and on from there. Mexico. Puerto Rico. Net mending on a shrimp boat. Deck hand. Mail carrier to South America. There were worlds and worlds I hadn't seen. I pictured myself in a silk scarf from a hawker's stall in Thailand, yellow fruit with a spiky skin and, inside, wet-tasting seeds. I could go anywhere I wanted, if I wanted.

One of the last times I'd sat in this very spot it had been late summer and Cody Black had been asleep. I'd tiptoed over and pulled the sheets back and run a fingertip over the crease along his cheek, marks the pillow made. His lips were open and I leaned down and sniffed his sleep-smelling breath and told myself that just maybe, maybe I loved this man. You can't love a living soul, Miracelle, he'd said to me, and sent me out into the world to learn who I was. *Miracelle Loving.* My whole history was in that name. Loving I'd never wanted, but searched for like it was the last thing I'd ever find. And here I was, back from searching for the Holy Grail of family and I'd filled in a blank or two or three inside myself, all right, but a hundred more seemed to follow. I was learning, I guessed, to live with the hollow places in my heart.

Nights like these I sat with what I'd saved from the pages Della and I had burned that night by the river. The words Russell Wallen had written to me the night he died.

> *Miracelle. You want the truth?*
>
> *I am no man of words and I've never believed in much but two fingers of whiskey and a straight line between here and there. And I can hear you asking. What line do you mean, Russell Wallen?*
>
> *The real truth?*
>
> *There's never been a straight line between any two souls in this world.*
>
> *I've known how to howl at the sky but not a sound ever came back but my own name. I've known how to grieve but never had a clue about what I'd lost until it was too late to ask. I've spit love out like something that I regretted as soon as it was gone. That's true, I swear it. Love chased me down. It was bigger than me. I fought it off, again and again.*
>
> *Still, I loved you.*
>
> *Didn't I?*
>
> *Miracelle, my own sweet girl.*
>
> *Let me tell you a story.*
>
> *What I have left you, baby girl, is tonight. I'm lying here in a pickup truck with no sounds anywhere but the way snow falls. The road is covered and the highways too. The whole world is waiting*

for the sun to come up, move across the snow. That's the only prom-
ise there is.
    Take the true road out.
    Make your heart your own.

That long Red Sari night I lay awake a long while, listening to my own breath. Where did breath go, after you died? Breath, traveling down back roads, down the narrow lanes of airways, into the dark caves of chests. I thought of Russell lying alone and waiting out the hours until morning, his last night on earth. *Breath leaves your body at night and goes out into the living space of the world.* When I finally slept, I dreamed of cowboys and cars. Thunderbirds and Chevys. A sunset redder than any that could really exist. I dreamed all their ghosts. Russell and Ruby, two-stepping across a diner floor at midnight. Della, her hands that knew an engine better than love. Hands reaching for other hands, those hands with stories I now know. Cody Black, his back tattooless, the skin new and fresh and waiting for its fine ink. Or them, Willy's Wonders. Natty-feathered birds taking flight into some strange, huge sky. Ruby Loving, her nails painted red. *Sweet one,* she said, as she stroked the top of my head as I slept. *You'll come around girl,* she said. *Oh, you'll be just fine.*

A ghost dream further back than that. Dream of the flat bare earth around Radiance and the house that used to be my grandfather's. Earth long before the dying trees, their branches barely tipped with green. How my mother used to play out there, her bare feet tough with summer. How her mother tossed pans of dishwater out the open door of the house that used to be. But that dream was still too new. There were a million others behind such simple ones of that family I'd never known. Time upon time. A hundred million years ago, layers of earth moved against earth. Swamps were alive. Seas and rivers were there, sand and clay and a hot heart fire, flames shimmying up and up at the center of everything. *The world,* my mother said, *already full of ghosts before it even began.*

Was it a dream or was it wishing when I finally slept deep? Dreamed of family, or what was left of one, become a mighty success. The Black Cat, moved east to Radiance, becomes a one-night-a-week performance hall for a once great fiddle player and on occasion his fortune-telling granddaughter. And Della? She fixes your ride for you, fixes engines of their miss. She fixes breakfasts and suppers, orders up and serves. And she owns a place that makes paper, too—song sheets and cards, menus and recipes, labels for perfume. Paper, she says, has no staying power—it can flare up, match to corner, corner to flame. But that, too, is right in this dreamed version of a family.

Awake or dreaming, I took all their ghost-hands. *Come awake, you little ones, come awake to the love always there.* Like it was floating from his house to this empty earth-place, the sound of my grandfather's bow and strings and voice. I danced every dance I'd ever known and more that came to me now, a revelation. I twirled and hummed along. I was the child I had never been and could be again with my own longing. I swung and do-si-doed by my own self. I took hold of notes I'd never imagined and flew with them around and around as the shadows of the room brightened, began to become first light. *Ruby. Della. Russell.* Dream or waking, my heart had danced with them and I knew for certain there were so many stories ahead. Ones about souls who love, ones who can't, and those who must, at last, come home.

It was August, hot as the dickens, and I sat the next morning for the longest while, just studying my own palm. If you looked at a palm the right way, you'd see mountain peaks, and I could even see a tiny little speck that was me in my Dodge Dart, climbing up and across the two peaks, toward the sky and to the other side of my hand and beyond. I could have predicted a road out for myself, but what I did instead was pick out a tank top and an indigo skirt with seahorses on it to wear to go see Cody Black at his shop.

Outside I moved against thick air and sat with the windows down and the door open until the car was aired out enough for me to hold the steering wheel. I read and reread the name and address on the back of the card Marvis had given me. I hadn't talked to Cody again since after the funeral at the Black Cat, so maybe the Cody I remembered wasn't even real. Maybe he'd ridden off into some Knoxville sunset where I could never go. Still, I found 13th Street, then cruised the block up and back before I saw the sign for Cody's shop.

Once I'd parked and dropped in enough quarters for two hours, I inched my way toward the large sign, one lit up, even in the daytime, with some light not of any earth I knew. It was smoke-purple and pink, and the closer I got, I realized that at the center of the sign was a forehead and an eye. The third eye, Cody had called it. I stood for a long time, thirty paces from the shop door, which opened and swung shut twice before I went inside. I'd heard about his world so often, I knew it without even opening the shop door.

Tattoo drawings covered the walls, the shoulders and arms and back shots, photos of recent customers who were becoming nearly famous for their sleeves and chests, their lips rings and tongue piercing photos thrown in for good measure. On the walls, month-by-month calendars of the most-tattooed woman, the most-decorated man. Bottles of ink, indigo and fuchsia and violent oranges, lined up next to cups of water and brushes, inviting as a child's art room, a painter's dream. Mats and massage tables. Padded chairs. The hum of needles, something Cody had always found soothing. A sound like a heartbeat and pipes swept me up as I walked inside, and I smelled peppermint and sage. The same light from the sign outside was everywhere, a softer, cooler version that felt like an ice cube moving slowly down my sweating summer skin. Two signs painted on cloth in another shade of purplish red were tacked on each wall, and they blew out and in from the overhead fans. *Let Your Body Head East. Dream Your Way Toward Unconquered Space.*

Cody. Standing beside a vinyl-covered table. Him and his tattoo gun and a woman draped in a white cover-up. She made a sound somewhere between a moan and a hum of pleasure as he made the final sweep of a long lilac line, the edge of an iris's petal.

I took a seat in one of the recliners on either side of the room. He worked with a focus I'd seen not long back, in the way my grandfather's hands stroked a fiddle with a bow. The kind of focus that started mid-chest, worked its way down a body to the feet that stood on the earth we all walked, then back up again to the heart, the throat, the center of the head. Cody said that holy places were inside our own selves and that we could find them with the touch of hands. My grandfather, for one. He touched strings and notes floated out, set free to soothe, to set you free, to remind you of who you are.

When I looked up, Cody had paused in his work and he was watching me. "You a customer?" he asked at last. "Or do I know you?"

"Could be a little bit of both." I held his look, reacquainting myself with the exact color of his eyes.

"That so?"

"Could be," I said again, and then I moved closer so I could see the iris Cody was etching on the woman's back. It blossomed like a living thing, a door to a soul stepping outside her own skin.

Acknowledgments

For this novel and its iterations over time, I am thankful for the sharp eyes and clear-headed comments of so many: Silas House, Heather Whitaker, Avery Caswell, Denton Loving, T.J. Sandella. Thank you for your advice, your votes of confidence, and your close reading. I owe much to other artists in my life, ones who know the power of friendship and the importance of supporting one another in our endeavors. I particularly thank my close women friends: Carlyle Poteat, Cindra Halm, Vicky Hayes, Gwendy Turnbull.

To all the good people at the University Press of Kentucky—they who have believed in this novel, labored over it with me in its editing —I offer my truest, most humble thanks.

Place has meant a great deal as this novel has evolved. Hindman and the Appalachian Writers' Workshop continues to be a homeplace I come back to in person and in memory. Teaching semesters as Visiting Writer at Hollins University, Gettysburg College, and University of South Dakota made space for these pages. And I am grateful to Charles and Cornelia Saltzman, whose farm in Aspers, Pennsylvania, became a necessary retreat.

Thanks always to family, both my ancestors and those still near and dear.

Above all, I am thankful to my partner, Johnny Johns, with whom I share love and a home, a safe place where words can flourish.